PERSUASION

It was better, he thought, to make a clean, swift break. She'd get over it . . . and so would he.

"I do like you, Amy," he said softly. "But I've been doing some thinking since then, and I, well, I don't think it's going to work out. You're just not my type."

She regarded him steadily. "I don't believe you."

He laughed nervously. "I'm sorry, but it's the truth."

"You're saying you're not attracted to me?" Her eyes, which had looked so luminous and soft before, were suddenly fired with angry glints. "Is that what you're saying?"

He wet his lips. "I, uh . . ."

Abruptly she stood. Then, taking him completely off guard, she walked over to him, put her arms around him, and lowered her mouth to his.

At the first touch of her lips, every good resolution he'd had went flying out the window. He groaned and crushed her to him. They tumbled back into the big chair. The kiss was open and wet and hungry. And once he started kissing her, he couldn't seem to stop . . .

TRISHA ALEXANDER

THE CONSTANT HEART

ZEBRA BOOKS
KENSINGTON PUBLISHING CORP.

ZEBRA BOOKS are published by

Kensington Publishing Corp.
850 Third Avenue
New York, NY 10022

First Printing: September, 1996
10 9 8 7 6 5 4 3 2 1

Printed in the United States of America

This book was a labor of love, and I owe thanks to many: Helen Breitwieser, agent extraordinaire, for believing in me; Ann LaFarge, editor extraordinaire, for her invaluable insights and suggestions; and the most wonderful writing buds on earth—Marilyn Amann, Carla Luan, Heather MacAllister, and Alaina Richardson. Thanks for keeping me on the right track.

This book is dedicated with love, to my grandchildren, who are keeping me young: Christopher Michael Howard, Ryan Alexander Kay, and Kaylee Ann Howard.

Prologue

Pregnant!

Amy Carpenter couldn't stop smiling. She tapped her fingers against the steering wheel in time to Bonnie Raitt's "Let's Give 'Em Something to Talk About" and grinned from ear to ear.

She knew she shouldn't be so happy. After all, this pregnancy was a bit premature, since her wedding was still eight weeks away. But she didn't care. Joy, like champagne, bubbled inside, giddy and irrepressible. She felt like shouting from the rooftops.

And her parents! They'd be thrilled. They wanted grandchildren more than just about anything. Of course, her mother would have preferred she wait until she was married, but she didn't think the fact that she and Sam had jumped the gun would matter much in the end. It was the baby that was important.

A delicious shiver raised goosebumps on her arms as she thought of her fiancé. Sam. *Oh, Sam, please be happy, too.* She told herself he would be. He wanted kids, and even though he'd said "someday" the one time they'd discussed the subject, Amy didn't think he'd mind if that "someday" was sooner than they'd anticipated.

She wished she could call him and tell him immediately. Unfortunately, where Sam was, there were no phones. She would have to wait until she heard from him again.

He'd originally expected to be back in Houston by now. Sam was a staff photographer for *World of Nature* magazine, and he'd thought this assignment to shoot the elusive snow leopards who made their home high in the Himalayas would take only a couple of weeks, a month at the most. But the snow leopards had proved more elusive than ever, and Sam had been in Nepal more than two months already.

It might not be so bad if she could at least talk to him regularly, but he was in a remote area, a three-day hike from base camp, so she'd talked to him only twice since he'd left.

If Amy had thought her married life would be like this—a long series of absences with no communication—she might not have been so eager to marry Sam, no matter how much she loved him. But he'd promised her he would do his best to avoid assignments that would keep him away longer than a week or two, and he had also promised he would take her along with him whenever he could.

Now that she was pregnant, she wouldn't be able to travel with him, as planned—at least, not until the baby was old enough to go, too, but that was okay. The trade-off was worth it. She was going to be a mother.

A mother.

Imagine.

Less than four months ago she'd despaired of ever finding the right man, and now she'd not only found him, but she was going to marry him over the Christmas holidays and have his baby in May. She could hardly believe her good fortune.

She smiled contentedly, her momentary unease

gone. As she braked for a red light, her big emerald engagement ring sparkled in the afternoon sunshine slanting through the windshield. Amy twisted her hand a little, admiring the rich color and fire of the stone, which was surrounded by tiny diamonds.

She loved the ring. It was so like Sam: out of the ordinary, a bit larger than life. She hated removing it, even to wash her hands.

She was still smiling as she pulled into the driveway of her parents' home, punched in the security code that would open the electronic gates, and drove around to the back of the property, where she lived in an apartment over the garage.

The first thing she saw was Justin Malone's dark green Toyota. She frowned. What was Sam's best friend doing here so early in the day? Justin and Sam worked together and had even lived together for a while. Several weeks ago, Amy had given Justin the code to the security gate because he was helping her paint the inside of the apartment while Sam was gone. Even though she and Sam were planning to find another place to live when he returned, Amy wanted to leave the apartment fresh and shining in case her parents decided to rent it to someone else. And Justin had insisted on giving her a hand.

Her unease deepened.

It was only 4:30. It wasn't like Justin to leave work so early. Since he'd been promoted to business manager at the magazine, he'd been working long hours. Amy had enjoyed teasing him about his diligence, saying she guessed that now he was "one of them" she'd have to be careful what she said in front of him.

Justin was fun to tease because he was so earnest

and serious. Too much so, Amy thought. She'd already decided that once she and Sam were married, she would try to find someone for Justin so he'd loosen up a bit. "The Quiet Man," Sam called him, always there, always the person you could count on.

She waved as she passed him, pulling her Miata into the garage. "Hi!" she said, as he walked toward her. "What a surprise! What're you doing here at this time of day?"

As he came closer, she saw a peculiar expression on his lean, angular face. His blue eyes, normally so bright and riveting, seemed shadowed and troubled, and he wasn't smiling.

"Hello, Amy."

His voice sounded odd, too—rough and strained.

Her smile slowly faded. Everything inside her went still except her heart. Something was terribly wrong.

"Amy," he said again. He reached for her, placing his hands on her shoulders and looking down into her eyes. "I—I've got some bad news."

No.

She shook her head. She wanted to put her hands over her ears. Whatever Justin was going to tell her, she didn't want to hear it.

"I came right over," he continued. "I didn't want you to hear about this on TV or over the radio."

Sam.

Please, God . . . please, God . . . please, God. She opened her mouth to speak, but no words came.

Justin's face was rigid and tightly controlled. Only his eyes betrayed his inner torment. "We heard an hour ago. Sam . . ." He took a long, shuddering breath. "Sam had a bad accident. He fell down the side of a cliff, and . . . and when the search party finally reached the place where they thought they would find him, his . . . his body was gone."

He swallowed hard, and the part of Amy's brain that still functioned normally noted in a detached way how his Adam's apple bobbed and how his dark hair, normally neat and well groomed, looked as if he'd been running his hands through it.

He squeezed her shoulders. "They . . . the authorities believe he's dead."

"Nooooooooo . . . noooooo . . ." Amy heard the keening sound, hardly aware that it came from her mouth.

"God, Amy, I'm so sorry."

Amy felt his strong arms go around her. She heard him continuing to talk, continuing to say comforting words, continuing to explain, but nothing he said mattered. "No, no, no," she moaned.

She tried to hold on. She tried to listen. To think. But she felt sick to her stomach and light-headed. A loud buzzing filled her head, and then there was nothing but blackness as she slumped against him.

PART ONE

SAM

One

The offices of *World of Nature* magazine occupied two floors of the Transco Tower in Houston. The building, sixty-four stories of faceted glass, was the third tallest in the city and the dominant piece of real estate in the Galleria area, dubbed the Magic Circle by Houstonians. A sleekly handsome Art Deco marvel of architectural design, on sunny days it seemed to smile benevolently down upon the retail shops and restaurants of the Westheimer/West Loop/Post Oak configuration. On overcast days, it seemed to rest its head among the clouds.

At night, its beacon made a languid 360-degree arc over the western end of the city and reminded those with more fanciful imaginations of a lighthouse warning away encroaching planes or birds. It was an upstart building, rising like a phoenix from the plains of suburbia, perfectly suited to the upstart city it graced.

On this muggy, insufferably hot Friday afternoon in July, the various departments of *World of Nature*, located on the twentieth floor, were all astir as a handsome, rugged-looking young man with strong, muscular legs shown to advantage in khaki shorts and hiking boots strode through the double doors leading from reception to the inner sanctum. His light brown hair was burnished by the sun to a shade of dark gold that perfectly complemented his tanned face and amber-flecked brown eyes. Deep dimples bracketed a brash smile that exposed very white teeth. Even a casual observer would immediately know that this man was completely comfortable in his skin.

The male employees of the magazine mentally shook their heads as they watched the women flirt and preen and strut in the newcomer's wake.

"Sam! You're back! Welcome home!"

Sam Robbins beamed at Rosie Pritchard, a cartographer who'd been with the magazine since its founding in 1972. "Hey, Rosie-Posey, how's it goin'? Did you miss me?" He ruffled her sleek black hair, then dodged her friendly punch on the arm.

"Oh, yeah," she said, with an exaggerated roll of her dark eyes, "I was counting the days. Couldn't hardly sleep at night, in fact."

"I've got a surefire cure for that," he said, winking. "Just name the time."

She laughed. "In your dreams."

"You're a hard woman, Rosie."

"Yeah, yeah, now get outta here. I got work to do." She shooed him away. But she was still smiling as he walked off.

Sam was smiling, too; he liked Rosie. He liked women of all ages, provided they had a sense of humor and didn't take themselves, or him, too seriously.

As he made his way to the photography department, people called out in welcome.

"Hi, Sam!"

"Hey, Sambo, heard you got some great shots in Alaska!"

"Well, if it isn't the Rogue, in the flesh!"

Sam returned all the good-natured greetings,

stopping to shoot the breeze for a few seconds with each co-worker. Finally he reached the office of his boss, Owen Church, the head of the photography department.

"He's waiting for you." Jeanne Linden, Owen's administrative assistant, inclined her head toward the open door, blushing and swatting him away as Sam dropped a quick peck on her cheek.

"Thanks, Jeanne." Sam tapped on the door frame before entering the big corner office.

"Sam! Come on in!" Owen was seated behind his mahogany desk, and he half stood to shake Sam's hand, then waved Sam to a seat. "The Alaskan shots are great." He chomped down on the unlit cigar that was as much a part of him as his wispy gray hair and gravelly voice. "Good job."

Sam felt a deep pleasure at Owen's praise. Of all the people he'd worked with over the years, he respected Owen the most. The older man had been with the Houston headquarters of *World of Nature* since he was twenty-two. He'd begun as a gofer for Monte Brewster, the nature-loving oil baron who'd started the magazine, and ended as the manager of one of the most elite sections, an accomplishment for which he was fiercely proud, and rightly so, Sam felt. Owen considered the photography department and its staff the way he would consider his children, if he'd ever had any.

He had given Sam his first break after Sam had moved to Houston eight years before—an assignment to photograph endangered wildlife along the Usumacinta River in Guatemala. He had liked Sam's work enough to offer him a staff job at the completion of the Guatemalan assignment. The job offer was a fantastic opportunity for someone who was only twenty-three. Sam still felt grateful, even

though he knew he was damn good at what he did
and had earned his place at *World of Nature.*

Owen leaned back in his swivel chair. "What're
your plans now? You going to take some of that vacation?"

"No. Not yet. I thought I'd wait and take some
in the fall." Owen had been nagging at Sam since
last summer to use some of the eight weeks of vacation he'd accumulated.

For a long moment, Owen didn't reply, just studied Sam with his shrewd, pale blue eyes. "I'm afraid
I'm going to have to pull rank on you this time,
son."

Sam frowned. "What do you mean?"

"I mean I'm ordering you to take your vacation.
At least six weeks of it."

Sam fought to keep his voice from betraying his
quick surge of anger. "I don't *want* to take a vacation."

"Whether you want to or not, I think you need
it."

Sam stared at his boss. Owen insisted that rest and
recuperation were a necessary part of any job. He
didn't understand that Sam didn't consider the
work he did to be stressful or taxing, nor did he
feel the need to get away from it. He supposed if
he were like most of the other staffers—with homes
and families—he might look forward to time off,
but Sam had no ties to speak of. And that was just
the way he liked it.

Owen carefully balanced the cigar on the edge of
a chipped glass ashtray that held paper clips and
other assorted odds and ends. "Tell me something,
Sam. Where do you see yourself going with your
career?"

"Going? I don't see myself going anywhere other than where I am."

"No aspirations to strike out on your own or become a manager or do a book?"

"Nope. I like things just the way they are. What is this all about, Owen?"

Owen hesitated before answering. And when he did, his voice had softened. "Look, you know how much I think of you. CeCe and I, we've talked about you a lot, and we both agree that if we'd had a son, we'd have loved to have had one just like you."

CeCe was a favorite of Sam's. Feisty and fiery, just as her red hair suggested, she was one of the kindest and warmest women Sam had ever known. He had often thought what a shame it was she and Owen had never had any children, because he knew how much they'd wanted them.

"And if you *were* my son," Owen continued, "I'd say the same things to you that I'm going to say now. I'm worried about you, Sam."

Sam started to interrupt, but Owen said, "Let me finish. Then you can talk. I'm worried because you don't seem to give a damn about anything, and as a result, you're taking too many risks."

Jesus Christ, Sam thought, *did Roger tell Owen about what happened in Alaska?* Roger Blakely was the researcher who had accompanied Sam on the Alaskan assignment.

"You know," Owen continued, "no wildlife photographer can afford to be impatient or to put himself in danger—not if he wants to be one of the great ones . . . or if he wants to live to tell about it."

"Come on, Owen, you know I'd never do anything *really* dangerous—"

"Just hear me out, okay?"

Sam slumped back in resignation. "All right."

"As your boss, I have a responsibility to make sure you not only get the best pictures you can get, but that you don't endanger your life or the life of anyone else you're working with in the process." Owen sighed. "Unfortunately, you *have* taken some needless risks in the past, which I excused by telling myself you were young, you'd learn. But now I've discovered you took another one in Alaska . . ."

Sam's jaw clenched, and the anger simmering below the surface flared into full flame. *Goddamn!* He'd wring Roger's neck when he saw him.

"And don't blame Roger," Owen said. "He has a larger responsibility than covering for you. He did the right thing when he told me what happened. Maybe if you had a family back here, as Roger does, you wouldn't take so many chances."

"Aw, come on, Owen, nothing happened! Roger's just an old lady! He's afraid of his own shadow, for Christ's sake!"

"Maybe nothing *did* happen, but it could have. Because you did something reckless in Alaska. You cornered that bear because you were either too impatient to wait and see if you could get the shots you wanted later, when you and Roger were out of harm's way, or you were too damned cocky to think that normal rules apply to you. Either way, I don't like it. It's only blind luck that everything turned out okay, but if you keep on like this, one of these days you won't be so lucky."

"Look, I'm sorry—"

"Saying you're sorry isn't good enough—not this time. I want you to take time off. I'd like you to take your full eight weeks, but I'll settle for four." Again his voice softened, and he leaned forward. "Sam, you have the potential to win a Pulitzer. But first you've got to learn the difference between calculated risk-taking and foolish endangerment."

Sam didn't trust himself to speak. He stood and walked over to the bank of windows and stared out at the afternoon traffic crawling along Westheimer and the intersecting West Loop. He had walked into Owen's office expecting congratulations and an exciting new assignment. Instead, he'd gotten a lecture.

"I know you're angry," Owen said. "But I want you to think about what I said. Think about what your goals are. And when your vacation is over, come in, and we'll talk about where you go from here."

After Sam left the office, Owen swiveled his chair around and gazed out the window unseeingly. He knew Sam was angry. Well, the kid would just have to get over it.

Owen sighed. If only he could knock some sense into Sam's head. Owen knew what drove Sam. He also knew, or thought he knew, what Sam's deep-seated fears were. Hell, if Owen had been born into the kind of situation Sam had been born into, if he'd had to scrounge on the streets from the time he was a little kid, if he'd been surrounded by pimps and prostitutes and drug pushers and addicts, if he'd been let down by all the people who were supposed to take care of him, maybe Owen would have the same kind of who-gives-a-shit attitude that Sam had.

But although Owen understood, although he realized that Sam had some kind of compulsion to thumb his nose at the conventional world as well as shout at the devil, Owen couldn't let him if it meant jeopardizing the work of the magazine or the lives of his co-workers.

He couldn't help smiling, though, as he remembered Sam's description of Roger Blakely. Roger *was* an old lady. He hated fieldwork. He much preferred to bury his nose in library archives or microfiche than to be a part of an on-site research team. Too bad he was so good at it.

No matter.

Sam was the one in the wrong, and he would either learn from this, straighten up, and fly right, or he wouldn't fly at all.

Sam forced himself to pretend nothing was wrong as he made his way out of the magazine's offices. But he was seething inside, and he decided he'd go to the running trail in Memorial Park and blow off some steam.

Normally he ran in the mornings, but he'd gotten into town late last night, then he and Justin had stayed up even later, talking and having a few beers. As a result, Sam hadn't crawled out of bed until eleven this morning, and by the time he'd unpacked and showered and shaved and had something to eat, it was already the middle of the afternoon.

It took him only ten minutes to get from the *World of Nature* offices to his apartment near the park. It was a stifling day, but Sam didn't mind. He didn't even run the 'Vette's air conditioner, just put the windows down and let the hot air rush through. He'd spent lots of time in jungles and tropical climates over the past eight years. His body was used to heat and humidity.

He got a kick out of the way his Houston friends complained about the heat. Most of them wouldn't survive two days in some of the places he'd been. They were soft and spoiled, going from their air-conditioned houses to their air-conditioned cars to their air-conditioned offices.

Sam shook his head, remembering his astonishment the first time he'd gone to Astroworld and discovered that its creator had even tried to air condition the outdoors. Only in Texas, he'd thought.

When he got to his apartment, he changed into his running shorts and shoes, then headed for the park. While he ran, he rehashed his conversation with Owen. He tried to get past his feelings of anger, but Owen's criticism rankled. Hell, any wildlife photographer had to take *some* risks. It went with the territory.

He felt like strangling Roger. Because of his big mouth, Sam had been grounded, like a misbehaving teenager. What in hell was he going to do for four weeks? He'd go nuts.

He was still mulling over the problem when he finished his run and slowly walked toward the parking lot. As he approached his 'Vette, he heard a faint sound, like a cry.

Frowning, he looked around.

There it was again. The sound seemed to be coming from under the thick Indian hawthorn bushes that bordered the lot. He turned and walked in their direction.

Sam parted the bushes and peered under them. Sweat rolled off his neck.

"Meowww . . ."

The muffled cry guided Sam as he finally located its source—a tiger-striped kitten, bedraggled and skinny. "Hey, fella," he said softly, "c'mere." He reached for it, and although the kitten meowed once more, it didn't resist as Sam pulled it out of its hiding place.

He cradled the kitten in his hands and stood. Poor little thing. It whimpered as he petted it and scratched behind its ears. Despite the heat, it was shaking all over. "Whatsa matter, fella? Did somebody toss you out on the streets? Huh? I know how that feels."

Sam knew he couldn't keep the kitten. He'd tried that once, with a puppy, and quickly discovered it was impossible to have a pet when you were away from home two-thirds of the time. In fact, that's how he and Justin had met. When Sam realized he would have to find another home for the pup, he'd put a notice up on the magazine's bulletin board, and Justin answered it. He'd taken the dog, and in the process, he and Sam had become friends—a friendship that had strengthened as the years had gone by.

Sam wondered what he should do about this kitten. It had obviously been abandoned, and if he left it, the little animal would probably starve to death.

He scratched its head gently. "Oh, hell, the least I can do is feed you. Then I guess I'll figure out something. C'mon, let's go. We'll be home in a few minutes. And who knows? If we play our cards right, maybe we can persuade Justin to take you, too!"

Two

The first pink fingers of dawn crept over the horizon at 6:28 Saturday morning.

Amy Carpenter had been awake for over an hour. She'd been having trouble sleeping lately. She was restless and would awaken several times during the night.

Lark DeWitt, Amy's best friend since first grade, kept telling her she just needed a good fuck, which always made Amy cringe. She hated coarse language, and Lark knew it, so just to be perverse and get Amy's hackles up, Lark said the "F" word every chance she got.

Maybe Lark was right, Amy mused, as she drank her third cup of coffee and nibbled on a bagel. She was sitting out on the second-floor deck, under one of the leafy red oak trees that ringed her garage apartment. For the past thirty minutes she'd been listening to a mockingbird call to its friends and enjoying the relative cool of the early morning air.

Maybe a lover was exactly what she needed. But there was a problem with that scenario: there was no one she could even imagine filling that role. Not that she hadn't had her share of possible lovers. Even now, Glenn would be delighted to step

in and do something about her sexual frustration—
if that's what this current itchiness was.

Amy frowned. She had to do something about
Glenn Wilhelm. She had mistakenly encouraged
him when he first began asking her out, because he
was nice, a fellow teacher, clean-cut and attractive.
She had talked herself into thinking he might grow
on her.

But after a few dates, she'd known the relationship was doomed to go no further. There were simply no magic sparks, no sparks of any kind, when
she was with him. She enjoyed his company. They
had fun together, but when she kissed him goodnight, it was like kissing a brother.

She couldn't imagine going to bed with Glenn.
Just the thought of having sex with him made her
cringe.

Yes, she definitely had to break it off completely.
Glenn was gone this week—off to Idaho to visit his
family—but when he returned and called her, she
would tell him, as gently as she could, that it was
best if they didn't see each other anymore.

She drained her cup and propped her feet up
on the deck railing. Would she ever meet a man
who made her feel those magical sparks her
mother had described?

Amy knew her parents' fondest wish was to see
her happily married.

"It's true that your father and I want you to be
safe and secure and that we want grandchildren
before we die," her mother'd said the last time
Amy had brought up the subject. "But we also want
you to be as happy as we've been. We don't want
you to settle for just anyone. Be patient, darling.
The right man will come along. And when he does,
you'll know it."

Amy wanted all that, too. In fact, she wanted a marriage exactly like her parents'. Faith and Alan Carpenter were the most in-love couple Amy had ever known.

She had heard the story of their meeting countless times: how it was "love at first sight," and how they immediately knew they were meant to be together always. "I took one look, and that was it," Faith had said, her eyes soft in remembrance.

The Carpenters had never spent a night apart, not even the night Amy was born. Her father had been by her mother's side throughout the birth, and he hadn't left the hospital until he could take her and their little daughter home with him.

Yes, Amy thought, her parents had set a shining example of what a marriage should be. Theirs was exactly the kind of relationship Amy wanted but had almost despaired of finding. Her standards were high, and so far no one had come close to filling them.

Amy continued to think about her deep yearning for someone to love, someone who would lift her to the stars and give her the children she wanted. Finally, as the sun began to climb, she realized it was getting late, and she'd better go inside and start getting ready for the day.

Although it was summer, and she wasn't teaching, she'd been doing some volunteer work at a nearby pet shelter. She'd started out by working two days during the week, but this past Thursday the director of the shelter asked her if she could possibly fill in today—Saturday.

"Beth moved to Tucson, so we're really short-handed," she'd said.

Amy agreed readily. She had no plans to go anywhere or do anything until her parents returned from Europe, which wasn't going to happen for several weeks. Even then, she had no concrete plans. Lark had been trying to talk her into taking a cruise, but Amy wasn't sure she wanted to.

Instead, she'd been toying with the idea of going to New York or perhaps Santa Fe for a week. She could immerse herself in museums and galleries, which would give her some fresh ideas to bring to her art classes and would be more relaxing to her than the enforced gaiety and relentless activities associated with the kind of cruise Lark was pushing.

After making her bed, showering, dressing, and feeding her cats, she left her apartment a little before 8:30.

It was such a pretty morning, she decided to put the top down on her little white Miata—a twenty-seventh birthday present from her parents in March.

By the time she reached the shelter ten minutes later, her vaguely restless mood had disappeared, blown away by the fresh air and blue skies. She smiled as she knocked on the shelter door and waited for Carl, one of the few paid full-time workers, to open up.

It was a new day. Anything was possible.

At 10 o'clock Saturday morning, showered and wearing clean army green shorts and an open-necked white cotton shirt, with his bare feet shoved into worn Docksiders, Sam put the kitten in a cardboard box and drove over to the shelter on Weslayen that Justin had recommended.

A few minutes later he reached his destination. The shelter was part of a seen-better-days, L-shaped strip mall, the kind that proliferated in Houston. The sign proclaimed the shelter to be PET HAVEN and took up the entire short leg of the L. There were two doors, one leading into the adoption center, one leading into an accompanying pet supplies shop.

Sam opened the door to the adoption center and a bell tinkled. The small reception area had a beat-up tile floor and a distinct animal smell. A symphony of barking greeted his arrival.

A few seconds later, a girl carrying a large black cat emerged from the back room. She smiled at Sam.

Sam took one look and his fingers itched for his camera. His photographer's eye rapidly took in the details of her appearance. She looked about seventeen—small, with a heart-shaped face, enormous green eyes, and a flawless complexion with just the barest smattering of freckles across her nose. Her hair, thick and dark and curly, was loosely tied back from her face with a narrow green ribbon, and she wore a jaunty green beret angled down over one eye. An oversized black T-shirt and black tights completed her costume. Long silver earrings in the shape of stars dangled from her ears and sparkled in the morning sunlight. She wasn't beautiful, Sam decided, yet she was totally captivating.

He was already imagining how he'd place her against a white backdrop with maybe a green park bench in the foreground. Maybe some bright red geraniums or azaleas to add a counterpoint of color. And that cat in her arms was perfect, too—a match with its black fur, green eyes, and silver collar.

"Hi," the girl said. "What've you got there?" Her voice was surprisingly husky.

"It's a stray I found. I can't keep it, and a friend told me to come over here and you'd take it." He couldn't stop staring at her. She had a wonderful

face—expressive and open and sweetly innocent.
And that smile!

"Oh, sure," she said, her gaze connecting with
his. "We'll take it." But for a long moment she
didn't move. Finally, with an obvious effort, she tore
her gaze away and put the black cat she'd been holding on top of the counter separating her from cus-
tomers, saying, "Now, you stay there, Jasmine." She
pulled a form from somewhere under the counter
and looked at Sam again. "Um, okay. Name?"

"I don't know."

She frowned for a second, then gave a throaty
little chuckle. "I meant you, not the kitten."

Sam grinned foolishly. She was enchanting. He
liked everything about her. The way she looked.
The way she talked. He especially liked the way she
laughed. Too bad she was jailbait. "Well, in that
case, my name is Sam Robbins. What's yours?"

Her eyes sparkled with good humor. "Nice to
meet you, Sam. I'm Amy." She pointed to her shoulder.

Belatedly he noticed she wore a name tag. It read:
Amy Carpenter. "Carpenter, Carpenter . . . are you by
any chance related to Jack Carpenter, the dentist?"

She shook her head. "Nope. Afraid not." She
continued asking questions and filling out the
form, and when she finished, she smiled again and
reached for the kitten. She petted it, saying, "We'll
find him a good home. Don't worry."

Sam knew it was time to say thanks and leave,
but he didn't want to, and he didn't think she
wanted him to leave, either. "You're doing good
work here," he said, stalling.

"Thanks."

"Do you work here full-time?"

"Oh, no. I just volunteer a couple of days a week."

He nodded. "Are you a student?"

"Actually, I'm a teacher."

"Really? You don't look old enough to be a teacher."

She eyed him for a moment, a smile hovering at the edges of her mouth. "I know. I get carded everywhere I go. But I'm twenty-seven. I've been teaching for five years."

Sam grinned. "In that case, I won't be considered a dirty old man if I ask you out, will I?"

"*Are* you going to ask me out?"

"How does dinner tonight sound? If you don't already have plans, that is."

She studied him thoughtfully. "I don't even know you. Maybe you're a serial killer."

"I'm perfectly harmless. Really. I'm a photographer, and I work for *World of Nature* magazine. Here. Look at my driver's license and my press card." He reached for his wallet. Suddenly, it was very important that she say yes. He couldn't just walk away without seeing her again.

She shook her head. "That's okay, I believe you. Serial killers wouldn't bother to bring an abandoned kitten to a shelter."

"Ted Bundy did," he pointed out.

She grimaced. "You just *had* to say that, didn't you?"

Sam laughed. "Sure you don't want to see my ID? Maybe check me out?"

"Well, after that remark, maybe I should." Then she smiled. "But I don't think I need to. I'm a pretty good judge of people."

"Well, then, what do you say?"

"Sure. I'd love to go to dinner with you tonight."

He knew his grin must look idiotic, but he felt ridiculously happy—out of all proportion to a simple acceptance of a dinner date. "What time are you through here?"

"We close at six."

"I'll be back," he promised.

"I'll be waiting."

Amy watched Sam Robbins fold his tall, muscular frame into a bright red Corvette. He waved before pulling out of the parking lot, and she waved back.

She knew that what she'd just done—accept a date with a man she had met only ten minutes ago, a man who really *could* be a serial killer—was foolishly impetuous, perhaps even dangerous.

Yet she hadn't been able to help herself.

He was the one.

She had known it the moment she'd gazed into those warm, golden-brown eyes. There had been an instant connection. An instant recognition. It was crazy. Ridiculously romantic. Totally improbable.

But it was also undeniable.

It was just as her mother had always said; when she met the right man, she would know it.

Her mother was right. Amy did know it.

He was the one.

Three

"You sound happy," Justin said. "Things must have gone well with Owen yesterday."

Sam broke off in mid-whistle. The reminder of the less than satisfactory meeting took some of the edge off his pleasure. "My good mood has nothing to do with work."

Justin held the back door wide, and as he did, Major, the part Lab, part mutt, bounded into the kitchen and skidded to a stop in front of Sam.

The dog barked joyously, and Sam gave him an affectionate head rub and knelt so the dog could lick his face. Once Major calmed down, Sam stood and walked into the kitchen of Justin's Highland Village town house and thought again, as he did every time he was here, how much the place reflected Justin's personality. It was filled with carefully chosen, comfortable furniture and was almost painfully clean and orderly. Even Major's water and food bowls, which sat in the corner, were neat, with no spilled dog food or slopped-over water.

Without even looking, Sam knew the pantry was stocked with neatly aligned food and so were the refrigerator and freezer. Sam thought of his own apartment—sparsely furnished with only the barest necessities, clothes thrown anywhere they landed, and the only food in sight a box of stale crackers and a few cans of baked beans.

Not for the first time, Sam pondered the phenomenon of their friendship—two such disparate personalities, opposites in every way.

"So what happened?" Justin said. "Did you win the lottery or something?"

"It's not that big a deal. I met someone new today, and I'm taking her out tonight, that's all."

"She must be quite a babe to put you in such a good mood." Justin walked over to the refrigerator. "You want a beer?"

"Sure." Sam pulled out a kitchen chair and straddled it.

Justin removed two bottles of Beck's from the refrigerator and handed Sam one. "So? What is she? A model? A dancer? An Oilers cheerleader?"

Sam grinned sheepishly. "Nothing like that. She works at the shelter. I liked her, so I asked her out." It was weird. Normally he would go into great detail about the women he met, but for some reason, he was oddly reluctant to discuss Amy. He hoped Justin would drop the subject.

"So you did take the cat to the shelter."

"Yeah," Sam said, relieved. "And you were right. They took him, no problem."

"Good."

"I just hope they can find him a home."

Justin nodded. After a moment, he said, "Since you've got a date tonight, I guess that means you're not going to Jessie's party."

Sam knew Justin's sister had a thing for him, which was flattering, because Jessie was attractive as well as nice. But he'd never followed up on any of her hints, because even if she hadn't been Justin's sister—which was reason enough to keep his hands off—Jessie was the kind of woman Sam avoided, the same way he avoided three-piece suits and management jobs. Jessie was the kind of woman who had marriage and picket fences written all over her.

"I forgot about her party," he admitted.

"She'll be disappointed."

"Tell her I'm sorry." Sam felt a momentary discomfort as Justin studied him in that unnerving way he had of looking right down inside you so that you felt as if he could read your mind. Or your soul.

Justin nodded slowly, his blue eyes reflective. "What about tomorrow? My mother said to bring you to dinner."

In the past, there was nothing Sam had enjoyed more than being with Justin's family, but this thing with Jessie had put a damper on his enthusiasm. Yet how could he refuse to go without explaining why? "Yeah, sure, I'd love to come."

"Good. That'll make Mom happy. She likes you. Don't ask me why. Doesn't have good sense, I guess."

Sam grinned and gave Justin the finger.

Then they both laughed, the slight tension introduced with the subject of Jessie now defused.

"How'd your meeting with Owen go?" Justin asked after a while. "Do you know what your new assignment's going to be?"

This, too, was uncomfortable territory. Sam wasn't ready to discuss his interview with Owen or the hint of an ultimatum in Owen's suggestions, not even with Justin. And Justin knew more of Sam's secrets than anyone else in the world.

"No, not yet," he said casually. "I think I'll take some vacation first."

"Really? Where are you going?"

"I don't know. I haven't decided yet."

"Want to go to Wyoming and do some fly fishing? I've still got two weeks vacation left."

Sam shrugged. "Hmm. I don't know. That might be fun." What the hell? Maybe he would. He had to do something to fill up the next four weeks. "Tell you what. Let me think about it tonight, and we'll talk about it tomorrow."

Amy washed her hands and applied lotion to make sure there was no lingering doggy smell. She brushed her teeth and her hair and freshened her lipstick. She also swiped at her T-shirt and tights with a lint brush she'd found in the supply cupboard. She wished she'd suggested to Sam that he pick her up later—at home—so she could have a shower and change her clothes, but it was too late now.

By the time she was ready and had turned the sign in the door around so that the CLOSED side was showing, Sam's Corvette was parked out front.

He looked great, wearing close-fitting jeans, a tan knit shirt, and brown boots. His sun-streaked hair gleamed in the afternoon light, and his eyes were an even richer brown than she'd remembered.

God, he was sexy. Just looking at him gave her a tingly feeling. The sensation reminded Amy of Lark's advice about what she needed, which caused her face to heat up.

"Right on time," she said, hoping he wouldn't notice how flustered she'd become. She ducked her head as he opened the passenger door for her.

"After our discussion about serial killers, I was half afraid you might have changed your mind," he said.

"Are you glad I didn't?" His smile and the way

he looked at her made her feel like the most attractive woman on earth.

"*Very* glad." He shut her door, walked around to his side, and climbed in. "Do you like Mexican food?" he asked, as he pointed the Corvette toward Richmond Avenue.

"It's my absolute favorite."

"Me, too. I know a little Mexican restaurant over on Kirby called Serafina's. They've got the best food and margaritas you ever tasted. How does that sound?"

Amy smiled. "I know Serafina's, too. I love it there."

Fifteen minutes later they sat opposite each other at one of the small, round tables filling the family-owned restaurant. A smiling young waitress in a brightly colored dress brought them a big basket of hot chips and a dish of homemade salsa, took their orders for margaritas, and promised to be back soon.

Sam attacked the chips enthusiastically, and Amy followed his lead. She was starving. She'd forgotten to pack a lunch today and had been reduced to eating peanut butter crackers from the vending machine. She couldn't leave when the shelter was shorthanded, as it had been today. She and the kennel attendant were the only workers there, and he didn't know anything about the paperwork involved in adoptions or animal admittance.

"So where and what do you teach?" Sam asked.

"I teach art at a neighborhood elementary school."

"You're an artist, huh?"

His smile really was one of the nicest she'd ever seen. And she loved his dimples. He reminded her of Jeff Bridges, all effortless charm and laid-back sexuality. "I'm an art *teacher,*" she corrected. "There's a big difference."

"What?"

For a moment, Amy wondered if he was just being polite, but after studying him, she realized he really wanted to know. "Well, an artist spends his time expressing himself and his feelings through his art. I think a true artist is compelled to create, just as a writer would be compelled to write or an actor to act. There's no *choice* in the matter." Then she laughed a bit self-consciously. "But why am I telling *you* this? You're a photographer. And photography is a creative art, too."

He nodded. "Yes. It is."

"Well, I'm not like that," she continued. "I love to paint and draw, but my real love is teaching kids to express themselves. It's the most wonderful feeling to know you've opened a child's eyes and introduced him to something exciting."

"I'll bet you're a great teacher."

"I hope so. I love teaching. It's all I've ever wanted to do." That wasn't quite true, but you didn't tell a guy you'd just met that your *other* objective in life was to get married and have kids. By now their margaritas had come, and she tasted hers. "Tell me about you. Since you work for *World of Nature,* I'm assuming you're a wildlife photographer."

"Right, although I've occasionally shot other things. Once I shot a volcano that was actively erupting."

"You must be very good." Amy knew that few magazines in the world were as well respected as *World of Nature,* and assignments with them were coveted.

"I am."

No false modesty on his part. She liked that. She

liked people who felt good about themselves and their work and weren't afraid to show it. Her father was like that. He was a brilliant cardiac surgeon—a trailblazer in his field who was invited to symposia and medical conferences all over the world. In fact, her parents were even now in Brussels, where her father would be presenting a paper on Monday.

"Are you based in Houston?" she asked.

"Yes. This is where I park between assignments. Not for long, though." He smiled. "I have itchy feet. In fact, what you were saying earlier—you know, about true artists being compelled to do their art—that's not exactly what I find the most satisfying about my work."

"Oh? What is?"

He shrugged. "The adventure . . . the excitement. In some ways, even the risks." Now his smile turned sheepish. "You know, man against the elements, that kind of thing."

His words sent warning signals to Amy's brain and diluted some of the pleasure she'd felt since meeting him. The last thing she wanted was to get involved with a man who would be gone all the time—a man who thrived on adventure and danger.

Maybe she'd been wrong. Maybe Sam *wasn't* the one.

"So you're one of those people who's always looking for a new challenge," she said.

"I guess you could say that."

Their food came. Sam had ordered chiles relleños—Poblano peppers stuffed with meat and cheese, a specialty of the house—accompanied by guacamole salad, rice, and refried beans. Amy, who knew how huge the servings were, had been a little more conservative and ordered the soft chicken tacos. Even then, she knew she'd never finish everything.

For a while, they didn't talk much except to comment an how good the food was.

Then Sam said, "Where do you live?"

"I have a garage apartment in River Oaks."

"River Oaks, huh? That's a pretty high-class neighborhood."

"Well, I teach close by, and the rent was right." Amy felt funny about telling him the garage apartment was actually on the grounds of her parents' home. She knew it was ridiculous to be embarrassed about it, but a couple of times guys she'd just met had given her an odd look when she'd told them— as if there might be something wrong with an adult woman who still lived so close to home.

On the other hand, telling Sam and seeing his reaction would be a good test. She'd find out if he really was the kind of person she thought he was. "To be honest, the rent is dirt cheap. The apartment is on top of my parents' garage."

"You must get along well with them," was his only comment.

"I do. They're wonderful. We've always been very close."

"You're lucky." His tone was flat, his eyes guarded, as if a shutter had come down, hiding whatever emotion lurked in their depths.

"I know." She waited, hoping he'd volunteer information about his own family, hating to press him. She knew instinctively that whatever he eventually revealed would not be positive

"You're wondering about me."

"Well, yes," she admitted. "But you don't have to tell me if you don't want to."

He shrugged. His eyes met hers squarely. "No

big deal. My father was a sailor who took off before I was born, and my mother died when I was nine." His voice was matter-of-fact, and his expression told her he didn't expect or want sympathy.

"That's tough," was all she said, but her tender heart ached for him. She thought about how loved and safe and secure she'd always felt. If she'd known nothing else in life, she'd known that her parents treasured her more than anything in the world and would always be there for her. That knowledge was the cornerstone of her existence. "Who raised you, then?" she asked softly. "A relative?"

His smile was wry. "Yeah. My cousin, the San Diego Welfare Department."

"Oh. I—I'm sorry. I shouldn't have asked."

He shrugged again, but now his eyes betrayed him. They were filled with a bleakness he couldn't hide. "I survived. It made me stronger. Hungrier. More determined. Tell you the truth, I'm not sure I would've been half as successful as I am now if I hadn't had to fight so hard."

Amy forced herself to keep her voice free of pity. She knew Sam Robbins would not want her feeling sorry for him. "Are you an only child?"

He hesitated, but only for a moment. "No. I have a younger sister. She was just an infant when we got placed with the welfare people. I haven't seen her in twenty-one years."

"Oh, Sam, why not?" she said, before she could stop herself. Amy had always wanted a sister or a brother, and she'd often thought about the kind of relationship she would have had with one if her parents had been able to have more children. She couldn't imagine a separation like the one he'd described.

"I don't know where she is. She was adopted a few months after our mother died."

"And the welfare people allowed you two to be split up?" Amy felt outraged for him. "And what about *her* father? Did he take off, too?"

"Nobody knew who her father was. Least of all, my mother," he said with a bitter twist to his mouth.

Oh, God, Amy thought.

"The child welfare people did what they thought was best. Holly was a baby and adoptable. I was nine years old and . . ." He grimaced. "I was a handful. I'd been in some trouble. Nobody wanted me, and I don't blame 'em."

How must he have felt? Amy's natural empathy and vivid imagination told her he had to have felt doubly abandoned and deeply lonely. And he'd been only nine years old. She fought to keep her expression free of her emotions but knew she hadn't completely succeeded by his next remark.

"Look, don't turn this into some kind of Greek tragedy. I'm glad Holly got adopted. The adoption gave her a chance for a better life. I've never felt resentful of that."

"Did . . . did you grow up in an orphanage, then?" Even the word made her shudder as images of Oliver Twist flashed through her mind.

"Foster homes," he said. Seeing her expression, he added, "Hey, come on, lighten up. It wasn't that bad. In fact, the last home I stayed in is the whole reason I'm a photographer today." A fond smile tipped his lips. "When I was twelve, I was sent to live with a photographer and his wife. Gus and Peggy were great. They were older and childless, and they took a shine to me. And when Gus saw how interested I was in what he did for a living, he started teaching me."

Amy smiled. That was better. His childhood had had *some* happy moments.

"This is getting boring, talking about me," he said. "Let's talk about you for a while. Where you went to school, and what you do for fun, and do you like to dance?"

"I went to St. John's High School, U.T. for my bachelor's degree, and the University of St. Thomas for my master's," she said, ticking the items off on her fingers. "I love to paint and draw, of course, and I like to read, swim, and walk. I adore movies and listening to forties music. And I *love* to dance! How about you?" Amy was already picturing them doing some romantic dance like the tango.

"I can't dance," Sam said sheepishly.

"Then why'd you ask me if I liked to?"

"The conversation was getting too maudlin."

All the bleakness had left his eyes, which Amy was glad to see. She chuckled. "Why dancing?"

"I've always wished I knew how to dance," he admitted. "It's my one failing."

If anyone else had said that, Amy would have thought how egotistical they were, but when Sam said it, it just made her want to smile. "Oh, really? Your one failing, huh?" His grin reminded her of some of her most mischievous and irresistible students. "Would you like to remedy that?" she continued.

"Did you have something specific in mind?"

It was Amy's turn to grin, and she totally ignored the inner voice that said she shouldn't do anything rash, that this might need some more thought, that maybe she really was being dangerously foolish.

Instead she said, "Yes, I do. Let's go to my place, and I'll put on some dance music and you'll have your first lesson."

"Now who could refuse an invitation like that?"

Four

Every city has its enclave where the very wealthy live. In New York, it's the tightly secured buildings along Fifth and Park Avenues; in Los Angeles, it's Beverly Hills and Bel Air; and in Houston, it's River Oaks.

River Oaks. Oil barons and Italian barons. Astronauts and former movie stars. The famous and the infamous.

As Sam followed Amy's little white Miata down the broad expanse of River Oaks Boulevard, past the five-million-dollar mansions with their sculpted gardens, he wondered who her parents *were*. When she'd said River Oaks, Sam had envisioned one of the streets on the fringes, not this prime center location.

He couldn't suppress a low whistle as she turned on Inwood Drive, drove about half a block, then pulled into the driveway of an enormous red brick Georgian home. After stopping to punch in the code for the electronic security gate, she drove on through, and he was right behind her.

"Holy shit," he muttered. "These people have some bucks!" For a few seconds, he wondered what he was doing there. Then he told himself not to get weirded out just because he and Amy might as well have been born on different planets.

Still, this kind of money was a bit intimidating. But what the hell, he wasn't planning on marrying her, or anything. They were just having fun together. They'd go up to her apartment, and she'd try to teach him how to dance—finding out soon enough how hopeless that was—and then, if he got lucky . . .

He smiled wryly. *Forget it, Robbins.* He might have known her only a few hours, but he was smart enough to understand that Amy wasn't the kind of woman who'd jump into the sack with some guy she'd just met. Not only that, from what she'd told him about herself, she might as well be wearing one of those marriage/picket fences signs, too. No, this was probably a one-shot deal, and sex wasn't going to enter into the picture.

Amy's taillights vanished around the back of the house, and Sam followed. It wasn't fully dark. Instead, the day had faded into the hazy lavender of twilight, and the house and trees were inky silhouettes against the muted sky. For the second time that day, Sam's fingers itched for his camera.

A four-car garage, partially obscured by dozens of huge leafy trees, loomed ahead. Amy opened the door at the far right with an automatic opener and pulled inside.

Sam parked his Corvette behind her. He didn't want to block anyone in, although the main house was dark except for outside lights flanking the front and back doors and lining the flowerbeds.

"Well, this is it," Amy said, walking toward him.

Sam looked around. The grounds of the estate seemed to go on forever, and the house was huge. "Good Lord, Amy, what does your father *do?* Own an oil company or something?"

She smiled. "No. Nothing like that. He's a heart surgeon."

It took Sam several seconds before comprehension dawned. He stared at her. "Is your father Dr. Alan Carpenter?"

"Yes."

Her father was world famous. Like Michael De-Bakey and Denton Cooley, Alan Carpenter was a pioneer in open-heart surgery and had perfected several techniques that he had demonstrated all over the world. He had operated on kings and Saudi princes, famous actresses and ex-presidents. Dr. Alan Carpenter! Jesus H. Christ. No wonder Amy was such a class act.

Good thing you have no serious intentions toward her, isn't it, Robbins? 'Cause you wouldn't stand a snowball's chance in hell . . .

"Do you mind if I collect my parents' mail before we go up to my apartment?" she asked, beginning to walk around to the front of the house, motioning for Sam to follow. "They're in Europe right now," she explained, "and part of my deal with them is that I take care of the house and mail and stuff while they're gone. They travel a lot."

Sam nodded, still a bit dazed by his discovery of Amy's identity.

After gathering the mail, they walked back to the garage, and Sam saw that there were outside steps leading up to the apartment.

"Come on," she said. "Let's go up."

When they reached the top, he realized that there was a wooden deck on the second level that appeared to go around three sides of the garage, although it was getting too dark to really see. He hadn't noticed the deck at first because when you stood at the bottom, the trees hid it from view. "This is nice. Like living in a treehouse."

He followed her inside, and as she snapped on lights, he looked around with pleasure. Even though he prided himself on the fact that he could be ready to go anywhere in an hour and could carry all of his important worldly possessions in a backpack and his camera bags, it didn't mean he couldn't appreciate a place like Amy's.

The main living area of the apartment had few interior walls that he could see. The different areas were defined by the placement of furniture and the judicious use of screens as well as a low counter that separated the kitchen from the living area. He noted the highly polished wood floors, the brightly colored rugs scattered about, the proliferation of wicker and light oak furniture, and the dozens of plants of every description and variety.

He noticed other things, too: speakers mounted in four different places high on the ceilings, hundreds of books overflowing two bookcases, a sturdy-looking easel in the far corner, and standing next to it, a tacklebox that looked as if it were filled with tubes of paint.

There were also cats, three of them: one sitting on top of the coffee table, one perched on the windowsill, and the third curled up against the cushions of a green and white striped sofa.

Sam walked over and petted the one on the coffee table, a salmon-colored long-haired beauty with huge topaz eyes.

"That's Delilah," Amy said, tossing her parents' mail on a rosewood bachelor's chest to the right of the doorway where it joined an already large mound.

Delilah purred and stretched, leaning into his hand.

"I think she likes me," he said.

Amy rolled her eyes. "Typical female," she murmured. "Stick a good-looking guy in front of her, and she's putty."

Sam grinned. "What's the black one's name?" He looked at the cat on the windowsill.

"That's Sheba. Isn't she beautiful? I got her at the shelter."

Sheba stared at Sam, then turned back to face the window, which reflected her haughty image.

"She *doesn't* like me."

Amy chuckled. "She doesn't like anyone."

"Not even you?"

"She tolerates me."

Amy took off her beret and tossed it at the big calico lying on the couch. "Hey, Elvis, move your fat rump off that couch. You know I don't allow you up there!"

The calico stretched lazily, then stood, arched his back, and lightly hopped down. He walked away slowly, his head and tail up in the air.

"Guess he told you," Sam said.

Amy laughed. "Honestly. They run the household."

"Yeah, I know."

"Do you have cats? No, of course, you don't. You're traveling all the time."

"I used to have a dog, but I had to find him another home."

Because she looked as if she felt bad for him, he said, "I get to see him all the time, though, because he lives with my best friend. So it's *almost* like having a dog of my own."

"What kind of dog is he?"

"Major is part Lab, but mostly Heinz 57 . . . like me."

"The very best kind," Amy said softly. Her eyes met his, and there was something about their expression that caused Sam's breath to catch.

For a long moment, nothing stirred except the current of emotion crackling between them.

Jesus, Sam thought. What's going on here? His throat felt suddenly dry.

Amy was the first one to look away. "Do you mind if I check my messages?" she said.

"No, go ahead."

She headed toward the telephone on the bar. Sam watched her. She walked like a dancer, sort of bouncing on the balls of her feet. She'd probably had years of ballet lessons, along with everything else that money could buy. He thought about his own childhood: about every spare penny going to feed his mother's drug habit. About all the times they wouldn't have eaten if not for the soup kitchen at the mission a couple of blocks away from their seedy apartment and his skill at panhandling . . . and other things.

Amy punched a button on her answering machine, and after a few beeps, a woman's slightly nasal voice said: *Hey, Amy, where are you? I thought we were supposed to go see that new Michael Douglas movie tonight. Call me when you get home.* The machine clicked off.

"Oh, no," Amy said, "I completely forgot . . . Lark's going to kill me." She turned, grimacing. "I've got to call her. I'm sorry."

"Hey, go ahead. I don't mind. I'll just sit here and pet Delilah. Or do you want me to go outside and give you some privacy?"

"No, of course not. I'll just be a minute."

Sam sat on the couch and reached toward the cat who still perched on the coffee table. He liked cats. His favorite animals to photograph were the big cats, especially tigers. They were so beautiful and sleek and strong. So completely sure they were superior beings. They walked as if they owned the earth.

"Hello, Lark?" Amy was saying behind him. "I know, I know, I'm sorry. I . . . well, I just forgot. I went out to dinner." Her voice lowered. "I *know,* Lark. I *said* I was sorry. Look, can I call you tomorrow?" There was silence for a few seconds, then, "Well, this isn't a good time for me to talk. I've got someone here."

Sam tried not to listen, but it was impossible not to. Because he was afraid she might be embarrassed, he got up and sauntered toward the easel. There was a painting in progress—a fairly faithful reproduction of a snapshot that was clipped to the top of the easel. Each portrayed three young women with their arms around each other. One of the women was Amy. The other two were a blonde who was a few inches taller than Amy, and an even taller woman with light brown hair. All three were dressed in shorts and T-shirts and were laughing as if they hadn't a care in the world.

The painting was nice but showed no spectacular talent. Amy had been honest rather than modest when she'd said she was primarily a teacher and not an artist. He wondered who the other two women were—was one of them the woman named Lark who Amy was still trying to appease?

Amy wrapped up her conversation and walked over to where he stood. "I'm really sorry about that." She inclined her head toward the phone and made a face. "Lark's my best friend, and normally she doesn't get mad easily, but she's really ticked off right now. I don't usually do things like that. I honestly don't know how I could have forgotten about her."

It was kind of ego-boosting to think that he'd been the cause of Amy's uncharacteristic lapse. Certainly, from the moment he'd laid eyes on *her*, just about everything else had been wiped from *his* mind. "It was my killer charm that did it," he said, trying to lighten her mood. "You just couldn't resist me."

She laughed, but he could see that some of the sparkle had disappeared from her eyes. Maybe he should go. "Do you want me to leave? You don't have to feel obligated to—"

"No, please, Sam, it's okay. This isn't your fault. I just feel bad. I've always hated those women who forget all about their girlfriends when a guy appears on the horizon, and I never thought I'd be one of them."

"Don't you think you're being a little hard on yourself? If this Lark is really your best friend, she'll get over being mad."

She nodded. "You're right. She *will* get over it. I'm just mad at myself, that's all."

"Speaking of your friend, is she one of the people in this painting?"

Amy smiled. "Yes. Lark's the one with the blond hair and . . ." Her eyes softened. ". . . The other one is Courtney Slavin . . ." She swallowed, her smile turning bittersweet. "Courtney and Lark and I . . . we all started out in kindergarten together. We became best friends, inseparable. Our mothers called us the three musketeers." Without warning, her eyes filled with tears and her lower lip trembled. "God,

I'm sorry. I—it's been two years. You'd think I'd be over it by now."

Sam touched her shoulder. "What happened?"

A tear rolled down her cheek, and she brushed it away. "Courtney died two years ago. She had breast cancer. Can you imagine? Only twenty-five years old, and she died of breast cancer! It was so awful. Her sister Christine, who was three years older, died of breast cancer, too, four years before."

"Jesus . . ." Sam didn't know what to say.

She sniffed and wiped her eyes again. "I'm sorry. I didn't mean to get emotional about it. It's just that sometimes . . . sometimes I think life can be so unfair. Courtney . . . she was so alive . . . so beautiful and so talented . . . she played the flute, and she had such a promising future . . . and then . . . just like that . . . she was gone."

Sam nodded. Sometimes things happened that way. He'd long ago given up trying to figure out why.

"I miss her a lot," Amy said. She seemed to have herself under control now. Her voice was steadier. "She and Lark were like the sisters I never had." She smiled. "Lark still is." She rolled her eyes. "But she won't be for long if I keep forgetting she exists."

"Send her some flowers tomorrow. She'll forget all about being mad." Flowers were Sam's solution to everything, as one disgruntled ex-lover had once said.

"That's a good idea. Now," she added brightly, "I *did* promise you a dance lesson, didn't I?" She walked over to a light oak entertainment center that divided the living area from the dining area and slid open one of the doors, exposing a rack of CDs. After sorting through them, she selected several, then opened another section and inserted the CDs into a player. The push of a few buttons started the unit, and within moments, music filled the air.

"I thought we'd start with a foxtrot," she said, smiling. "It's the easiest dance to learn." She held out her arms.

"I'm warning you. This is about all I know. How to hold a woman when you dance," Sam said.

"At least you know that much."

She felt good in his arms, even though she was shorter than he usually preferred. Her head only came up to his chin, but that was okay, he decided. Her body felt surprisingly strong, the back muscles firm under his palm. Her fragile air was deceptive, he was beginning to discover.

"Okay, now, here's the basic step. One . . . two . . . one and two." She demonstrated, moving to her left on the count of one, then to the right, then nudging him forward while she took two backward steps. She continued to count, and at first, he felt awkward and his steps were too big, but within minutes he got the hang of it, and soon they were circling the room.

"You're doing well," she said, looking up.

"I can't believe I'm really dancing."

Her smile was infectious. "It's fun, isn't it?"

"Yes." What was the most fun, though, was holding her like this. Feeling her body up against his, feeling the firmness of her breasts and her legs. Smelling the light flowery scent she wore and the faint trace of lemon in her hair. He wanted to draw her even closer, tuck her head under his chin, and slow down their steps, but he knew that kind of thinking was dangerous. Yeah, sure, he could probably seduce her, if he pushed it, but he wouldn't like himself very much if he did. Amy was obviously one of those women who played for keeps.

They danced for a long time. One song segued into another. Most of the tunes were old ones. Sam recognized a lot of them because Peg, his best foster mother, had loved music from the thirties and forties and played it all the time. He even knew the words to many of the songs and started singing to "Nevertheless."

"You *know* this music?" Amy said, drawing back so she could see his face.

"Uh huh." He told her about Peg.

Amy's smile was filled with delight. "You're the first man I've ever known who actually knew this music."

After that, they sang along together. Her voice was a true contralto and blended nicely with his baritone. They sang "Nevertheless" and "You'll Never Know" and "I'm in the Mood for Love" and dozens of others. Twice Amy changed CDs. Sam knew it was getting late and he should be going, because the longer he stayed, the more dangerously and foolishly attracted to Amy he became.

As a song finished, Sam reluctantly said, "You're probably getting tired; I should go."

"No, I'm not tired at all. I could dance all night." She moved closer, and Sam's breath caught. A new song began, and Amy smiled up into his eyes.

He sang along with her, caught in the spell woven by the romantic music and the warm, enchanting woman in his arms.

Instead of dancing, they swayed together, bodies close, gazes connecting. Sam's heart beat faster. Something was happening here. Something exciting. Something scary. Something dangerous.

They sang the rest of the song, Amy letting Sam carry the melody while she sang soft harmony, their voices weaving together perfectly.

The song ended.

They stopped swaying and looked deep into each other's eyes.

Amy's eyes were filled with something potent, something that Sam no longer had the will to resist. He lowered his head and she raised her face simultaneously.

Their lips met. Softly at first. A kiss of exploration.

She made a sound, halfway between a sigh and a moan, her breath soft and sweet.

Sam's arms tightened around her, and he deepened the kiss, feeling an immediate response from her.

His last coherent thought was, *Oh, boy, am I in deep shit now.*

Five

Amy had often wondered if there was something wrong with her—if she was frigid—because sex had never given her the kind of satisfaction other women claimed to get from it.

Now, thanks to Sam, she knew she wasn't.

As Sam kissed her, every nerve ending quivered, every part of her strained toward him. She twined her arms around his neck and pressed close to him. All thought disappeared, leaving only primal urges and stripped-bare defenses.

She wanted him.

The knowledge ripped through her. She wanted him in ways she had never believed possible.

The kiss went on for a long time. One kiss became two, two became three. They must have come up for air, but if so, Amy wasn't aware of it. Afterward she would never know what had caused her to suddenly begin to think again—to realize that if they were going to stop, she must be the one to say so. Otherwise, the only place these kisses would end was Amy's big bed.

That realization gave her the strength to do what she knew she must. The next step was too serious to take without some thought to the consequences.

Heart thundering, she regretfully pulled away. "Sam, I'm sorry, but things are going too fast for me."

He looked as stunned as she felt. He pushed his hair back from his forehead and frowned in bewilderment. "Jesus, Amy," he muttered. "I never intended to hit on you."

"I know you didn't," she said softly.

They stood awkwardly for a few seconds, evading each other's eyes. Now that they were no longer kissing, Amy felt confused and embarrassed. Her actions tonight were so unlike her.

"I think I'd better go," Sam said. His voice sounded rough.

"Yes." Amy desperately wanted to see him again. She *had* to see him again. She slowly met his gaze. "Sam—"

"Amy—"

They spoke simultaneously. Both broke off and laughed self-consciously.

"You go first," he said.

"No. You go first," she said.

"Okay. I, uh, I had a great time tonight."

"Me, too."

He hesitated, and her heart fell. He wasn't going to say anything about seeing her again.

"I'll call you tomorrow," he finally said.

Her heart soared. "I'd like that."

Silence fell between them once more. Amy knew he wanted to kiss her again, but she was afraid if he did, he would never leave. She wasn't sure she had the strength to resist this powerful force a second time.

But he seemed to understand how she felt, or maybe he felt the same way. He leaned over, gave her a light kiss on the cheek, and said, "I'd better get going."

Amy walked outside with him and stood on the deck as he lightly ran down the stairs. There was a full moon, and it illuminated the grounds below, silvering everything it touched. Stars studded the jet-black night, and all around her night creatures stirred while a chorus of cicadas provided background music. Amy breathed in the warm, scented air and thought about how even the most ordinary sounds and sights were magical tonight.

When Sam reached the bottom of the stairs, he turned and looked up. He raised his hand in farewell, eyes gleaming in the moonlight.

Amy smiled and raised her hand in return.

And then he did something that caused her to stop breathing. He began to whistle the opening lines to "Always," the notes pure and clear and completely unmistakable.

In that instant, Amy knew she'd been right. He might not know it yet, but this man was her destiny.

At midnight, Justin decided to call it a night. Although all his friends, except Sam, were at Jessie's party, Justin wasn't enjoying their company the way he normally would.

He felt restless and dissatisfied. He looked around. Everyone else seemed to be having a wonderful time, drinking and eating, laughing and talking, dancing and flirting. One couple was necking in the corner. Hootie and the Blowfish blared from Jessie's CD player. Yeah, everyone except him was having a blast.

Justin kept remembering the gleam in Sam's eye as he'd told him he'd met someone new. At this very moment, after a single date, Sam was probably in the woman's bed, having charmed the pants off her in just hours.

How did Sam do it? Okay, he was good-looking. And he could talk to women effortlessly. But he certainly didn't offer them what they all—Justin's sisters included—professed to want: a steady, stable, serious relationship that would lead to permanent commitment.

And yet any woman Sam had ever wanted he had easily conquered.

Justin couldn't understand it. He would never understand it. And for some reason, tonight he felt vaguely resentful of Sam's prowess.

"Hey, big brother, why so pensive?"

Justin turned, smiling down at Jessie. Of all his sisters, she was his favorite. She looked nice tonight—her short black tank dress complementing her dark hair, fair skin, and blue eyes. For probably the thousandth time, Justin wondered why some guy hadn't snapped Jessie up long before now. "I don't know. I was just thinking."

"About what?"

"Things. Sam."

At the mention of Sam, the brightness in her eyes dimmed slightly. "Where *did* the great adventurer go tonight?" she asked, her voice studiedly light and casual.

"He had a date."

Jessie nodded, looking away.

Silence fell between them.

"Jess . . ."

Slowly her eyes met his.

"Sam's not the settling-down kind. He never will be."

Her smile was wry. "Don't you think I know that?"

"Than why . . . ?"

"Why?" She laughed, but the sound was hollow and forced. "Why does anyone fall for someone who doesn't know they're alive? Because we're idiots, that's why!"

She looked away again, but not before Justin caught the sheen of tears in her eyes.

He squeezed her shoulder. "Let's go outside. The noise in here is getting to me."

Wordlessly, they walked out to the front of her town house, which was one of sixteen that formed a U around a central park-like area studded with tall oaks and carefully tended flower beds. The sweet smell of jasmine filled the humid air. They sat on her moonlit front stoop, and Justin put his arm around her.

"Sam's crazy," he said softly.

"Uh huh."

"He *is*. He'd be damned lucky to get you. Any man would be damned lucky to get you."

"Yeah, sure." She sniffled, brushing her hand against her eyes.

Justin could feel the tremor snaking through her. "C'mon, Jess. This isn't good. You've got to forget about him."

"I know, but saying it is easier than doing it. I just . . . I don't know . . . from the moment I met him, I couldn't seem to help myself." She bowed her head. "I'm okay when he's away. I hardly think about him, in fact. But then he comes home again, and I just fall apart. I-I'm so hopelessly in love with him."

At that moment, Justin wanted to strangle Sam. He knew it wasn't Sam's fault that he wasn't interested in Jessie, but it didn't make any difference. Jessie was hurting, big time, and Sam was the cause of that pain.

"I'm like you," she said. "Neither one of us gives his heart lightly. And when we do, it's tough to reclaim it."

She was referring to the one time he'd been seriously in love, his senior year in college. Marilyn had been everything he'd ever looked for in a woman: smart, pretty, generous, warm-hearted. After one date, he'd fallen hard.

Unfortunately, she hadn't returned his feelings. She'd tried, he knew she'd tried. But after they'd been seeing each other a couple of months, she told him she thought it would be better if they stopped. "I like you, Justin," she'd said gently. "I like you a lot, but I don't feel, you know, *that* way about you."

It had taken him nearly a year to get over her. It had been one of the bleakest years of his life. He had confided his feelings to no one except Jessie.

"My brain knows that until I let go of Sam, I'll never be able to fall in love with someone else, and I'm trying, I really am," she continued. "If only he *would* get serious about someone. If I knew for sure that he was not available—" She broke off, sat up a little, and squared her shoulders. "Enough of this. I'm just feeling sorry for myself. Wishing for something I can't have." She turned her gaze to him. "What about you? You dating anyone?"

"Nope." He chuckled. "I'm too picky, that's my problem. The women I meet—if they like me, I don't like them."

"It'll happen; just be patient. The right person will come along."

"I hope she hurries. I'm not getting any younger."

"Oh, that's true, you're a real old fogy."

They both laughed, and Justin was relieved to see that Jessie had pulled herself together. "Listen, Jess, I think I'm going to take off. Do you mind?"

"No, you go ahead. I'll see you tomorrow. And Justin? Thanks for listening."

"Any time," he said, kissing her cheek. "Any time at all."

All the way home, Justin thought about his conversation with Jessie. He was still thinking about it when he unlocked his back door and walked into the kitchen. Major, who'd been sleeping right next to the door, stretched and gave Justin a lazy "Woof" in greeting.

Justin couldn't help comparing the almost-offhanded welcome to the wild joy the dog had exhibited earlier today when Sam had come.

He shook his head in half-amusement, half-annoyance. *I've had the goddamned dog for nearly seven years, taken care of him when he was sick, fed him, petted him, been here through thick and thin, and he still likes Sam best!*

There was a lesson there somewhere.

Amy couldn't sleep. She was dying to talk to Lark or her mother. But it was too late to call Lark, and she certainly wasn't going to call her mother in Brussels.

Yet she *needed* to talk. She needed to tell someone she trusted about the amazing thing that had happened to her today.

After tossing around for an hour, she got up, showered, dressed, and headed for her easel. Although painting by artificial light wasn't nearly as satisfactory as painting by natural light, she could do it. Painting soothed her. When she felt stressed or worried about anything, picking up her paintbrush and losing herself in a painting always calmed her. She'd tried to describe the feeling to her mother once, but it was hard to put into words. The best she'd been able to come up with was, "It's like being enveloped in a soft, pink cloud. Everything else fades away, and I feel at peace."

Amy painted until 6, then finally stood, stretched, and touched her toes a few times to loosen her cramped muscles. She put on a pot of coffee and while it was brewing, changed into shorts and a T-shirt and her Reeboks. When the coffee was ready, she took a cup out to the deck and watched the sunrise and listened to the birds. By seven she had headed out for a walk.

As she walked the quiet neighborhood streets, she thought about Sam and everything they'd said and done the previous night. Even the memory of the kisses they'd shared was enough to send a plume of heat curling into her belly. Maybe it would be safest if she didn't think about the kisses, especially since she knew it wouldn't be wise to rush into a relationship with him. But oh, she wanted to. She wanted to more than she'd wanted anything in a long, long time.

Still thinking about Sam, at 8 o'clock, she turned toward home. As she climbed the steps to her apartment, she could hear the phone ringing. Maybe it was Sam. She raced up the remaining steps. "Oh, damn! Don't hang up!" Fumbling with her key, she finally got it inserted in the lock and opened the door.

Once she was inside, she made a final mad dash

toward the phone and yanked up the receiver. "H'lo." She was breathing hard.

"Amy?"

"Mom!" *You idiot. Of course, Sam wouldn't call you this early* . . .

"Is something wrong? You sound funny."

"No, no. I'm just out of breath. I was out walking and ran up the steps when I heard the phone."

Amy chuckled, mentally shaking her head at her mother's needless concern. "I'm fine. In fact, I'm great! And I'm so glad you called. I really wanted to talk to you. I've met this terrific guy and . . well, I couldn't wait to tell you about him."

"Oh? Now, that sounds important."

Amy smiled. "Yes. Very important."

"Well, come on, tell me. Who is he, and how did you meet him?"

Amy explained, ending with, "And it all happened just the way you said it had happened with you and Dad. I took one look and I just knew Sam was the one. I couldn't say this to many people, because it would sound silly, but I knew *you'd* understand."

"Well, yes, I do, but—"

"But what?"

Her mother sighed. "Just be careful, darling, won't you? Don't jump into anything. Give it some time. Get to know him before . . . well, you know . . ."

Amy frowned. "I'm not sure I understand. Haven't you been saying I'd know when I found the right man?"

"Yes, darling, but your father and I were introduced by mutual friends. I already knew about his family and his background. It was *safe* for me to fall in love so quickly. It's a little different in this case, don't you think? You really don't know this young man at all, and I don't want you to be hurt."

"There's no need to worry. Sam wouldn't hurt me."

Her mother sighed again. "I'm sorry, Amy. Perhaps he's every bit as wonderful as you think he is. Just promise me you'll be careful."

Amy started to say she wasn't a child. She started to say she was perfectly capable of making her own decisions and that she wasn't gullible or stupid. She was smarting from her mother's lack of confidence in her judgment and confused by Faith's about-face.

But she said none of these things. Her mother loved her. She had Amy's best interest at heart. *Besides,* said a tiny part of Amy's brain, *she could be right.* Pushing away the traitorous thought, Amy said, "Don't worry. I'll be careful. Now, tell me about your trip. How's Brussels? Did Dad knock 'em dead?"

For the rest of the conversation, Faith recounted their itinerary of the past week, and Amy passed on several messages that she'd received on her parents' behalf. Just before they said goodbye, her mother said, "Are you seeing this young man again today?"

"I think so. He's going to call me later."

"And how long will he be in Houston?"

Her mother's question was sobering. Amy had been trying not to think about the fact that Sam would be leaving again, probably fairly soon, and might be gone for weeks or even months. She had no idea how long an assignment might take. He had talked a little about his work, but he hadn't described any specific assignment in detail. "I'm not sure," she finally said.

"I see," was all her mother said in return.

That *I see* said a lot, though, Amy mused, as she hung up the phone. An awful lot.

She was still thinking about her mother's cryptic comment when she finally reached Lark later that morning. "You still mad at me?" she said, after Lark gave her a sleepy "hello."

"Totally pissed," Lark mumbled.

Amy grimaced. "Seriously?"

Lark said something else unintelligible, then more succinctly, "No, I'm not mad at you anymore. However, I do need a strong jolt of caffeine before I can talk with my usual scintillating wit and intelligence. So how 'bout if I go get some coffee, then call you back?"

Amy smiled. "Even better, why don't you roll out of bed and throw on some clothes and come over here? I'll have coffee and breakfast waiting for you."

"You got a deal."

Twenty-five minutes later, Lark's hot pink Amigo pulled into the driveway.

"So what's for breakfast?" she said, as Amy greeted her from the top of the steps. "Sackcloth and ashes?"

Amy grinned. "Would you settle for French toast and bacon?"

"Honey, I'd *kill* for French toast and bacon!"

The two young women hugged as Lark reached the deck. Amy grinned again as she took in Lark's appearance. Her short, blunt-cut blond hair looked like it had been struck by a tornado, and her white shorts and red T-shirt were so wrinkled, it was obvious she'd probably plucked them out of a laundry basket where they might have been sitting for days. She wore no makeup, and her feet were shoved into well-worn sandals.

Lark was a flight attendant for Continental, and on the job she was meticulously groomed, efficient, and organized. At home she was a complete and utter slob, the exact opposite of Amy. She was proud of being a slob, too. She reveled in it. Once, when Amy had asked her how she could stand living in such clutter, she'd said, "It's friendlier that way," and oddly, Amy had understood what she meant.

They went inside, and Amy poured Lark a mugful of coffee while she cut up fresh strawberries and put the French toast in the skillet. The smell of bacon, cooked and being kept warm in the microwave, permeated the kitchen.

"C'mon, tell me about him," Lark said, perching on one of Amy's barstools. Her large gray eyes were bright with curiosity. "He must be something, to make you forget about me."

"He's wonderful," Amy said softly.

Lark raised her eyebrows. "Wonderful, eh? Wow. How'd you meet him? What does he look like? Spare no details." Lark grinned, the tiny gap between her two front teeth giving her an impish look.

For the second time that morning, Amy talked about Sam. By the time she'd finished, breakfast was ready, and they sat down at Amy's round table. "I know it sounds corny," Amy finished, meeting Lark's gaze and gearing herself for her friend's teasing, "but it . . . it was love at first sight. He's the one, Lark. I just know it."

But Lark didn't return her smile, and for a long moment, she didn't answer, either. She took another bite of her French toast, chewed it slowly, and thoughtfully studied Amy's face. "Did you sleep with him?"

"*Lark!*"

"Well, *did* you?"

"No."

"Good."

Amy shook her head. "You know, even though

we've been friends forever, and I think I know you better than anyone, you continually surprise me."

Lark paused with her fork in midair. "What? You thought I would've encouraged you to have sex with some guy you'd just met?"

"Well, you're always telling me what I need is a good, you know . . ."

"Fuck, Amy. The word is fuck," Lark said dryly. "And the fires of hell will not leap out to get you if you say it." Lark put down her fork. "And, yeah, I do think you need to get laid, but that doesn't mean I think you should do something stupid."

"*You've* gone to bed with a guy on a first date," Amy pointed out.

"Yeah, but I'm different. I'm tough, and you're not. I don't expect hearts and flowers and engagement rings, and you do. I go into things with my eyes open, and you wear rose-colored glasses."

Amy had no answer for Lark's logic, because she knew her friend was right.

"You see things the way you think they should be," Lark continued softly, "the way you *want* them to be, and I see things the way they are."

"Maybe that's true, but sometimes you just have to trust your heart."

"Amy, listen to me. What do you know about this guy, anyway? Just what he told you, right? Well, maybe he's the slickest con artist on the face of the earth."

"He's not!" Amy protested. "I *know* he's not."

"Fine. Okay, let's forget about that for now. Let's say he's everything he said he was, completely honest. Even so, he's obviously a here-today, gone-to-morrow type. I m an, hell, Amy, look at what he does for a living! The guy's constantly on the go, traveling all over the world."

"People can change," Amy said stubbornly, trying not to think about Sam's words. *I have itchy feet. I like the adventure, the excitement, the risks . . .*

Lark sighed. "Maybe. But they usually don't."

"You're so cynical." Amy didn't want to have doubts. She didn't want to think about her mother's warning and now Lark's.

"Listen, if you'd had a mother who'd been married three times and a stepfather who put the moves on you one night when your mother was out playing bridge with her buddies, and you spent most of your working life saying 'thanks, but no thanks' to married fly-boys who forget they're married the moment they say goodbye to the little woman, you'd be cynical, too."

Amy couldn't think of anything to say in response. She knew she'd led a sheltered life compared to Lark, but she refused to believe the worst about people.

"Just be careful, will you?" Lark said. "If you want to go out with him again, fine, have fun. If you want to have sex with him, fine." She grinned. "Have even more fun." Then the grin faded. "Just don't give this guy your heart until you're sure he won't trample on it, okay?"

"God, you sound just like my mother."

"Don't try to change the subject."

"Okay, okay, I'll be careful," Amy agreed, but inside, she knew it was too late. It didn't matter what her mother had said. It didn't matter what Lark had said. And it didn't even matter what Sam had said.

Amy had already lost her heart to him.

Six

Sam picked up the phone at least six times Sunday morning, then replaced the receiver without making a call. The last time, he banged the receiver down, saying "Shit" under his breath.

He'd never been in this kind of dilemma before—wanting to call a woman, wanting to see her again, yet knowing it would be a mistake. Usually, when he met someone he knew wasn't his kind of woman, he just steered clear of her.

Amy was different.

Amy was everything he knew he should avoid. In addition to being the marrying kind, she was a wide-eyed innocent. He reminded himself that even if she hadn't been the type to expect more than he was capable of delivering, he didn't mess with any woman who didn't know the score. He wanted no scenes and no broken hearts when he walked away.

Do the right thing. Stay away from her, no matter how much you'd like to see her again. You can't afford to get involved. Remember, everything you decided about Jessie applies to Amy.

But he kept thinking about her. He hated that she would think he was a complete jerk, after say-

ing he'd call and then not calling. Ah, hell, so what
if she did? Except for his ego, did it really matter
what Amy thought? Wasn't it better that she *would*
think he was a jerk? That way, she'd be angry for
a while, then she'd forget all about him.

He kept telling himself all this as he got ready
to go to Justin's for Sunday dinner, and by the time
he pulled into the driveway of the big old house
in the Heights, he had almost succeeded in con-
vincing himself that as far as Amy was concerned,
he'd done the only thing he could do.

"Sam!" Claire Malone, Justin's mother, gave him
an exuberant hug and a kiss on the cheek. "It's
wonderful to see you again." She pulled back to
study him. "You look terrific, as usual. Come on
in. The kids are all back on the sun porch." Her
blue eyes shone with pleasure and her smile was
wide and welcoming.

Claire Malone was the woman Sam would have
picked if he'd been able to choose his mother. Intelligent, honest, generous, and loving, she was
everything a woman should be.

He smiled down at her. "How's my favorite girl?
Did you miss me?"

She laughed. "Flatterer! *Of course* I missed you.
We *all* did." She linked her arm with his and led
him to the glassed-in sun porch that ran the entire
width of the house and overlooked the tree-filled
backyard. A chorus of voices greeted him as they
crossed the threshold.

Sam shook hands with Stephen, Justin's younger
brother, said hello to Lisa, Stephen's wife, and patted the head of Ryan, their two-year-old, whose face
lit up as he cried, "Tham!"

"Hey, slugger, how's it going?"

Then Sam turned his attention to Justin's sisters.

"Hey, Susan, looking good . . . how're the wedding plans coming?"

Susan flushed with pleasure.

"Hey, Katie, I hear you made the dean's list. Congrats."

Katie grinned, and they exchanged high fives.

"Good to see you again, Win," he said to Winston McNally, Susan's fiancé, who returned his greeting with a pleasant smile and handshake.

The last person he acknowledged was Jessie. "Sorry I missed your party last night, Jess."

"It was a good one," she said lightly, but her blue eyes lingered on him as he accepted a beer from Justin.

The conversation moved at a lively pace, with Susan resuming a story she'd been in the middle of recounting when Sam arrived. He sipped his beer, listened, and watched. Every time he was with Justin's family, he marveled at how much they looked alike. All five siblings had thick, wavy hair, almost black, and the brilliant blue eyes of their mother.

"Sure and they've got the map of Ireland stamped on their faces," Claire had once laughingly said in the Irish brogue she could effortlessly affect.

Sam wondered what it would be like to have a heritage you could trace back hundreds of years. He didn't have a clue about his own. All his mother had ever told him was that her father had been a coal miner, a brutal man who'd beaten her mother "just for the hell of it."

"When I turned sixteen, he started on me," she'd added, her brown eyes turning hard. "And that's when I decided I wasn't stickin' around to be his next punching bag."

She had escaped her West Virginia home as soon

as she could scrape together enough money for her bus ticket. Sam wasn't even sure if Robbins was really her name. He suspected she might have changed it.

"So, Sam, you home for a while now?" Stephen asked.

Sam shrugged. "Yeah, I'm taking some vacation."

"Sam and I may go to Wyoming to do some fly fishing," Justin said.

"Really? You lucky dog," Stephen said.

Lisa poked him in the ribs. "Don't act like you never go anywhere."

"I don't. I'm completely henpecked."

"I'll give you henpecked," Lisa said, but her remark lacked bite. She pretended to swat at her husband, and Stephen laughed.

The good-natured talk flowed effortlessly. Sam continually marveled at the way the Malones actually liked each other and liked being together. Even Winston, who wasn't officially a part of the clan yet, had blended in perfectly.

After a while, they all moved inside to the dining room. As always, dinner was excellent. Claire was a good cook, and she enjoyed cooking for her family. Sam stuffed himself on roast pork, oven-fried potatoes, salad, corn, and fresh green beans. He traveled so much that he could never get enough of good home cooking.

When he finally settled back, sated, he saw that Jessie had been watching him. There was an expression of longing on her face that she quickly masked. He felt a sharp stab of guilt, even though he had nothing to feel guilty about. He'd never led Jessie on. He'd never even *dated* Jessie, for crying out loud. The most they'd ever done was dance together when a bunch of them had gone out to the clubs, and once Sam had driven her home early from a party because she hadn't been feeling well.

For some reason, the guilt about what he didn't feel for Jessie segued into the guilt he couldn't completely banish because of his treatment of Amy.

Jesus! Forget about Amy.

"You're awfully quiet today, Sam," Katie said. "Tell us about Alaska. Is it true there are about ten guys there for every girl?"

Sam smiled. Katie was a favorite of his. She was more light-hearted than Justin and Jessie, and smarter and more interesting than Susan and Stephen. He had a feeling Katie would probably break a few hearts in her lifetime. "I'm not sure about the exact ratio."

"Hmmm, maybe I should transfer up there," Katie said.

Jessie rolled her eyes. "Is that all you ever think about—guys?"

"What else is there?" Katie countered, smiling mischievously at Sam. "And don't pretend you *don't* think about guys, because I know you do."

"Oh, you don't know *anything*," Jessie said.

"Oh, yeah? Well, I know you're hung up on somebody, because I heard you and Susan talking one day."

"You're crazy, Katie." Jessie's protest sounded strained, and she avoided meeting anyone's eyes.

"Oh, c'mon, quit pretending. Tell us who he is and when we're going to meet him," Katie pressed.

Two bright spots of color rode high on Jessie's cheeks. "I am not hung up on anybody."

Sam squirmed uncomfortably.

Susan darted a look in Sam's direction.

"Oh, no?" Katie continued, laughing, teasing,

completely oblivious to the undercurrents. "Then why is your face red?"

"Katie . . ." Claire said warningly.

"Did I tell you that Jennifer is going to be able to come to the wedding, after all?" Susan broke in. She gave Katie a dirty look.

"What did *I* do?" Katie said.

Sam decided life would be a lot simpler if he swore off women completely.

Amy hung around the apartment all day, but Sam didn't call.

At first, she made excuses. Something must have come up. Something unavoidable. He would call her when he got back. Probably this evening.

But evening came and went without a call. By 10 o'clock, she knew there wasn't going to be one.

She couldn't understand it. She couldn't have misinterpreted what had happened between them the previous night. She knew he wanted to see her again.

Then why hadn't he called?

She couldn't sleep. She kept thinking about him, wondering why she hadn't heard from him.

On Monday she was scheduled to work at the shelter again. Before she left for work, she changed her answering machine message. Instead of the usual "I can't take your call just now, please leave a message," she recorded, "I can be reached at . . ." and left the number of the shelter.

All day long, every time the phone at the shelter rang, she held her breath, sure it was Sam.

It never was.

She rushed home, even though she had planned to go to Texas Art Supply and restock her dwindling store of watercolors. She told herself he hadn't wanted to call her at work, that there would be a message for her at home instead.

There wasn't.

Very near tears, she wondered what she could do. Normally, in a situation like this, she would simply blow the guy off. She had no use for men who said one thing and did another. But this was not a normal situation. Down deep, she knew something had happened. Something that had kept Sam from calling her.

She bit her bottom lip, blinking furiously. She wouldn't cry. She would *think!* She simply *had* to see him again. That's all there was to it. She wasn't willing to let him go without some kind of effort, because what had started between them yesterday was too special.

They were meant to be together . . . she knew it.

Okay, so what are you going to do about it?

She toyed with the idea of calling him. She even went so far as to look up his number in the telephone directory, then replace the directory without writing the number down.

No. Telephone calls could be so unsatisfactory. She wanted to see him. To see the expression on his face and in his eyes. If he was giving her the brush-off, she would force him to do it in person.

The thought that he might be caused an ache in her chest and those stupid tears to well again.

You're being ridiculous. You know that, don't you? You just met this guy. He can't possibly mean that much to you already.

But he did! He did.

Her mother and Lark had been right to caution her against jumping into anything, but where Sam was concerned, Amy could no more stop the way she felt about him than she could stop breathing.

They were meant to be. And if he didn't yet realize it, she would have to show him.

She absently petted Delilah, who had jumped up on the kitchen table and was rubbing against her. But before she did anything, she needed to figure out why he hadn't called her. Was he afraid? From the way he'd talked at dinner the other night, she sensed he wasn't a person who would trust others easily. Growing up the way he had, she was sure he'd be wary of close relationships.

Was that it?

Was he scared of getting close to her? Scared of allowing himself to care? Did the emotions unleashed between them Saturday night frighten him off?

Amy looked at the clock. It was only 7 o'clock. Abruptly she stood. If she wanted him, she was going to have to take the initiative. Her decision made, she headed for her bedroom and her closet.

Her whole future rested on this encounter. She wanted to look her best.

Sam prowled restlessly around his apartment most of the day Monday. He couldn't seem to settle down to anything. He kept thinking about Amy. Maybe he should at least call her and . . . and what? Tell her he was sorry? Tell her it just wouldn't work out? She'd probably think he was a conceited jerk who attached a hell of a lot more importance to himself than she did. What was the big deal, anyway? All they'd done was kiss. For all he knew, she hadn't given him a thought since.

Forget about her, Robbins. She's trouble . . . go to Wyoming instead . . .

After stewing most of the day, he made up his mind. What the hell. The trip would do triple duty—take his mind off the problem at work, force him to relax, and get him away from Amy and the temptation to call her.

He would call Justin and tell him. He had just punched in the telephone number when his doorbell rang. "Now what?" he muttered, slamming the phone down. He was getting damned tired of these door-to-door solicitors. His apartment complex had a big sign posted at the entrance, but these sales types just ignored it.

He strode over to the front door and yanked it open. "Look, I'm not inter—" He broke off, momentarily speechless. "Amy?"

"Hello, Sam." She didn't smile.

He ran his fingers distractedly through his hair, completely disconcerted. She looked unbelievably sexy and desirable in a short red sundress and strappy red sandals that showed off narrow, graceful feet and red-tipped toes. Her hair, instead of being tied back, the way it had been on Saturday, drifted around her bare shoulders in a glorious, shining cloud.

Desire—unwanted, unbidden—leaped to life. He willed himself to ignore it. "This is a surprise."

"I know. I had to talk to you," she said.

"Okay. Uh, c'mon in." As she brushed past him, her scent filled his head, and the desire to touch her was so strong he clenched his fists. "You want a Coke, or something? A beer?"

"No, nothing."

Sam scooped up the magazines and clothes and books littering his brown leather sofa and cleared a space for her to sit. He sat on the arm of the only other chair in the room as she perched on the edge of the sofa.

She looked at him for a long moment, her green eyes huge and luminous. "Why didn't you call me, Sam?" she finally asked in a quiet, steady voice.

Her directness disconcerted him, but he struggled not to reveal it. He shrugged. "No real reason. I just got busy." Jesus, but he felt like a jerk.

"Busy," she repeated.

"Yeah, look, I'm sorry. I meant to call you, but you know how it is . . ."

"No," she said slowly, "I guess I don't know how it is." She swallowed. "I—I thought you liked me. I thought we had something special going. But I guess I was wrong."

Her composure had slipped, and Sam saw an unmistakable glint of hurt in her eyes. Something constricted in his chest. More than anything, he wanted to get up and take her into his arms. He wanted to slide his fingers into that thick, shining hair that fell so appealingly around her face and onto her shoulders. He wanted to taste again the warmth of that sweet, soft mouth. He wanted to nuzzle his face into the hollow of her throat and inhale the fresh, flowery fragrance she wore. The urge to do all these things . . . and more . . . was so powerful, he almost couldn't withstand it.

Yet somehow he did.

Somehow he hardened his heart. *No way.* No matter how much he wanted to, he couldn't. Indulging his desire to be with her, to make love to her, would only hurt her more in the long run. Better to make this a clean, swift break. She'd get over it . . . and so would he.

"I do like you, Amy," he said softly. "We had a

great time Saturday night. But I've been doing some thinking since then, and I, well, I don't think it's going to work out. You're just not my type."

She regarded him steadily. "I don't believe you."

He laughed nervously. "I'm sorry, but it's the truth."

"You're saying you're not attracted to me?" Her eyes, which had looked so luminous and soft before, were suddenly fired with angry glints. "Is that what you're saying?

He wet his lips. "I, uh . . ."

Abruptly she stood. Then, taking him completely off guard, she walked over to him, put her arms around him, and lowered her mouth to his.

At the first touch of her tongue, every good resolution he'd had went flying out the window. He groaned and crushed her to him. They tumbled back onto the big chair. The kiss was open and wet and hungry. And once he started kissing her, he couldn't seem to stop. His hands seemed to have a life of their own.

He kissed her again and again, running his hands over her body, lifting the hem of her dress and cupping her tight little bottom. When he slipped one hand between her legs, she gasped. The sound galvanized him. He reached for the zipper on the back of her dress, and she responded by tugging his shirt out of the waistband of his pants.

He knew he should stop. He knew this was madness. Complete madness. But trying to stop what had begun between them was like trying to stop a tornado with your bare hands.

He managed to tug the sundress down, exposing her bare breasts. His heart pounded as he filled his hands with them. They were small and perfect.

She moaned when he took one nipple into his mouth, drawing on it.

From then on, Sam was completely lost.

Their lovemaking was swift and urgent. There was no subtle foreplay, no slow building of desire. The desire was there, full blown, raging between them like an out-of-control forest fire.

There was also no rational thought. All Sam knew was that he wanted this woman. He wanted her more than he'd ever wanted any woman before.

Before long, the chair they were in was too uncomfortable and unaccommodating, so Sam lifted her up and carried her into his bedroom. He laid her on the bed and shucked off his shorts, T-shirt, and briefs. Before he lowered himself beside her, some semblance of sanity made him ask, "Are you sure?"

"Oh, yes. I'm sure." She held out her arms.

Minutes later, he was thrusting deep inside her. In some part of himself, he wanted to slow down. He wanted to make this first time between them special. But his need was too intense. When he felt her spasm around him, crying out his name, he could no longer hold on. He exploded into her, and as the powerful sensations pummeled him, he knew they had started something that might be completely impossible to stop.

"It'll be better next time, I promise."

Amy smiled lazily. "So you've decided I'm your type, after all?" she teased. In all of her twenty-seven years, she had never felt this way. Making love with Sam was incredible. It was everything she had ever imagined it could be. *He* was everything

she'd ever imagined he could be. He was everything she'd ever wanted.

She sighed with happiness and deep contentment.

He cupped her left breast, rubbing the nipple
until it perked into a hard little nub. "Don't be a
smart ass."

"Why don't you show me right now?" she murmured.

"Show you what?"

"You know. How much better it can be." She
couldn't believe this was she, Amy Carpenter, talking this way. She'd never talked this way to a man
before. Of course, she'd never felt this way about
a man before. Totally shameless. She tightened her
arms around him, feeling the hard contours of his
back, the muscles moving beneath the surface of
the skin.

"Oh, I'll show you, all right." His mouth moved
slowly down her body as his fingers delved, finding
the exact spot that ached to be touched.

They didn't talk again for a long time.

Seven

For the next two weeks, Amy walked around in a dizzying haze. Years from now, she would look back on these magical days and nights and remember them as a perfect time.

Everything she did and saw and smelled and tasted and touched was clearer and brighter and richer and more intense. Her body was on sensory overload, and she reveled in it.

She and Sam spent every moment they could together. After that first night in Sam's apartment, where they'd awakened the following morning to no food in the refrigerator and barely enough coffee to brew a pot, they'd spent most of their time at Amy's place. Gradually, Sam's belongings had appeared. His bathrobe joined her bathrobe on the hook at the back of the bathroom door. His toothbrush and shaving supplies joined her toothbrush and cosmetics on the bathroom vanity. His clothes and his camera equipment joined her clothes and her art supplies in the closets and cupboards.

They couldn't seem to get enough of each other. He would no sooner walk in the door than they were tearing off their clothes and heading for her bed. Sometimes they didn't even make it to the bed. Sam joked about it, saying, "we've got to stop doing this on the floor, it's killing my back."

Amy was deeply in love . . . so in love that it almost hurt to look at Sam. Even hearing his whistle as he came up the stairs outside could make her knees go weak and her chest tighten.

Sam hadn't said he loved her, but Amy knew what he felt down deep, even if he didn't yet. She also knew he would eventually realize what his feelings for her were . . . and then he would say the words.

She could wait.

In the meantime, she would just enjoy being with him, laughing and talking and making love.

They had so much fun together.

They went to movies and ate hot dogs dripping with mustard and huge bags of buttered popcorn, then came back to her apartment and shed their clothes and slipped into her bed, where they whispered and laughed and made unhurried love.

They swam naked in the moonlight in the backyard pool and made love standing up in the warm water. Amy liked it so much, she wanted to do it again and again.

They went to Astroworld one day and rode every single roller coaster and stuffed themselves on junk food and stayed late to watch the fireworks.

One night they got all dressed up—it was the first time Amy saw Sam in a suit, and she couldn't believe how handsome he looked—and went to Brennan's. They sat at a window table and drank wine and ate turtle soup and warm spinach salad and baked red snapper stuffed with crabmeat and tiny shrimp and finished off the enormous meal with the best crème brulée Amy had ever tasted. Afterward they came back to her apartment and put on some of her forties music and danced close together until they couldn't stand it anymore, then they went into her bedroom and slowly undressed each other and made love.

On Friday of their first week together, they drove to New Orleans, where they stayed in one of the small, luxurious hotels in the Quarter. That first night, they sat outside on their tiny balcony and absorbed the decadent charm of the city. Amy had been to New Orleans before, many times, but that night she saw the city through new eyes. There was something elemental and darkly sensual about the atmosphere, something she knew would add another dimension to their lovemaking that night.

On Saturday they walked the narrow streets—Bourbon and Royal and Chartres and St. Peter's. They gazed into shop windows and bought junk souvenirs and a poster of Jackson Square that Amy just had to have. They drank hurricanes at Pat O'Brien's and listened to jazz at Preservation Hall. They rode the trolley out to the Garden District and ate oyster po'boys and jambalaya. They danced at Tippitino's and Amy laughed so hard she got the hiccups. They ended the night at the Café Du-Monde where they gorged themselves on warm beignets and chicory-laden coffee.

Sunday morning they went to Mass at the St. Louis Cathedral. Amy wasn't Catholic, but Sam was.

"Well, I was baptized a Catholic, but I don't go to church much," he said, grinning down at her. "Sure you want to go?"

"Yes." At that moment she'd have followed him anywhere.

They talked about everything and anything. They discovered they both liked to read thrillers. Sam was amused. "I'd've pegged you for romance novels," he said. "Or poetry. Yeah, highbrow poetry."

"What a chauvinist remark!" Amy said, trying to maintain a stern expression, but not succeeding very well. "Although I do like poetry. Especially Emily Dickinson."

"Figures." But he smiled when he said it.

Amy tried to get Sam to talk about his childhood, but he always changed the subject, and she didn't push him. She figured when he was ready to tell her, he would. He loved hearing about her childhood, though, and asked her dozens of questions.

"Were you lonely as a kid?" he asked one night after they'd watched a couple of rented movies, shared a pizza, and made love.

Amy shook her head. "I always wanted a brother or sister, but I was never *lonely*. I pretended my dolls were people. What about you? Were you lonely?"

He didn't answer for a long moment, just lay staring at the ceiling with his arms crossed behind his head. "Yeah, I was lonely."

Amy longed to put her arms around him, yet knew that in moments like these, he'd reject any overture that hinted at pity. She vowed he would never be lonely again. She would fill up every empty place in his heart, and gradually, he'd forget about those long ago days of his childhood.

One night, he did talk about Gus and Peggy, the foster parents who had made such a difference in his life. "They were hippies in the sixties, anti-Vietnam, peace marchers, the whole bit," he said, "and even though it was the late seventies when I lived with them, they were still kind of out of the mainstream."

"Tell me about them."

"Gus is a photographer, mainly of portraits. He's

retired now, but back then he specialized in children. He was great with them, too. Probably because he has a kind of Santa Claus look about him—you know, hearty laugh, twinkly eyes, bushy hair and beard."

Amy could tell by the fond smile on Sam's face that he had related to Gus in the same way the other children had. "What about his wife?"

"Peggy? She's great, too, but in a different way. She's one of those tall, thin women who always have a tan and a cigarette dangling from their mouths. She wore Mexican dresses and sandals and long turquoise earrings and she was a writer—still is, I guess. I don't think she's ever made much money writing, but she'd find these odd people and she'd write about them. Once in a while she sold her stories to local papers and magazines." He grinned. "She wrote a story about me once."

"She did? Did it ever get published?"

He nodded.

"Do you have a copy of it? I'd love to read it."

"Somewhere. I'm not sure where."

"What was it about her that you liked so much?"

He turned to look at her, his gold-flecked eyes thoughtful. "You know how most people love to talk? Well, Peggy was just the opposite. She loved to listen." After a moment, he reached over and curled a lock of Amy's hair around his finger. "You're like that, too. It's one of the things I like best about you."

Tenderness flooded Amy. In that moment, she wanted so much to tell him she loved him, but she knew she couldn't . . . not yet. He wasn't ready. Instead, she wrapped her arms around him, and soon she was lost in his kisses.

* * *

The only discordant note in the idyllic days was the return of Glenn Wilhelm. He called within hours of arriving in Houston after a three-week trip to his hometown in Idaho.

"Oh, hi, Glenn," Amy said, wishing she hadn't been such a coward earlier in the summer when she'd first realized she wasn't interested in pursuing the relationship. "You're back. Did you have a good trip?"

"It was great, but I sure missed you."

Amy grimaced.

"I can't wait to see you," he continued. "Can I come over tonight?"

"I'm sorry, Glenn, but I have plans."

"Oh. That's okay. How about tomorrow night?"

"Um, Glenn? I . . ." She closed her eyes. She knew she shouldn't be doing this over the phone, but she also knew it wasn't fair to let him go on thinking they had any kind of future together. "Listen, something's happened while you were gone. I . . . I've met someone."

"You've met someone?" he echoed.

"Yes."

He was silent so long, she began to wonder if he was still there. Finally she said, "Glenn, I'm sorry. I—" Oh, shoot. Why was she apologizing? There had been nothing between them. They'd only dated a few times. It wasn't like they were going together or anything.

"I guess I'll see you when school starts," he finally said, his voice strained.

"Glenn . . ." She started to say she was sorry again, then stopped. She was just making things worse.

After she hung up the phone, she could've kicked herself. Surely she could have handled that better than she had. She stewed over the conversation for a while, but then Sam called, and soon everything else was driven from her mind.

Sam knew he was playing with fire. He also knew that eventually, someone was going to get burned—and that he should do something about it. Yet each day, no matter what his good intentions had been, he did nothing to clarify his relationship with Amy.

He couldn't.

When he was away from her, he'd think, today I'll tell her we have to cool it. I'll tell her I'm just not the settling-down kind. And then he would see her—eyes filled with happiness, smile lighting her face, soft lips parted in a "hello" kiss, and he'd forget all about his intentions. All he wanted was to take her into his arms and make love to her.

When Sam made love to Amy, he felt things he'd never felt before. Things that scared the hell out of him. Things he wasn't sure what to do about.

One day, while Amy was working her regular shift at the pet shelter, Sam and Justin had lunch together. Suddenly, surprising even himself, Sam said, "You ever been in love, Justin?"

Justin nodded and told Sam about a girl he'd met in college. "Why'd you ask? Don't tell me you've fallen for someone!"

Sam shrugged.

"Well, *have* you?" Justin pressed.

"Ah, forget it. I don't know why I asked."

Justin grinned. "I can't believe it. You *are* in love. Hallelujah, praise the Lord. Sam Robbins, love-'em-and-leave-'em Robbins, break-their-hearts-and-hear-them-cry Robbins, is in *love*. Miracles *do* happen."

"Will you wipe that shit-eating grin off your face?"

Justin laughed. "Sorry. I can't help it. I never thought I'd see the day. So who is she?"

"It's that girl . . . you know . . . the one I met at the shelter. Her name's Amy. Amy Carpenter."

"Well, c'mon, tell me about her."

So Sam did. "I don't know what to do," he said, when he'd finished.

"You've only got two choices. Marry her, or break it off for good."

That night, long after Amy had fallen asleep in his arms, Sam thought about Justin's words. *Marry her or break it off for good.* Black or white. Justin was right. No wonder Sam had been unable to tell Amy they needed to cool it. Cooling it wasn't an option. Cooling it was in a gray zone, a zone Amy would never accept.

He knew he had to decide, and soon, because if he chose to break it off completely, the longer he waited, the harder it would be.

And not just for Amy.

On Wednesday of her second week with Sam, during a telephone conversation with Lark, Lark said, "Amy, are you *sure* you know what you're doing?"

"I've never been surer of anything."

There was an audible sigh. "So when am I going to meet him?"

Amy felt a twinge of guilt. She'd neglected Lark shamelessly the past ten days. "How about tonight? We'll all go out for Mexican food."

"Sure you don't want to ask Sam if he minds first?"

"Of course not. We'll meet you at Serafina's."

* * *

Lark looked different than she had looked in the now-completed painting sitting on Amy's easel. It was more than just a different hairstyle, Sam decided. She had some harder edges than she'd had when she was younger. You could see them in her eyes and mouth, sense them in her no-nonsense handshake and don't-mess-with-me stance.

Her get-up shouted her independence and disdain for anyone's opinion: faded and patched cut-offs paired with heavy black boots studded with silver and a skin-tight black tank top that clearly defined her nipples. Her blond hair stuck up every which way and her big silver earrings were mismatched. One lobe sported a huge starburst, the other a long dangle of fruit.

In contrast, Amy wore a neatly pressed pair of white walking shorts, a dark green silk blouse, and white sandals. Her hair was swept back with a white headband.

Lark gave Sam a long, assessing look as they were introduced.

"Do I pass inspection?" he said lightly.

Her smile was challenging. "The jury's still out."

Amy rolled her eyes. "Don't mind Lark. For some reason, she thinks she needs to protect me."

"Somebody has to," Lark said.

"Oh, Lark . . ." Amy gave Sam a conspiratorial smile.

Sam didn't blame Lark for having reservations about him. She obviously cared about Amy. They'd been friends most of their lives. He was an unknown quantity. In her shoes, he'd be wary, too.

They ordered margaritas. When their waitress left to fill their orders, Lark said to Sam, "Amy tells me you're a photographer for *World of Nature* and that you just got back from Alaska."

"Yes."

She reached for a chip. "So you're between assignments right now?"

"No, I'm on vacation."

"Oh." She chewed thoughtfully. "A long vacation?"

"Kind of. Four weeks. I report back to work the tenth of August."

"And then you'll get another assignment."

He smiled. "Yes."

"Where will it be, do you know?"

"No. Not yet." He avoided Amy's eyes. They had studiously steered clear of this subject. "It could be anywhere."

"How long do the assignments generally last?" Lark said.

"Two, three weeks. Sometimes longer."

"That long." She looked at Amy. "Boy, and I thought I traveled a lot, but at least I'm only gone a few days at a stretch."

"Lark's a flight attendant," Amy said.

"Traveling for longer periods of time is actually easier," Sam said. He refused to let Lark's questions irritate him. In fact, they amused him. She was acting like a surrogate parent. Perhaps, in the absence of Amy's own parents, she felt she needed to.

"Easier on you, maybe," Lark said, giving Amy another pointed look.

Sam thought it might be better to let that comment pass without an answer. Until he had made his decision about the future—and whether he wanted it to include Amy—he wouldn't be drawn into this kind of discussion.

"Sam and I went to Rockefeller's the other night

and saw Asleep at the Wheel," Amy said, in a bright voice that was an obvious ploy to change the subject. "They were great."

Lark smiled and continued nibbling at chips. She took a long swallow of her margarita, her large gray eyes meeting Sam's over the rim of her glass. "You haven't met Amy's parents yet, have you?"

"No."

"They won't be home until a week from Monday," Amy said.

"I'm looking forward to meeting them," Sam lied. He wasn't looking forward to meeting them at all. He was sure the Carpenters would not be happy about his association with Amy—another complication if he wanted to make their relationship more permanent.

As if she'd read his mind, Amy said softly, "My parents'll be crazy about you." Under the table, her hand crept over to squeeze his leg.

He smiled down at her. Amy. She was a complete romantic. She saw things as she wanted them to be. It was one of the things he liked most about her— that trust and unbridled optimism. Sometimes, when he was with her, he even began to believe in the basic goodness of people. Unfortunately, the very qualities that made her so refreshingly appealing were also the ones that made it difficult to get her to face reality . . . or to prepare for trouble.

For a while, the talk turned to more impersonal topics, and Sam was grateful for the reprieve. He leaned back against the leather booth and listened to the two women, interjecting a comment now and then. They discussed the current heat wave, agreeing that they were already sick of summer, though it was only the third week of July; Lark's job and how much she hated it, and the career change she was considering; a mutual friend and her marriage woes; and two current movies.

Their waitress came and they ordered another round of margaritas. Their food was served, and they ate and continued to talk casually.

Amy asked about Lark's mother.

"The bloom has worn off the rose," Lark said.

"So soon?" Amy said.

"Yeah, well, you know my mother." Lark looked at Sam. "Mother's working on her third marriage, and I don't think this one is going to 'take' any better than the first two." Her smile was wry. "Trouble is, she has lousy judgment. She goes for the type with killer charm and movie-star good looks, instead of the type with staying power." Her eyes met Sam's coolly.

Despite the fact he'd decided he was amused by her self-appointed role as Amy's protectress, Sam was beginning to get a little pissed off by Lark's relentless jabs. He stared back, and was gratified when she was the first one to look away.

After they'd finished their dinner, Amy said, "I'm going to the ladies'." She looked at Lark.

"I don't need to," Lark said. When Amy was out of earshot, she said, "She's terrific, isn't she?"

"I think so."

Her gaze pinned him. "Tell me something, Sam, are you serious about her, or are you just screwing around?"

He didn't answer for a long moment. When he did, his voice was even, his temper under tight control. "I don't think my relationship with Amy is any of your business."

"Well, I'm making it my business. See, the thing is, I love Amy. She's special. Really special. And she's also the best friend I have in the world. I don't want to see her get hurt."

The control slipped a notch. "And you think I do?"

"I don't have any idea whether you do or not. I do know, though, what kind of life you lead, and I don't think it's conducive to happily-ever-after."

"You don't know anything about me," he said stiffly.

"That's why I asked if you were serious about her."

Their gazes locked. "I care about Amy," he hedged.

"Good. Glad to hear it."

She didn't look glad. Her expression said she didn't trust him a bit, that she classified him in the same category as the men her mother had married.

Hell, maybe Lark was right. He wasn't sure he had staying power, either. Right now, he wasn't sure of anything.

"I just want to say one last thing, Sam," Lark said, "and it's this, if you *do* hurt Amy, you'll be sorry."

Amy wondered what Lark and Sam were talking about while she was in the ladies' room, but later, when they were alone, he didn't say anything, and she didn't ask. All he said was, "Has Lark always been like that?"

"Like what?"

"You know—tough. Cynical."

"She's always been tough. When we were little, she used to get in fights with boys all the time." Amy smiled, remembering. "But the cynical part, that's been a slow, steady kind of thing that started when her parents were divorced."

"Hit her hard, huh?"

"I didn't think so at the time. She acted as if she didn't care, but looking back, I can see that she did."

"How old was she?"

"We were fourteen."

"Parents can really screw up their kids," Sam said.

"Yes. The older I get, the more I realize what wonderful parents I have." She snuggled closer to him.

In answer, he just put his arms around her and kissed her lightly. "And they produced a wonderful daughter."

The day before Amy's parents were scheduled to return, Amy went through their house, making sure the maid had given it a thorough cleaning and that everything smelled fresh and welcoming. Once she was satisfied that it looked the way it should, she turned her attention to her own apartment.

She decided it might be a good idea to put away anything that screamed out Sam's presence. After all, her parents would find out soon enough that he spent most nights with her, but there was no sense rubbing their noses in it. They might be sophisticated and modern in many ways, but where she was concerned, they were still very old fashioned and traditional.

She felt ridiculously nervous. She couldn't imagine why. Her parents would adore Sam, she was sure of it.

But what if they don't?

She paused in the act of dusting. "Well, they'll just *have* to accept him," she said aloud, "because he's the one I want, and he's here to stay."

Eight

"I'll be glad to get home, won't you?"

Faith Cameron Carpenter smiled at her husband, who sat next to her aisle seat in first class. "You know I will. Three weeks is too long."

Alan had presented a paper in Brussels at the European Cardiac Surgeons' conference during the first week they were away, and because their thirty-eighth wedding anniversary fell the following week, they had decided to expand their trip to include Ireland and a visit to Faith's sister in Dublin and then France, where they'd spent their honeymoon. They'd had a wonderful time, but home was home. Faith was tired of living out of suitcases and eating rich food and sleeping in unfamiliar beds. Besides, she missed Amy.

That was the trouble with having only one child. A mother tended to obsess.

As if he'd read her mind, Alan said, "This new fella Amy's dating sounds serious."

"Yes, he does." Each time Faith had talked to Amy in the past two weeks, her daughter had seemed more and more in love.

"What's bothering you, darling? I thought you were eager for Amy to meet someone."

Faith gave her husband a sidelong look. He knew her so well. Even the slightest change in her tone of voice or the subtlest nuance alerted him to her feelings. It had always been this way. She sighed. "I know, but I'm not sure this young man is the *right* someone. However, I'm reserving judgment until I meet him."

"What is it about him that concerns you?"

"I don't know . . . a number of things, I guess."

"Like what?" Alan pressed.

"Well, he's apparently rootless, with no family to speak of. And God knows what kind of background." She met her husband's eyes. "I know this will make me sound like a snob, but I was hoping Amy would marry someone more like her. More like *us.*"

Alan frowned. "Marry? Is she talking about marrying him?"

"Not in so many words, but I know Amy. That's what she's thinking."

"But she hardly knows him."

"I know."

Alan lapsed into a thoughtful silence. Then he reached over and took her hand, giving it a gentle squeeze. "Don't worry, darling. Amy's not stupid. If she's fallen in love with this young man, he must have the right stuff. And if, for some reason, he doesn't, we'll talk to her. She's very sensible, you know."

Faith nodded and gave him a reassuring smile, but she knew how fast common sense could fly out the window when the heart was involved. Not to mention hormones. No, if Amy was set on marrying Sam Robbins, nothing she or Alan could say would make any difference. The best Faith could hope for now was that Sam was worthy of Amy's love . . . and that he returned it.

Amy waited impatiently just beyond the Customs checkpoint in the International Terminal at Intercontinental Airport. According to the arrival monitor, her parents' Air France flight should have landed by now. She kept her gaze trained on the double doors where the arriving passengers would emerge. There had been a steady trickle of incoming travelers, but she knew these were stragglers from a flight that had landed about fifteen minutes earlier.

She couldn't wait to see her parents, not only because she'd missed them, but because she was so excited about them meeting Sam. Not that the meeting would happen immediately. No, she and Sam had talked over breakfast this morning and decided that he would make himself scarce this afternoon. But tonight he would come over and they would all have dinner together at her parents' house.

Amy had already made all the preparations—putting together a chicken casserole and fixing a salad and buying fresh bread from the French Bakery. She'd also baked a banana cream pie—her father's favorite.

She'd laughed at herself when she'd realized what she was doing. She told herself her parents didn't need bribing. They would love Sam. But she'd made the pie, anyway.

"Come on, come on," she murmured. She hated waiting. It was such a monumental waste of time.

A few seconds later, the double doors burst open and dozens of people poured through. Amy stood on tiptoe and searched the faces. There they were! She waved, but they weren't looking in her direction. And then her father turned his head. Amy knew the moment he spied her, because his face lit up with a big smile and he said something to her mother. Then they were both waving at her.

Faith was the first one through Customs, and she and Amy hugged hard. As always, her mother smelled of Joy and the expensive English soap she favored. Amy smiled. Anyone else who'd just spent long hours traveling would smell tired and stale, but not Faith. She looked as lovely, as always, too—her dark blond hair smooth and perfectly styled in the short, breezy cut she'd worn the past few years, her makeup muted and impeccable, her clothing neat and attractive. No one looking at her would guess she was sixty-two years old. She could have passed for at least fifteen years younger.

"What're you laughing about?" Her mother's green eyes, the exact shade of Amy's, shone with gentle humor.

"You," Amy said happily. "You never change."

"Well, I'm certainly not going to change in just three weeks abroad."

"Where's a broad?" Amy's father said, giving them both a mock leer.

Faith laughed. "Alan!"

Amy grinned as her father bent down to envelope her in a bear hug.

"Hi, Sunshine," he said, using his childhood pet name for her.

Amy knew it was silly to get emotional, but she couldn't help it. There was a lump in her throat as she returned his hug. She loved both her parents, but her brilliant father, as tall and handsome at sixty-five as he'd been as a young man, was her hero. She adored him.

When, as a teenager, her girlfriends had complained about or made fun of their fathers, Amy had always remained silent. She had known her friends would not understand the way she felt; they would think she was a geek. Of all her friends, only Lark knew the depth of Amy's feelings for her father. Lark had once confessed that of all the differences between them, Amy's relationship with her father was the one thing Lark envied.

"We missed you," he said.

"I missed you, too," Amy said.

Faith watched as Alan and Amy embraced. She had always known her daughter harbored special feelings for her father, but that knowledge had never bothered Faith. On the contrary, she had always felt a deep satisfaction and contentment over Alan's and Amy's close relationship. It was comforting to know that if something should happen to her, Alan would have Amy.

Today, though, a shadow of concern clouded the pleasure she normally felt when she saw the love between her husband and her daughter. She knew the concern would not be erased until she had met Sam Robbins and assured herself that his advent into their family would not cause problems or upset their close-knit harmony.

Her worries niggled at the back of her mind all through the forty-minute drive from the airport. She was careful not to let Amy know she was worried, though, even as Amy bubbled over about Sam.

"He's coming over tonight," she said, her eyes shining. "We're all having dinner together."

Faith gave an inward moan. As eager as she was

to meet this young man, she wasn't sure she was up to it today.

"That's okay, isn't it?" Amy said, an anxious note in her voice.

"Of course," Alan said. He slanted a look at Faith. *Back me up,* it said.

"Well, I am a little tired from traveling, but yes, darling, of course it's okay," Faith said. "We're just as eager to meet him as you are to have us. I'll just squeeze in a nap before he comes."

In the flurry of unloading their luggage and getting it into the house, the subject of Sam was temporarily dropped. But once all the suitcases were carried upstairs and the three of them were in the kitchen—Alan leafing through the pile of waiting mail and Faith drinking a glass of cold water—Amy said, "Now, Dad, about tonight . . . I don't want you giving Sam the third degree, okay?"

Alan looked up and chuckled. "And why not? That's a father's job."

"Because I don't want Sam to feel uncomfortable. If there's something you want to know about him, ask me now."

Faith's concern deepened as she carefully studied Amy—the first chance she'd really had to do so. There was a radiance about her that practically shouted out how far Amy's relationship with Sam had progressed. If her daughter wasn't a woman who was deeply in love as well as completely and thoroughly fulfilled sexually, then her name wasn't Faith Cameron Carpenter.

"Okay," Alan said, with typical good nature. "Where's he from, who are his parents, how much money does he make, and are his intentions honorable?" He winked at Faith.

Amy grinned. "He's from San Diego originally,

but he's lived in Houston for eight years; his parents are dead—well, his mother is dead—Sam's not sure about his father; he makes a *lot* of money; and as far as his intentions go—we haven't discussed that subject yet." Her eyes softened. "But I'm not worried, and I don't want you two to worry, either."

Faith fought to keep her face free of her thoughts. "But you're serious about him, aren't you?"

"Yes." Amy met Faith's eyes, then turned to her father. "Please don't worry, Dad. I know Sam loves me. He's just cautious, that's all. He doesn't have the example of happily married parents, like I do, so he's a little leery of that kind of commitment. But he'll eventually want to get married. I know he will."

Faith told herself to quit borrowing trouble. Perhaps everything Amy believed was true. So she returned her daughter's smile and prayed that Amy was right and that Sam Robbins wouldn't let her down.

Sam wished he didn't feel as if he were a side of meat soon to be inspected by a government agent. He hoped Amy appreciated the lengths he'd gone to, getting ready for the meeting with her parents.

The first thing he'd done was shop for new clothes. Normally he just went to Banana Republic or Oshman's or the Gap. Today he'd gone to Dillard's and bought a pair of ridiculously expensive DKNY slacks in a soft shade of honey and a collarless dark brown Ralph Lauren shirt. He'd even sprung for a new pair of shoes—supple brown leather Gucci loafers that he sure hoped he'd have a reason to wear again.

Next he went to a salon in the Galleria and had his hair cut, and then—thinking, what the hell, might as well go the whole hog—he had a manicure, too. The entire time he was sitting at the manicurist's table, he hoped he wouldn't see anyone who knew him.

He was half amused, half disgusted with himself. Why was he going to so much trouble to make a good impression on Amy's parents? If they couldn't accept him as he was, then they weren't the kind of people he wanted to be around.

Sam drove to Amy's, arriving at exactly 7:30. The security gates were open, and he drove to the back, automatically parking behind the door where he knew Amy kept her Miata. It felt odd to walk around to the front of the big house instead of climbing the steps to Amy's apartment. And for the first time since he'd met Amy, he didn't whistle "Always," the song he'd come to think of as theirs.

Standing in front of the heavy double walnut doors that marked the entrance to the Carpenter home, Sam took a deep breath, told himself he had nothing to be nervous about, and rang the doorbell.

Amy opened the doors instantly, and he knew she'd been watching for him. As always, he experienced a little kick of pleasure as he smiled down at her. She looked beautiful in a softly flowered pink dress with a low scooped neck and full skirt. She smiled back and raised herself on tiptoe to kiss him. He held her close for a brief moment, inhaling the subtle mixture of fragrances that clung to her: wildflowers and jasmine and sunshine. He released her reluctantly.

"You look great," she said.

"So do you."

She took his hand. "Come on. My parents are in the living room."

As Sam entered the elegantly furnished room, the first person he saw was Amy's mother. Seated in a yellow silk wing chair near the marble fireplace, Faith Carpenter was the epitome of grace and beauty in a simple black dress and double rope of pearls. She had a smooth, barely lined face with classic bone structure. Her eyes were striking— large and luminous, and filled with intelligence. Her gaze stayed steadily on Sam's, and he had the unnerving feeling that she was probing deep, unearthing all of his secrets in the process.

Amy introduced them, smiling proudly. Faith smiled and held out her hand, but did not rise.

"Hello, Sam," she said. "I'm so happy to meet you." Her voice was cultured, soft, and carefully modulated. The thought flashed through Sam's mind that if he were to look the world over, he would never find a woman more unlike his own mother than Amy's mother.

"It's nice to meet you, too." Because she made him feel uneasy, he did what he always did in such situations: he turned on the charm, flashing her his hundred-watt smile, the one Claire Malone once said could charm even the wee people, who weren't easily beguiled.

Something flickered in the depths of Faith's eyes, but her expression revealed nothing except a pleasant welcome.

Then Amy turned to her father.

Sam's first impression of Alan Carpenter was that this was a man who would command attention and respect wherever he went. Even if Sam hadn't known the older man was an eminent cardiac surgeon, he would have known Alan was important.

Everything about him—his stature, his expression, his shrewd brown eyes, his clothing, his handshake—said this was a man who was confident of his place in the world.

Alan was thinking along the same lines as he shook Sam's hand. Although he'd decided to take a page from Faith's book and reserve judgment, he couldn't help being drawn to the boy. Sure, he was a bit on the cocky side, as evidenced by that brash smile he'd given Faith a few moments earlier, but he had a good, solid look about him, and he had a direct, honest gaze. Alan believed you could tell a lot about a man by his eyes.

"Nice to meet you, son," Alan said warmly.

"Thank you, sir. It's nice to meet you, too."

"We were just having a cocktail," Faith said. "Would you care for one?"

"Or you could have a beer," Amy interjected, looking at Sam with her heart in her eyes.

It almost hurt Alan to see that expression on her face. He wanted to tell her to be careful, to tread softly and slowly, but he knew she never would. Amy jumped into every situation with both feet—eagerly and joyously. She put everything on the line and expected everything in return. And she'd rarely been disappointed, because it was hard for anyone to resist her. Alan had seen even the most jaded and disagreeable people brought to their knees by the sorcery of Amy's personality.

Once Sam was settled on the turquoise brocade sofa with a Baccarat tumbler of scotch in his hand and Amy sitting next to him, there was a long moment of silence, then both Alan and Amy started talking at the same time.

"Tell Sam about your adventure in Dublin—" Amy began.

"So you work for *World of Nature*—" Alan began. They both broke off, laughing.

"Yes, sir," Sam said. "I've worked for them since moving to Houston."

"That's a class magazine." The boy must be good, because *World of Nature* could afford to be choosy. Amy was probably right . . . Sam probably *did* make a good living. "What kind of assignments have you had?"

As Sam talked about photo shoots in Alaska, Argentina, and the Everglades, Alan listened and studied the way Amy and Sam related to one another. He liked the way Sam unselfconsciously held Amy's hand. He also liked the way Sam smiled down at her when she occasionally interjected a comment. There was tenderness in his gaze, a look that said his feelings for her ran deep.

Alan tried to catch Faith's eye, but her gaze remained fixed on Sam.

After about thirty minutes, they headed for the dining room, where Elsa, the Carpenters' longtime maid, had been called in for duty.

Throughout Amy's excellent dinner, Alan continued to study and evaluate Sam. As the minutes ticked by, he felt more and more reassured. Several times, he exchanged glances with Faith, hoping that she, too, was being won over, but her eyes still contained a kernel of reserve. Well, she'd always been more cautious about people than he'd been. She'd come around, eventually; Alan was sure of it.

By the time Alan's favorite, banana cream pie, was served, most of his misgivings had disappeared.

"The pie's great," he said, smiling at Amy. "The whole meal was great."

"Yes, Amy, everything was wonderful," Faith said.

"Thanks." Her eyes twinkled with amusement as they met Sam's. "This is where I'm supposed to say I made everything from scratch and really impress you."

"I *am* impressed," Sam said. "My idea of cooking is opening a can of beans."

"I suppose," Faith said, "your rather nomadic lifestyle is the culprit, because I'd imagine an intelligent man like you could learn to do anything he wanted to. Just how often *are* you home, say, in any given month?"

Sam met her gaze squarely. "Depends. Sometimes I've had as long as two or three weeks between assignments. Sometimes only days."

"Only days . . . that must be hard on the men who are married . . ."

It didn't take a genius to see what Faith was driving at. With anyone else, Sam might have gotten his hackles up, but after all, this was Amy's mother. "I'm sure it is," he answered evenly, although the truth was, he hadn't thought about the subject much. Now he wondered how the married staffers—the ones who traveled a lot—*did* manage to keep their spouses happy and their marriages working.

Suddenly, Sam realized he had a lot more to think about than simply whether or not he wanted to marry Amy. He also needed to think about the way he lived and the work he did and whether he was willing to give it up or make compromises, because Faith's not-so-subtle message had clearly shown him that there was no way he could have both Amy and his current lifestyle.

Nine

"So how'd the big meeting go?" Lark asked the following day. She and Amy were having lunch at a favorite sandwich shop in the Montrose area. When the weather was cool, they always asked for one of the sidewalk tables, but today the temperature was hovering at a hundred degrees, so they sat inside.

"Wonderful," Amy said. "Dad really liked Sam. Of course, I knew *he* would. And Mother, well, I think she likes him, but you know her. She's more cautious where I'm concerned." She smiled fondly. "Dad tends to indulge me."

"No kidding," Lark said dryly. She wondered what the Carpenters really thought. Knowing Amy's parents—especially Faith—Lark was sure they had as many reservations about Sam Robbins as she did. Probably more. How could they not? Despite the fact that he was good-looking, charming and intelligent, he still wasn't in Amy's league.

Most important, Lark had a gut feeling about him. No matter what he'd said the other night at Serafina's, she was sure he would eventually let Amy down. People couldn't just change their natures. They might change their behavior temporarily, but eventually they went right back to being who they were. "So where's this relationship going? You two talk about anything yet?"

"No, not yet."

Amy's complacency frustrated Lark. Sometimes she wanted to shake Amy. Lark knew it was futile, but she wished that just this once Amy would at least *think* about the possibility that things might not turn out the way she wanted them to. At least then, if Sam took off the way Lark expected he would, Amy wouldn't be completely blindsided.

"Quit worrying about me, Lark," Amy said. About to say something else, she stopped as their waiter approached with their food.

As soon as the man left, Lark said, "I know what you're going to say. You're a grown woman, you can make your own decisions, you don't need me or your parents or anyone else hovering over you. I *know* all that."

"So stop, okay? It's all going to be *fine*. You'll see. Now," Amy continued brightly, "tell me about your date Saturday night. How was it?"

Lark rolled her eyes. "Awful. I swear, I'm never going on another fixed-up date again. Never."

"That's what you said the last time," Amy pointed out. She took a small bite of her chicken salad.

"I know, but I mean it this time." Lark ground fresh pepper onto her omelet before sampling it.

"What was so awful about it?"

"What wasn't? He was one of those I've-done-everything-and-I-know-everything guys—you know the type. Anything you talk about, they've done it, only better."

Amy shook her head in silent commiseration.

"And you should have seen him when we got to my place. Suddenly he'd grown about six hands, which were everywhere. I finally wrestled him off me. Geez! I *hate* that. A guy takes you out for one lousy dinner and he thinks that gives him carte blanche to jump your bones. Or worse, he thinks he's so fucking irresistible you just can't *wait* for him to jump your bones!"

"Lark," Amy said mildly.

"I know, watch my language. But it's *true*, Amy. I don't know where all the nice, ordinary guys are. You know, the polite, sweet, considerate guys. The ones who don't even try to kiss you goodnight on a first date. That's the kind of guy I want to meet. Not these idiots who think every woman is sexually frustrated and hot to trot." Lark expelled a noisy sigh. "I want an old-fashioned Prince Charming, that's what I want—and honey, he doesn't exist."

"Yes, he does," Amy said, her eyes going all soft. "Sam's like that."

"Oh, shit," Lark said. "I'm sick of talking about men, especially when you're so gooey-eyed and impossible. Let's talk about something else. Have you seen the new Daniel Day-Lewis movie yet? Now *there's* a guy to die for . . ."

Two days after Sam met Amy's parents, he got a call from Owen Church, asking him to come to his office whenever he got a chance. It was Wednesday of the fourth week of Sam's vacation. At the summons, a quicksilver excitement raced through his veins. Maybe Owen was ready to give him a new assignment.

Sam called Jeanne, Owen's assistant, who said Owen had time to see him at 9 o'clock the following morning.

Promptly at 9 A.M. Sam presented himself.

Owen studied him for a few seconds before saying, "You look good, Sam. Rested. Relaxed."

Sam smiled. "I feel good."

Owen waved him to a chair. "You been thinking about our conversation?"

"Yes. I've been thinking about it a lot."

"Made any decisions?"

"Maybe." Sam hesitated. "One thing I do know is that I owe you an apology."

Owen's eyes widened slightly.

"You were right about me taking an unnecessary chance in Alaska. Trouble is, I don't know if I can change."

Owen studied him thoughtfully. "Let's put it this way, son. You *have* to change. If you don't, one of two things will happen. Either I'll have to fire you, or you'll get hurt . . . or worse . . . you won't live to tell about it."

Sam wanted to protest that Owen was exaggerating. Hell, he wasn't even sure he'd meant the apology, but he'd felt he had to offer it, or Owen might start giving some other shooter the best assignments. So he wisely kept his lip buttoned.

"What's it going to be?" Owen said. "You going to begin playing by the rules?"

"I'll do whatever I have to do to keep my job— you know that, Owen."

The older man smiled. "That's what I wanted to hear." He lifted a file from his desk. "What do you know about the snow leopards of the Himalayas?"

Sam's heart leaped. He was almost afraid to believe what Owen was saying. "I know that very few people have ever been able to get close enough to study them and that very few photographs have been taken of them."

"We've contracted with Ira Morgenstern to do a cover story on them."

Ira Morgenstern was a wildlife biologist, the best in the business. Sam had worked with him once, a couple of years ago, on a big cover story about wild-life in the rain forests of Suriname. It had been the kind of experience a man never forgot. Morgenstern was the consummate professional, but he was also more daring than most, certainly more daring than other scientific types Sam had worked with. His willingness to push the envelope had challenged Sam and helped him produce some of his best work.

"He's asked for you to be his photographer." Owen tapped his fingers against the manila folder. "This is the file containing Ira's preliminary research. I suggest you study it carefully tonight and see if you want this job."

By now Sam could hardly contain his excitement. "Hell, Owen, I don't need to read the file to know I want the assignment. Any shooter worth his salt would want this assignment."

"This won't be an easy shoot," Owen warned.

Sam grinned. "So what's your point?"

Sam headed straight for Justin's office after leaving Owen's.

"Hey, look who's here," Justin said, looking up and grinning as Sam walked into the room. "I thought you were still on vacation."

"I am. I just came in to see Owen." Sam quickly told Justin about the new assignment. "Great, huh? This is the kind of shoot that comes along only once in a lifetime."

"When are you leaving?"

"As soon as Morgenstern can finish getting things

set up. Owen said it'll take a few weeks, but I expect to head out sometime around the middle of August." He grinned like an idiot, the elation he'd tried to contain in Owen's office spilling over, making him feel like shouting. "I'm in the mood to celebrate. Let's go to Treebeard's for lunch. My treat."

Justin moaned. "If I eat that much at lunch, I'll be falling asleep by three o'clock, and I can't afford to do that. I've got too much work with end-of-the-month ERs and billing. How about dinner instead?"

"Can't. I'm taking Amy to dinner—" Sam broke off. "But, hey, come with us. Amy won't mind." The thought of Amy sobered him momentarily. They still had not talked about the future, but now, with this assignment, Sam could no longer put it off.

Justin smiled. "I've been wondering if I'd ever get to meet her. Sure, I'd love to come."

"Good. Let's meet at Pappadeaux's about six-thirty, try to beat the crowd."

"Great."

"Uh, just one thing . . . don't say anything about this assignment of mine. I'd rather wait and tell Amy later, when we're alone."

"Sure," Justin said.

For some reason, Sam felt uncomfortable. There was nothing in Justin's steady blue gaze that was accusing, but Sam couldn't help feeling that Justin didn't approve of something.

As Sam left his office, Justin shook his head. Poor Amy. Justin knew exactly what was about to happen to her; he'd seen it happen dozens of times. Sam was getting ready to shake loose, and he'd probably do it tonight. No wonder he didn't want Justin to say anything about the Himalayan assignment. He didn't want to create a scene in the restaurant.

At least Justin wouldn't be a reluctant witness to the dumping scenario. Still, he couldn't help feeling sorry for the unknown woman. She had lasted longer than most of Sam's conquests, but Justin guessed that would be small comfort when she ended up in the same place.

Justin almost wished he weren't going tonight. His desire to meet Amy had had to do with the fact that he'd thought Sam might be getting serious this time—after all, Sam had passed up fly fishing for her and he'd all but admitted he thought he'd fallen in love with her—but down deep, Justin had known better.

Sam had only one real love: his work, which, translated, meant adventure, excitement, freedom. A serious relationship would impinge upon his freedom and curtail the adventure and excitement.

Jessie was lucky, Justin decided, as he turned his attention back to a report on second-quarter advertising revenues. Getting involved with Sam ultimately meant only one thing to a woman—a broken heart.

Justin had arrived at the popular Galleria-area restaurant early, but the parking lot was already full. To the admiration and envy of other wannabe restaurateurs, the Pappas family had the Midas touch. All their restaurants were highly successful, and Pappadeaux's, their Cajun seafood entry into Houston's fiercely competitive market, was no exception.

Most of the wrought-iron tables dotting the courtyard were already filled with casually dressed patrons of all ages. After putting his name on the waiting list, Justin walked back outside and looked around.

Spying an empty table near the back, he headed toward it.

The courtyard was a noisy place. Water splashed from a central fountain, Dixieland music blared from the loudspeakers mounted on the walls, and kids—sensing their parents wouldn't mind a little horseplay outside—giggled and chased each other.

Justin ordered a Bloody Mary and watched for Sam. A few minutes later, he spotted him and stood and waved. Sam grinned and headed for Justin's table.

Amy wasn't at all what Justin had expected. Sam generally went for tall blondes—the breezy California-girl type—the kind who, on the surface at least, knew the score.

Amy was completely different. And it wasn't just that she looked different. Justin could see the difference in her eyes, in her smile, in the way she looked at Sam, even in the way she talked.

He couldn't take his eyes off her. Sam introduced them, she said how happy she was to meet him—her soft, green eyes glowing as she met his gaze—and Justin said something back, but he had no idea what it was was because he was thunderstruck.

She was wonderful. She was perfect. She was exactly the kind of woman Justin had always dreamed of finding. No wonder Sam was acting so out of character. No wonder he'd thought he was in love. No wonder he was still seeing her, long past the point where he normally broke off a liaison.

She was also beautiful—not in a perfect cover-girl way, but in a fresh, girl-next-door way that was much more appealing.

After they were all seated, Amy turned her friendly gaze his way and said, "Sam tells me you two met when he was looking for a home for his dog. That's funny, isn't it? Because he and I met when he was looking for a home for a cat."

Justin answered her in a daze. And that's the way it was for the entire evening. The three of them talked and laughed and ate and drank, but Justin wasn't really conscious of any of it. He was on autopilot, functioning like a normal human being, but his mind and senses were totally captivated by her.

He kept trying to direct the conversation back to her. Sam hadn't told him much about her, and Justin wanted to know everything. He found his opportunity after Amy had asked him what he did at the magazine and he'd told her. "What do you do?" he asked.

"Me? I'm a teacher."

As Justin questioned her and Amy answered, Sam listened, amused. It was obvious to him that Justin was completely dazzled by Amy. But hell, that was no surprise. Why wouldn't he be? Amy was irresistible. She seemed to like Justin a lot, too, but then again, Amy liked everyone.

Watching her charm Justin, Sam felt a swell of pride. Any man would be proud to be with her . . . but she belonged to him.

She belonged to him.

In that instant, he knew there was no decision to make as far as Amy was concerned. The decision had been made for him.

She belonged to him. They belonged together.

Always.

That night, there was an intensity and depth to their lovemaking that frightened Amy, because she wasn't sure what it meant. She had been trying not to think about Sam's going away, but she knew he soon would be. His vacation was nearly over. Only two more days, and then he'd have a new assignment and he'd be gone.

She told herself it didn't matter. He'd be back. A temporary absence wouldn't change anything between them. He wasn't leaving her forever.

But as their lovemaking climaxed and he brought her to a shattering peak, Amy's response was tinged with desperation, and a silent prayer ran through her mind even as she shuddered in the throes of passion. And afterward, as she lay in the warm circle of Sam's arms, his lips pressed against her forehead, one hand caressing her belly, she said the prayer over and over: *Please, God, don't take him away from me . . . don't take him away from me. . . .*

The following morning, Amy's fears of the night before seemed groundless and silly, just the way childhood nightmares had seemed in the bright sunlight, and by the time she'd had her breakfast she was once more her normal, optimistic self.

Sam left at 9 A.M. saying he'd be tied up most of the day with errands and shopping, so Amy filled her day with shopping and errands of her own.

She finished up early and still had enough time to give the apartment a fast cleaning and do a load of laundry before she had to get ready for the evening. By seven, she was showered and dressed in a cool white eyelet sundress and white sandals and waiting for Sam. She sipped at a glass of wine and idly glanced through her new *Vanity Fair*. She'd barely gotten through the Letters to the Editor when she heard his car in the driveway. The anticipation of seeing him brought a quickening of her pulse and a smile to her face.

She heard the thunk of his car door, then light footsteps bounding up her outside stairs. As usual, he was whistling their song.

And then her door opened. For a moment, he stood framed in her doorway, the late afternoon sun burnishing his hair and turning his pale green shirt and khaki pants golden. He grinned, and she felt a rush of love so powerful, so stunning, she could hardly breathe.

She knew it would always be this way, that all he would have to do was enter a room and she would be putty. That any absence, no matter how brief, would make his return seem like a glorious gift.

For a moment, he didn't move. His gaze clung to hers, then in three long strides he banished the distance between them.

Taking her face between his hands, he looked deep into her eyes, then kissed her with a sweetness that made Amy tremble. Afterward, he held her close and murmured, "God, you feel good."

She kissed his neck. "You, too," she whispered.

"Let's sit down," he said. "I've got something to tell you."

She didn't have time to speculate, to feel fear or any other emotion as he took her hand and led her to the couch. They sat, and he put his arm around her and tipped her face up with his free hand. Softly, almost shyly, he said, "I love you, Amy."

The most incredible joy flooded her. He had finally said what she had known all along. He loved her. He *loved* her. She touched his cheek. "Oh, Sam, I love you, too. So very much."

Their gazes clung for a moment, then he kissed

her again. She closed her eyes and savored the feel of him, the taste of him, and the knowledge that now everything would be the way it was always meant to be.

Then, in a moment Amy knew she would never forget, he reached into his pocket and removed a small gray velvet box. He handed it to her.

Fingers trembling, she snapped open the lid. Nestled inside on a bed of satin was a large emerald surrounded by a dozen diamonds. It was exquisite.

Speechless, Amy looked up.

Sam smiled tenderly. "With your eyes, I knew you had to have an emerald. Will you marry me, Amy?"

"Oh, Sam!" she cried, throwing her arms around his neck. "Nothing would make me happier!"

After another lingering kiss, he removed the ring from the box and slipped it on her finger. It was a perfect fit. Amy was astounded. "How did you know what size to get?" She raised her hand to let the ring catch the sunlight, and it nearly blinded her with its brilliance.

He grinned sheepishly. "I sneaked that little silver ring of yours out of your jewelry box."

"Oh, Sam . . . that was so sweet . . ." She felt her eyes fill with tears.

"Hey, what's this?" He touched her cheek. "Why are you crying?"

She sniffed. "I don't know. I guess because I love you so much. I loved you from the first moment I saw you, and even though I told myself you'd eventually realize we were meant to be, maybe deep down, I was afraid."

In answer, he just pulled her closer and kissed her again. And again. And then, hand in hand, they headed for her bedroom, everything else but how much they loved and wanted each other driven from their minds.

Later, she lay in the circle of his arms, and they talked. He told her about his new assignment and what a spectacular opportunity it was. "I'm going to miss you, though."

"I'll miss you, too." Her voice was subdued.

Sam looked at her closely. "Amy, it's not going to be easy . . . being married to me. Your mother was right. My job keeps me away a lot of the time."

"I know, I've thought about that, but, well, after we're married, can't I go with you?"

Sam smiled. "Some of the time, yes, but there will be many times you can't. This assignment in Nepal, for instance, would not be one where I'd encourage you to accompany me. However, I've been thinking about this, too. From now on, I'll try not to take many of these kinds of assignments, and if I do, I'll try to keep them short." This was the compromise he had finally settled on, and he hoped she would accept it. "Can you live with that?"

She sighed and traced lazy circles on his chest. "It's not perfect, of course, but . . . yes, I can live with that." She reached up to caress his cheek. "I'd rather live with that than live without you."

"Amy, I do love you," he murmured, tightening his arms around her.

They kissed deeply, and Sam could feel his body stir again. His hand moved slowly down her arm, her hip, and then around to cup her buttocks. She groaned and pressed closer to him.

A long time afterward, Amy said, "Sam . . . I want you to promise me something."

"What?" he said with his lips against her forehead.

"I know your work carries risk, and that you like that aspect of it—the danger and the excitement—but I couldn't bear it if anything happened to you. So I want you to promise me you won't take any chances."

He kissed the tip of her nose. "I know how to take care of myself."

"That isn't what I asked you. Please, Sam. Do you promise?"

"Tell you what. I can't promise I won't take *any* chances, but I do promise I won't take any *unnecessary* chances. Does that make you happy?"

Amy wanted to say more, but she knew it would be useless. Sam was not the kind of man to be bound too tightly. She wasn't even sure she'd love him as much as she did if he were. Smiling, she traced the outline of his mouth with the tip of her forefinger. "Yes. That makes me very happy."

Ten

The moment Faith saw Amy's face, she knew. Her daughter's smile was blinding.

"Mom, Dad . . ." Amy held out her left hand. "Sam and I are engaged."

Something clutched at Faith's heart, and for a moment she couldn't speak. A kaleidoscope of images swirled through her mind: Amy, five years old, lower lip trembling as Faith and Alan made a solemn ceremony of burying their sixteen-year-old cat, Tomasina; Amy, adorable in a starched white pinafore and patent leather Mary Janes, starring as Alice in her elementary school production of *Alice in Wonderland,* causing her parents to fairly burst with pride; Amy, enchanting in a filmy sea green chiffon dress the night of her senior prom. So many milestones. And now, another—this one the biggest of them all.

Slowly, Faith lifted her gaze from the beautiful ring to her daughter's glowing eyes. She knew she must be careful. She had grave reservations about Sam, but she mustn't let Amy see them . . . not yet. Not until she'd decided what, if anything, she should say. Above all, she didn't want to alienate her daughter. "Oh, darling," she managed to say quite calmly, "how wonderful."

She and Amy hugged, then Faith turned to Sam. "I'm still a bit stunned."

"I am, too," he said, leaning over to kiss her cheek.

After Alan hugged and kissed Amy, he clasped Sam's shoulder and said, "Welcome to our family, Sam."

"Thank you, sir." Sam's expression was appealingly tender as he looked down at Amy.

Faith, still overcome by emotion, tried to get herself under control. She had never dreamed she would feel this way—so ridiculously close to tears—she, who was always so firmly in command of every situation. To cover her agitation, she said, "Why don't we all go into the living room, where we can talk in comfort?"

By the time they were settled, Faith was once again self-possessed.

"Sam and I have talked about it," Amy said, "and we've decided we want to be married December nineteenth."

"So soon!" Faith said. "But why?"

"The Christmas holidays are the only time I'll have off for a honeymoon."

"But Amy, that's only four and a half months away. I don't know if we can—"

"Mom, we don't want to wait."

Faith was not accustomed to being interrupted, but she hid her irritation. "I don't think you understand how much there is to do. What I started to say was, I don't know if we can get everything ready that quickly."

"We just want a simple, small wedding," Amy said. "So it shouldn't take that long to prepare."

"But darling, we have so many friends, and their feelings will be hurt if they're not invited to your wedding." Faith looked at Sam. "I'm sure Sam does, as well."

"There are no more than a dozen people I care about inviting," Sam said. He reached for Amy's hand, and they exchanged a look.

"We want to be married over the Christmas break," Amy said firmly.

Faith thought fast. Perhaps she wouldn't argue this point. She'd learned a long time ago that one picked one's battles. If she conceded on the date of the wedding, it would probably be easier to get Amy to agree on the number of guests later—that is, if the wedding actually took place. "All right," she said briskly. "Christmas it is. Oh, dear, I just remembered . . ."

"What?" Amy said.

"Your father and I are going to China for two weeks in October. Perhaps I shouldn't go."

"No, Mom, don't cancel your trip. It'll all work out. I'm going to have a lot of free time in the next few weeks, because Sam will be leaving soon on a new assignment." Amy smiled at him, her heart in her eyes. "I'll miss him, but I'll use the time to good advantage."

"Where will you be going, Sam?" Alan asked.

As Sam told them about the upcoming shoot in Nepal, Faith only half listened. Her mind was busily selecting and discarding ideas for the wedding and reception. Amy would be married at St. John's, of course. The Carpenters had belonged to the parish since before Amy's birth. Faith hoped the date was open. Amy didn't realize how far ahead people planned. And the reception would be at the River Oaks Country Club, where Faith and Alan had been members for more than twenty years. She'd better call both places in the morning and nail down those dates. She refused to think about what she'd do if one or the other couldn't accommodate them.

Her mind turned to the wedding party. She was sure Amy would want Lark as her maid of honor and wondered who else her daughter would choose. Since Courtney's death, Amy hadn't formed any other close friendships. There was always her cousin Hannah—the daughter of Alan's only sister, Marian—but she and Amy had never been close. Still, she was Amy's only female relative of her generation. Faith decided she would talk to Amy about Hannah. The girl was lovely and would make a beautiful attendant, just as Amy would make a beautiful bride.

Faith wondered if Amy would want to be married in her wedding dress, which had been carefully preserved, or if she'd want a dress of her own. Knowing her daughter, she'd probably love the idea of wearing her mother's dress. Suddenly, Faith was filled with excitement. Despite her reservations about Sam, planning a wedding would be such fun! And no matter what Amy said, Faith was determined to have the kind of wedding that would be a fitting showcase for the daughter of Alan Carpenter.

She smiled in satisfaction and turned her attention back to the conversation.

"Sam has promised that this shoot will be his last long one," Amy was saying. "He's also promised to take me with him whenever he can."

Faith carefully kept her expression and tone neutral. "But aren't some of your assignments dangerous, Sam?"

"They can be, but I wouldn't take Amy anyplace

dangerous. You don't have to worry about that."
Once again, he and Amy exchanged a smile.

"You've always gone everywhere with Dad," Amy
pointed out.

"I know, but accompanying your father to London or Brussels or even New Delhi is not the same
as trekking in the Himalayas or in some tropical
jungle," Faith said.

"Sam has already said he won't take her anyplace
dangerous," Alan said.

Faith laughed softly. "I know. I'm being a mother
hen, aren't I?"

Amy got up and came over to Faith, leaning over
to hug her. "It's okay, Mom," she said softly. "I
know you're just concerned because you love me.
But everything is going to work out beautifully.
You'll see."

"If this is what you want, Amy," Lark said the
following morning, when Amy called her to tell her
the happy news, "I'm glad for you."

"This is *exactly* what I want, and I also want you
to be my maid of honor," Amy said. "Will you?"

"You know I will."

"Oh, Lark, I'm so happy! And I can't wait to
show you my ring. Do you want to meet for lunch
today?" Amy held out her hand to look at her ring
again. Prisms of light danced on the ceiling as sunlight fired the stones.

"I wish I could, but I've got a dentist's appointment at noon. How about if I stop by afterward?
Unless Sam's going to be there, of course . . ."

"It wouldn't matter if he *was* here. But he's not
going to be, so don't worry."

"Good. See you about two."

After hanging up, Amy thought about Lark and her obvious antipathy toward Sam. Surely Lark would begin to like Sam better, now that he and Amy were going to be married. She just had to get to know him, that's all. And once she did, how could she help but think he was wonderful?

Amy hugged herself. She was so happy. She had everything she had ever wanted. Her life was perfect. And she knew it would only get better. Everything, absolutely everything, was going to be wonderful from now on.

Justin's initial reaction to Sam's news was shock. His second was envy. "I never thought I'd see the day," he said, recovering from both nicely.

Sam grinned.

Justin clasped Sam's shoulder. "I'm happy for you, man. She's a great girl."

"Thanks."

"When's the big day?"

"December nineteenth."

"Wait'll I tell Mom. She always said if the right woman came along, she'd change your mind about marriage." Fleetingly, Justin thought of Jessie. No matter what she'd said about it being easier to forget about Sam if he was committed to someone else, Justin knew this news would come as a blow.

"I want you to be my best man," Sam said.

"I'd be honored."

"Something else . . . would you keep an eye on Amy while I'm gone? I'd like to give her your phone number to call if she needs anything."

"Sure, no problem."

"I know you're halfway in love with her yourself,"

Sam said, a teasing twinkle in his eyes, "so make sure you remember whose girl she is."

Justin felt his face heating and inwardly cursed.

Faith didn't have a chance to talk to Amy until late the following afternoon. When she heard Amy's car pull into the driveway, she put down the book she'd been reading and walked to the back door.

"Hi," she said, as Amy walked out of the garage.

"Hi."

"Where've you been all afternoon?"

"Lark and I went shopping." Amy smiled. "I asked her to be my maid of honor."

"I thought you might. Listen, do you have a few minutes? Why don't you come in and have a cup of tea with me?"

Ten minutes later, the two of them were settled in the sun room, a laden tea cart in front of them. Faith poured them each a cup of the English tea she preferred, then settled back onto the chintz loveseat. She chose her words carefully. "Darling, I had a very hard time falling asleep last night."

Amy chuckled. "I can imagine. What were you doing? Going over the guest list for the wedding?"

"Nooo, not exactly."

Amy's smile faded as she studied Faith's expression. "Is something wrong?"

"I am worried about something," Faith said.

"Something to do with the wedding?"

Faith hesitated. "Shall I be very honest with you?"

"Yes, of course."

"All right then. I . . . I'm troubled by your engagement. I'm not sure you really understand what you're letting yourself in for by marrying someone like Sam."

Amy stiffened. "Someone like Sam? Just what does that mean?"

"Amy, darling . . ." Faith put down her cup. "Please don't be angry. Sam's a lovely man. He is. I can easily see his appeal. He's attractive and charming and very engaging, but he's . . . well, he's not exactly the kind of man who is good husband material."

"If you're talking about his job, I told you, we've discussed that."

"It's not just his job. It's . . . it's everything. His background. His upbringing. Everything."

Amy stared at her. "I never thought you were the kind of person who judged someone by his background," she finally said.

"I don't, not really. But background does shape us. You know that." Even though Amy had only told Faith a little of Sam's history, that little was enough. "We bring our life experiences to everything we do. To all the choices we make."

"I don't care about Sam's background. I know what kind of man he is. He's good and decent and caring."

"I'm sure he is, but you must admit he's not exactly our kind of pe—"

"Our kind of people! I—I can't believe you said that." Amy stared at her mother as if she'd never seen her before. "I love Sam, Mother," she said tightly. "And I'm marrying him, whether you approve or not."

"Oh, Amy . . . I'm sorry." Faith had known, before she'd uttered a word, that Amy wouldn't listen. Still, she'd had to try. "I didn't mean anything by what I said. I *do* like Sam, a lot. It's just that I want the best for you. And I want you to be happy." She laid down her teacup and reached over to hug her daughter.

Amy resisted for only a moment. Then she hugged Faith back. "You don't have to worry. I *am* happy. Sam is all I'll ever want or need."

The next couple of weeks flew by, and before Amy knew it, it was her last night with Sam before he was to leave for Nepal. A few days earlier, she had started painting his portrait. She'd hoped to have it finished before he left, but it was slower going than she'd imagined and she was only about half done.

"How much longer do I have to sit here?"

Amy chuckled. Sam was as bad as the kids she taught. He hated sitting still. She dabbed a bit more ocher onto the canvas, blending it with the pink and white already there to try to find the exact flesh tone she wanted. "Just a few more minutes, okay?"

He grumbled under his breath, but he kept the pose.

Amy dropped her brush into a jar of turpentine and sighed. "All right. The rest will have to wait until you get back."

"Finally," he said, getting up and stretching. He crooked his finger, his eyes filled with lazy heat. "Come here."

Amy sighed and closed her eyes as his arms enfolded her. Their kiss was long and deeply stirring.

"I've been wanting to do that for the past hour," he said, holding her close.

"Um." She nestled against him, wishing she could make this day go on forever. "I'm going to miss you."

In answer, he tightened his arms around her. "I'll miss you, too."

She drew back a little so that she could look into his eyes. "Not enough to stay home, though."

For a moment, his eyes clouded, then he smiled. "You wouldn't want me to."

"No," she admitted. "I know how important this assignment is to you. But Sam, I've been thinking . . . if we have a family, I won't be able to travel with you, and—"

"Amy, quit worrying," he said, interrupting her. "That's not going to happen for a long time, and when it does, we'll work it out."

Later, as Amy lay in Sam's arms, listening to his deep, even breathing, she told herself Sam was right. Why worry about the distant future? As he'd said, when a problem arose, they'd find a way to work it out. Right now she had to concentrate her energies on the upcoming wedding and getting ready to go back to school for the fall semester.

And on getting through the weeks Sam would be gone without missing him too much.

The next morning, she refused to be sad, even when it was time to say goodbye.

"Before I go, I have something for you," Sam said. "It's out in the car."

While he went outside, Amy dug out the gift for him she had hidden away.

His smile was tender as she carefully undid the red ribbons on the foot-square box.

"Oh, Sam," she whispered, lifting the delicate cloisonné music box from its nest of tissue paper. "It's beautiful!"

"Open the lid," he said huskily.

Amy had to blink back tears as the pure notes

to "Always" floated in the air. And then she could hold them back no longer.

"Amy, sweetheart, don't cry . . ." He brushed away her tears.

"I can't help it. It's so beautiful. And I can't believe you found it. Where *did* you find it?"

"Jacobson Gallery. I went in to look at those Camellia Sturgis paintings. I thought I might get you one—"

"Oh, my God, Sam, you could never afford a Sturgis!"

"I know that now," he said. "Anyway, they had these music boxes, six different ones. I thought they were nice and I started lifting the lids and listening to the songs. I couldn't believe it when I heard this one."

"It's an omen."

His smile was tender, indulgent.

"I have something for you, too. It's not nearly as nice as what you gave me, but . . ." She handed him her gift, a photo of herself encased in plastic and hanging from a sturdy chain. She watched him anxiously. What if he didn't like it?

She needn't have worried. He grinned and immediately put the photo around his neck. "I won't take it off until I come back," he promised.

Amy swallowed. This was it. It was time for him to go. He drew her into his arms and they exchanged one last kiss, then he hugged her and said, "Good—"

"No, no, don't say goodbye," Amy said. "I hate goodbyes. I never say goodbye to anyone."

"I love you," he whispered. "I'll see you soon."

And then he was gone.

The last thing Amy heard as he bounded down the steps was his clear whistle.

Eleven

Shiva Singh held his breath.

It looked as if Sam Robbins, the charming but foolish American photographer who had refused to listen to his warning, might make it to the ledge. He had managed to climb almost a quarter of the way down the steep face of the cliff, which loomed several thousand feet above a narrow gorge.

Shiva Singh had tried to dissuade him from going. He had pointed out that the cliff was too dangerous, the possible rewards too uncertain. Shiva Singh was not a gambling man, but if he had been, he would have said the odds were not in Sam Robbins's favor.

Yet the stubborn photographer had insisted. "I may not get another chance," he'd said. "I'm tired of waiting. That's all we've done for weeks is wait." He'd smiled his charming smile, his brown eyes twinkling with good nature. "I told you, Shiva, I'm getting married soon. I can't hang around out here forever." He'd laughed and winked, and then he'd held up the picture he wore around his neck, of a laughing-eyed, dark-haired woman.

"Yes, I understand your feelings. She is very beautiful," Shiva agreed. But he knew, as any good

Sherpa guide knew, that what the American had proposed was too risky.

But what could he do? He couldn't physically restrain the American, even if he'd wanted to. Sam Robbins was at least four inches taller and thirty pounds heavier than he.

The trouble had all started yesterday, when Robbins had sighted a female snow leopard entering a cave about halfway down the cliff. After that, there was no stopping him. "I'm not blowing this opportunity," he'd said.

No matter what Shiva Singh said, Robbins wouldn't listen. He wouldn't wait until the other members of the team returned from the base camp where the scientist, Morgenstern, was recuperating from a bad case of influenza. He wouldn't be patient and see if his carefully hidden solar-powered cameras would capture any photographs of this leopard and any others who were known to inhabit the region.

Stoically, Shiva Singh had sighed and said, "If you will not be persuaded otherwise, I will go, too."

"No," Robbins had said, as he'd snapped on a telephoto lens. "You stay here. You know the drill. In case anything should happen, there has to be someone to go for help." He smiled. "Not that anything's going to happen."

Shiva Singh had finally agreed. And so here he was, watching and praying.

And there Robbins was, clinging precariously to the face of the cliff, his heavy camera strapped behind him as he inched his way down.

He was almost there!

Shiva Singh permitted himself a small, relieved sigh.

And then, just as Shiva Singh thought everything

was going to be all right, Robbins gave a startled cry.

Shiva Singh's heart leaped into his throat as he peered over the side and saw the photographer slide down the cliff, gathering momentum as he fell, bouncing over the rocky terrain until he disappeared from view.

After a few stunned seconds, Shiva Singh propelled himself into motion. It would take at least five hours to get back to the base camp, where he could radio for help. Then another five hours to get back. And who knew how long before a rescue team would show up.

With a heavy heart, Shiva Singh started the trek back to camp. It really didn't matter how long it took for the rescue team to come, because he was fairly certain of what they would find when they reached the bottom of the gorge.

No one could have survived that fall.

PART TWO

JUSTIN

Twelve

The first hint of autumn had finally arrived after months of nonstop ninety- and one-hundred-degree heat. All over the city, Houstonians were enjoying the bright, cloudless day and the refreshing seventy-degree temperature.

In neighborhoods large and small, mothers and nannies walked their small charges in baby carriages and strollers or watched them at boisterous play on swings and slides and jungle gyms. Windows and patio doors were opened wide to the silky breeze, and for once, the steady hum of air conditioners was absent, replaced by sounds of human voices, TV sets, and stereos.

The tennis courts were getting a workout, too, filled with trim, tanned women, fit seniors, and the few men who'd managed to finagle the day off. They energetically whacked balls and returned serves and reveled in the glorious weather.

Children of all ages looked longingly out the windows of their schoolrooms, wishing the schoolday were over so they could be outdoors, riding their bikes or skateboards or rollerblades. If it had been spring, teachers would have called the malaise that gripped their students—and themselves—spring fever.

In Memorial Park, joggers had hit the trails early,

and even now, at 2 o'clock on a Wednesday afternoon, there were dozens of people running along the paths. Beyond the trails, on the grassy expanse of lawn, a smattering of couples lay on blankets under the tall oaks, their radios playing softly.

Justin wanted to be outdoors, too. A month earlier, he'd been promoted to business manager of the magazine, and ever since, he'd been working sixty-hour weeks. He didn't mind. The new position was a challenge, and he wanted to do well. But today he couldn't wait for the day to be over. He had plans to play tennis after work with his brother, Steven. Which reminded him that he had not called Steven to tell him what time they had the court.

He reached for the phone, and just as he did, Owen Church walked through the open door. Justin returned the receiver to its cradle, a feeling of disquiet inching through him as he noted Owen's somber expression and the unfamiliar pallor of his complexion. "Hi, Owen," he said slowly. "Is . . . something wrong?"

Owen nodded, his face grim. "It's Sam. He's had an accident." His voice was even rougher than usual.

"An accident! Is . . . is he all right?"

Owen swallowed, and his eyes, normally so clear, looked as if someone had reached behind them and switched off the light. He sank into the leather chair in front of Justin's desk. As he visibly worked to calm himself, Justin had a glimpse of what Owen would look like as a very old man.

"We don't know. He's disappeared," Owen said slowly. "And the Nepalese authorities fear the worst. They . . . think he's dead."

"No!" Justin shook his head. "No." Shock caused

the blood to roar to his head. "I—I can't believe it."

"Jesus, I know. I didn't want to believe it, either. But the police didn't hold out much hope."

"But . . . but what happened?" This was a mistake. It had to be a mistake. Sam couldn't be dead.

"Sam's guide said he was climbing down a steep mountain face thousands of feet over a gorge. He wanted to get a shot of a leopard who had disappeared into some kind of cave on the side of the mountain." Owen bowed his head. "I told him not to take chances. *I told him.*" He took a deep, shuddering breath and slowly met Justin's eyes. "The guide warned him, too, but he didn't listen. Somehow he lost his footing and fell. The guide couldn't even see him, let alone get to him. He had to go back to their base camp and radio for help. It was days before the search party was able to reach the area, and when they finally got there, the only trace of Sam they found were his smashed camera and . . . bits of skin and blood." This last was said in a mangled whisper.

Justin stared at Owen, the horrible images created by Owen's words swirling in his head. Ordinary office sounds surrounded them: the click of nails against a computer keyboard, the whir of the copy machine next door, the muted ring of telephones. The rest of the magazine was going about its business, oblivious to the catastrophe unfolding only a few feet away. "Wh-where was Morgenstern when this was happening? And the other guide? I thought there were two guides."

"Morgenstern was running a fever, so he was back at the base camp. The other guide was with him."

Justin still felt shell-shocked. He knew that once the shock wore off, he would begin to feel the pain and loss. Right now, everything still seemed unreal. "But . . . is that it? I mean, surely the searchers are still looking . . . ? Hell, Owen, Sam could be wandering around, hurt and dazed and lost. If it took days to get to the place where he'd landed, he could have gone miles by now."

Owen's expression was compassionate as his eyes met Justin's. "From what I was told, anyone who'd fallen those thousands of feet wouldn't be in any shape to walk anywhere." His voice softened, roughened. "We have to face it, Justin. Sam was probably dead before he hit bottom."

"Then . . . then why wasn't there a body?" The pain wanted to break through. It was right there, hovering, ready to pounce. *Sam . . .*

Owen swallowed. Hesitated. "Cats . . . wolves . . any number of animals could have gotten to it."

A wave of nausea hit Justin. He closed his eyes.

"Someone has to tell his fiancée," Owen said softly.

Amy!

Jesus, God in heaven, how could he have forgotten about Amy? "I—I'll tell her." His voice sounded as if it belonged to someone else. He stood, leaning against the desk as his legs threatened to give out on him. Images of Sam—laughing and telling him to take care of Amy while he was gone, saying, "But just remember who she belongs to!" and Amy, as she'd looked yesterday evening, when Justin had helped her finish painting the apartment, happily talking about her wedding and how she couldn't wait for Sam to come home— those images burned in his brain.

He couldn't even begin to imagine how Amy was going to feel. *Oh. Jesus.* This news would devastate her.

Her parents were away, in China. And that friend of hers that she talked about so much—Lark. She wasn't in Houston, either. Amy had mentioned yesterday that Lark would be gone until Friday, "So this is a perfect opportunity for me to get all my wedding invitations addressed," she'd said, eyes sparkling.

She would have no one to lean on, no one to help her through this. Except him.

Justin had almost forgotten Owen's presence as all these thoughts careened through his mind. It wasn't until Owen stood and walked around the desk to touch his shoulder, saying, "You sure you're okay?" that he remembered.

"I—I'll be all right," he said. He had to be all right. He couldn't afford to indulge in his own sorrow and loss. Right now, the only important person was Amy. For her sake, he had to be strong. His gaze met Owen's. "There's no doubt about this, is there? I mean, Jesus Christ, Owen, I wouldn't want to tell Amy this if there was any chance at all Sam is alive."

"There's always a chance," Owen said gruffly, "but the authorities don't hold out much hope. The man I talked to said if nothing more is found by the time the first snow falls, they'll call off the search."

Justin nodded. He looked at the clock on the wall. It was 2:30. Amy usually got home from school about 4:30. He needed to be there, waiting for her, when she arrived. But he still had some time. Maybe he could find her friend Lark. Even if she couldn't get back to Houston tonight, she could probably manage to be there tomorrow morning. He would get his secretary to call Continental and track Lark down.

"You going to see Amy now?" Owen said.

"She won't be home for another couple of hours, and this is not the kind of news I want to tell her at school. I'm going to see if I can locate her best friend. Get her back to Houston."

Owen nodded. "That's a good idea. That poor kid. She's going to need her friends. Do you know how to get in touch with her parents?"

"I wish I did, but I haven't got a clue."

Owen squeezed Justin's shoulder again. "I know this is going to be tough, son. You want me to come with you?"

For a moment, Justin was tempted. But Amy didn't know Owen. She'd only met him once, when Sam had taken her to the office a few days before he'd left for Nepal, and the meeting had been brief. "Thanks, Owen, I appreciate the offer, but it . . . I think it'll be easier for her if it's just me."

"All right. Call me if you need me."

"I will."

Owen hesitated, then put his arms around Justin, giving him a quick, hard hug. The rare show of emotion was nearly Justin's undoing. He managed to hold on, knowing that this was only the first of many tests of his strength that he would have to endure in the next days and weeks.

Then Owen left. And before Justin did anything else—talked to his secretary, called his mother, anything—he said a silent prayer, asking God to give him the strength to get through it all.

Justin arrived at Amy's a few minutes before four, just in case she should get home earlier today. He opened the security gate and pulled around to the back, parking at the far side of the driveway.

For the next thirty minutes, he sat on the steps and waited. Peaceful sounds permeated the air: birdsong, a dog barking nearby, the hum of tires when a car passed by, someone playing scales on a flute, and far in the distance, the muted sound of a siren. Sounds people take for granted. Sounds Sam would never hear again.

Dappled sunlight made a constantly shifting pattern against the wood of the stairway and garage. A few feet away, a squirrel cocked its head before racing lightly up the trunk of one of the red oaks shading the garage. Lining the driveway, well-tended beds of impatiens and begonias added touches of scarlet and rose to the surrounding green . . . sights and colors Sam would never see again.

Justin put his head in his hands. *Sam, why weren't you careful? Why?* Hot tears scalded his eyes, but he forced them back. He wanted to throw something. Hit something. Do something. But all he could do was wait.

A few minutes after 4:30, he heard the security gate opening. His heart began to pound, and his hands felt sweaty. He stood, walking over to his car on unsteady legs. *Take it easy* . . . He took several deep breaths and wiped his palms on his pants.

Amy's little white Miata came around the house. He saw the surprise on her face when she realized he was there. She opened the garage door and waved gaily as she drove past.

Slowly, feeling like an old man, Justin walked toward her. She looked so beautiful, so happy, and so completely unsuspecting as she climbed out of the car, her brightly colored gauze skirt swirling around her legs, her arms filled with paraphernalia from school. Although her eyes held a question, he knew she had no idea that in only minutes he was going to break her heart and completely destroy her world.

"Hi! What a surprise! What are you doing here this time of day?" she said, smiling at him.

"Hello, Amy." His stomach clenched, and his throat felt as if it were filled with sawdust; it was all he could do to get the words out.

Her smile slowly faded.

"Amy . . ." He walked forward, put his hands on her shoulders and looked down into her eyes. "I—I've got some bad news."

He felt the tremor snaking through her. She shook her head. Her expression said it all. Whatever it was he was going to tell her, she not only didn't want to hear it, she was already denying it.

"Amy," he said again. And then he told her, as gently as he could. "I—I came right over. I didn't want you to hear about it on TV or the radio."

Her eyes. God, her eyes.

Her mouth twisted. Her face blanched. The school supplies slid to the ground. *"Noooooo . . . noooooo . . ."* Her head moved from side to side.

The terrible sound tore at his heart. "God, Amy, I'm so sorry. So sorry." He pulled her into his arms, fighting back his own agony. For a moment, she clung to him, moaning and saying "No" over and over again. And then, taking him off guard so that he almost couldn't keep her from hitting the ground, she fainted.

When Amy regained consciousness, she was lying on her bed. She frowned, confused. She didn't remember going to bed. And it was light out. Was she late for work? She turned to look at her bedside clock and saw Justin. His eyes were closed, and he was sitting in her rocking chair, which had been moved from the living area and was now positioned only inches away from the bed.

In a rush, everything came back to her, and with it, agonizing pain. *Sam!* Justin had said Sam was missing, probably dead. A hot knife of pain sliced through her, searing, excruciating, unbearable. A sound erupted from her mouth as tears gushed from her eyes.

Justin jumped, his eyes popping open. "Amy . . ." He moved to the edge of the bed and reached for her hand. "It's okay, I'm here, I'm here," he said in a singsong voice as if she were a child who'd had a nightmare.

It *was* a nightmare. It *couldn't* be true. Sam couldn't be dead. Sobs racked her body as she moaned and writhed.

Justin pulled her into a sitting position and held her, saying over and over again, "It's okay, it's okay."

But it wasn't okay. And it would never be okay again. Justin knew it, but he didn't know what else to say. So he kept murmuring useless platitudes and smoothing her hair and rocking her in his arms. She cried for a long time, but gradually, her sobs lessened until they became an occasional deep shudder.

Finally she disengaged herself. When she looked up, her face was ravaged. "J-Justin? Are . . . are they *sure?*"

Justin grimaced. There was no way he was going to tell her what Owen had said about Sam's body. And yet, it wouldn't be a kindness to her to hold out too much hope. "They're pretty sure, Amy," he said gently. "There's very little chance Sam could have survived."

"But they haven't *found* him," she said.

"I know, but—"

"If they haven't found him, maybe that means he's wandering around, trying to find his way back to camp."

She'd used almost the same desperate words Justin had spoken earlier when he'd wanted Owen to reassure him. "Amy, the chances of him surviving such a fall are practically nil."

"Then why didn't they find his body?" she insisted.

Justin stared at her. She wasn't going to let it alone. "Remember, it—it's the wilderness," he said slowly. "There are animals . . ."

Her face contorted, but she didn't cry again. Instead, she sank back, curled herself into a ball, and closed her eyes. Justin sat there wondering what to do. After a few moments, he squeezed her arm. "I'll be close by if you need me."

Amy heard him, but she didn't answer. She couldn't answer. She was consumed with pain. It had invaded every corner, every crevice of her body. *Sam . . . Sam . . .* How could he be gone? How could she go from such exhilarating happiness to such unendurable pain? She had been ecstatic as she'd driven home today. Now he would never know about the baby.

Their baby. She moaned. Their baby. The baby they had conceived with such passion, with such love.

He would never see it.

Never touch it.

Never hold it.

Oh, God, oh, God, oh, God . . .

How could she bear it? Sam . . . Sam . . . Sam . . . gorgeous Sam. His laughing face. His beautiful golden-brown eyes. The way his eyelashes grew. That tiny little bump on his nose. The way he felt, hard in some places, soft in others. The way he smelled: masculine, sexy. Never again. *Never again . . .*

After a very long time, completely spent and exhausted, she fell into a restless sleep. Several times she moaned or whimpered, and each time, Justin would walk quietly over to the bed and look down at her. He'd have given anything to have been able to take her pain onto himself. Anything to have spared her this misery.

He remembered how Sam had asked him to take care of her. "I'm trying, Sam," he whispered. "I'm trying."

It was only then, in the silence of the night, with Amy's cats the only witnesses, that Justin allowed himself to cry for the loss of the man he'd loved, too.

Thirteen

Lark paid the cab driver and allowed the door-man at the Marriott Marquis to help her out. She pushed her way through the revolving doors and walked past the security desk and around to the circular bank of elevators.

Lark always stayed at the Marquis when she went to New York. She liked staying in the heart of the theater district, so that most nights she had no need of a cab. Tonight, though, she'd met Terry Gruber, an old friend from flight attendant school, and they'd gone to Terry's uncle's Italian restaurant in the Village.

Feeling pleasantly full and with a slight buzz from the wine they'd drunk, Lark hummed "Someone to Watch over Me" while the glassed-in elevator whizzed her to the sixteenth floor. She hadn't been able to get the song out of her mind since seeing *Crazy for You* the night before. She felt relaxed and contented and glad she'd decided to take a few days vacation after her last, particularly grueling, shift.

Too bad Amy hadn't been able to come with her, she thought, as she headed toward her room. Amy loved New York—the galleries and museums and theaters. The two friends had visited the city often in the past and always enjoyed their stay. But even if Amy hadn't been teaching and unable to take time off, she still had too much left to do to get ready for her wedding.

Lark had mixed emotions about Amy's getting married. She was glad for Amy, but she also knew things would never be the same. They were already changing. But that was inevitable, Lark supposed. *Maybe I'll get lucky one of these days and meet the man of my dreams, too . . .*

Reaching her room, she unlocked her door and walked inside. She tossed her purse on the bed and kicked off her heels, sighing with relief.

Her gaze settled on the bedside phone. The red message light was on. Idly wondering who had called, she picked up the remote and clicked on the TV, selecting the in-house channel. There was only one message: *Call Justin Malone at Amy's apartment, no matter how late you get in.*

What in the world? Justin Malone? Lark knew who he was, but she'd never met him. Lark couldn't help smiling. Amy really liked Justin and kept hinting that maybe Lark would, too—a hint Lark had pointedly ignored. She'd had enough disastrous fixed-up dates to last her a lifetime.

Why was Justin Malone calling *her*? Had something happened to Amy?

She picked up the phone.

It rang only once before a low, masculine voice answered.

"Justin? This is Lark DeWitt."

She listened—disbelief, shock, then concern for Amy flooding her in rapid succession. When he was finished, she said, "I'll get there as soon as I can.

Do you want me to call you back when I know what time I'll get in?"

"Yes."

For the next hour Lark tried not to think about anything except the arrangements necessary to get her to Houston. But once that task was accomplished and she'd called Justin back, she could no longer keep from thinking.

She closed her eyes and fought the tears that threatened. Crying was so useless. It was weak and self-indulgent, and it changed nothing. She had learned that hard fact a long time ago. Crying wouldn't do Amy any good, and right now, Amy's welfare was all that counted.

Oh, God, poor Amy. She'd been so happy the past few months, her happiness like a golden aura, shimmering around her, touching everyone in her sphere.

This would shatter her, completely devastate her. And as if Sam's disappearance wasn't bad enough, it had happened when both her parents and Lark were away.

Please, please, let everything be okay. Let him be found. Don't let this happen . . .

Lark shivered, although the room wasn't cold. She was terribly afraid that all the prayers on earth wouldn't be enough to put Sam and Amy back together again.

Alan's hand shook as he replaced the receiver. He stared at the closed bathroom door. Beyond, he could hear the water running. Faith was taking a shower, getting ready for their day.

He bowed his head.

There would be no sightseeing today. Instead, in

a moment, as soon as he had himself under control, he would pick up the phone and make arrangements for them to go home.

But first he had to break the terrible news to Faith. He refused to allow his thoughts to go beyond the immediate task. He sat on the side of the bed. He felt sick.

After a bit, the water stopped.

Five minutes later, the bathroom door opened and Faith emerged, drying her hair with a towel. She took one look at his face and said, "What's wrong?"

"Come here, darling." Alan patted the bed next to him. When she was seated beside him, he put his arm around her. "It's not good news."

Her beautiful eyes—Amy's eyes—didn't waver. "Tell me."

Afterward, she put her arms around him, and they held each other and cried for their daughter's lost dreams.

Claire Malone couldn't sleep. She kept thinking about Sam and Justin and Sam's fiancée, Amy. Claire hadn't yet met Amy, but she'd heard all about her from Justin, who thought she was wonderful. Claire's heart ached for Amy. For all of them. They'd lost someone they loved.

Claire's eyes filled with tears as she remembered Jessie's reaction. The poor kid had fought so hard to control herself, but she hadn't been able to. She'd collapsed, weeping, into Claire's arms. Claire held her and wished, not for the first time, that she could take a child's pain away.

"I—I loved him," Jessie sobbed.

"I know." Claire smoothed Jessie's hair. Why was

life so hard? Why did good people have to get hurt?

When Jessie's tears finally abated, she wiped her eyes and in a thick voice said, "Is Justin with Sam's fiancée?"

Claire nodded.

"Do you think there's anything we can do?"

"I don't know. Justin said he'd call tomorrow."

"Let me know. I—I want to help."

The other kids had taken it hard, too, especially Katie, who had adored Sam. Tears streamed down her face. "It's not *fair!*" she cried.

"No. It's not," Claire agreed. The unfairness of life was one of the hardest lessons anyone ever had to learn. She remembered how angry she'd been after she'd gotten over the first desolation of her husband's untimely death. She'd railed at the unfairness of it all, furious with the fates that had stolen Sean away from her. In the end, though, there was nothing to do but accept . . . and go on.

All these thoughts, and more, refused to stop churning in Claire's mind. Finally, at 4 o'clock, she gave up trying to sleep. Rising, she tiptoed into the bathroom—she didn't want to disturb Katie—and splashed water on her face, then reached for her robe. She would go downstairs, fix a pot of coffee, and mix up a meat loaf and put it and some potatoes into the oven to roast. When that was done, she'd bake some brownies. Later this morning, she would take the meal over to Amy's apartment.

Food wouldn't take away the pain, but perhaps it would help Amy to know that people cared.

At the very least, preparing something for Amy and Justin would make Claire feel better.

* * *

At 4:30, Justin tried to sleep on the bed he'd fixed up on Amy's couch. He had just checked on Amy, and although her breathing was shallow and uneven, she was sleeping.

He had done everything he could think of—located Lark and spoken to her, gotten the number where Amy's parents were staying in Beijing and managed to get her father on the phone, talked with his mother and several co-workers at the magazine. He had called Owen Church and let him know how Amy was doing. He'd found the cat food and put fresh food and water in the cats' bowls. He'd even managed to get Amy to take a few bites of the chicken soup he'd fixed. And tomorrow morning he'd call Amy's school and talk to her principal and explain what had happened. Surely they'd be understanding. Justin couldn't imagine Amy being in fit enough shape to go back to work for at least a week.

He couldn't think of anything else.

He closed his eyes. He knew he needed to sleep, at least a few hours, to be in any shape to help Amy get through tomorrow. He wondered what time Lark would get in. She'd said she thought the first flight out would be at 8 A.M. She might get to the apartment as early as 12:30.

He turned on his side, trying to get comfortable. Just then, he heard a cry. Leaping up, he disposed of the distance between the couch and Amy's bedroom area in a half-dozen long strides.

As he came around the screen that served as a divider, he saw that Amy was sitting up, clutching her stomach. Her face was contorted with pain. "Justin," she gasped.

"What? What is it?"

And then he saw the blood.

His heart stopped.

"Oh, Justin, c-call 911. I . . . it's the baby . . ."

The baby!

Stunned, he grabbed for the phone at her bedside, nearly knocking it over. He punched in the emergency number, managed to answer the dispatcher's questions. In the meantime, Amy had stuffed her pillow between her legs, obviously trying to staunch the flow of blood. Her face had drained of all color and her eyes looked enormous and were filled with fear.

"An ambulance is on its way," the dispatcher said.

Justin hung up. He reached for Amy's hand and squeezed it. "They're coming. Can you hold on by yourself for a few minutes? I have to go down and open the security gates so they can get in."

Amy managed to nod.

Justin raced outside, down the steps, and around to the front of her parents' house. He punched in the code, then tore back to Amy's apartment.

The nine minutes it took for the ambulance to arrive were the longest nine minutes of Justin's life. He held Amy's hand and tried not to look at her terrified eyes and kept telling her over and over again to hold on. His mind swirled with the knowledge that she had been pregnant with Sam's child. If only he'd known! Yet what could he have done differently? They'd had to tell her about Sam. They couldn't have kept the information from her.

He looked at the clock. Seven minutes had gone by.

Where in God's name *was* that ambulance?

Finally it came and the paramedics took over. Justin watched helplessly as they ministered to Amy, then loaded her onto a stretcher and put her into the ambulance.

Christ, she was so white! And she looked so little lying there. Fear, dark and suffocating, clogged his throat. He'd have given anything if her parents had been there.

"You want to ride with us?" one of the paramedics said.

Justin shook his head. "I'll follow you in my car."

"Okay. We'll see you there."

For the second time that day, Justin prayed, but this time he wasn't praying for strength. This time he was praying that the tiny life Amy carried inside her would survive.

Pain, like a red cloud, closed around her. No matter where Amy went, it followed her. She kept trying to get away from it, but it was relentless.

She moaned.

"It's okay, sweetie. I've got something that'll help."

Hands were lifting her torso, rolling her onto her side, swabbing her hip. Then, a sharp prick.

And finally, blessed oblivion.

Justin paced up and down the corridor. What was going on? Why didn't someone come and tell him how Amy was doing? She'd been there for nearly two hours, and he knew nothing. He glanced at his watch: 6:30. When he looked up again, one of the nurses was approaching him. "Mr. Malone?"

"Yes?" he said eagerly.

"Mr. Malone, is Miss Carpenter, um, is she your

. . . was she carrying your baby?" said the nurse, whose name tag identified her as Marianne Zeller.

"No, no, she's a friend. How is she? Is she all right?"

Her gray eyes were kind. "She's going to be all right, but I'm afraid your friend lost her baby."

Justin grimaced. Christ, wasn't it bad enough she'd lost Sam?

"Where's the father? Is he out of the picture?"

Justin nodded bleakly. He quickly explained the situation. "Can I see her?" he asked.

"You can go into her room, but she's sleeping. We gave her morphine. It knocked her out, which is the best thing right now."

Justin followed the nurse down the hall and around a corner. He was relieved to see that Amy had a private room. Just as the nurse had said, Amy slept. She looked so fragile . . . and so young. Her hands lay at her sides. The left one was hooked up to an IV. Her face had no color at all, and her hair, normally so shiny and curly and full of life, lay dull and lifeless.

Justin sat down next to her bed and laid his hand gently on top of hers. In that moment, he'd have given anything to be somewhere else. He didn't want to be the one to tell her about the baby. Yet what choice did he have? He certainly couldn't let one of the nurses or doctors do it.

Without warning, a violent anger seized him. God damn Sam! He should be here. He should never have left her. If he hadn't left her, none of this would have happened. If he hadn't left her, Justin wouldn't be sitting here now, waiting for Amy to awaken so that he could deal her another blow.

In that moment, he hated Sam. In fact, if he'd had Sam there, he'd have cheerfully strangled him.

But Sam wasn't there.

And he'd never be there again.

Amy knew before Justin ever said a word. She saw the truth in his eyes. She'd lost the baby. The knowledge sat on her chest like a heavy block of steel, making it hard for her to breathe.

"Amy, I'm so sorry." He stroked her hand.

She closed her eyes. Oh, God, it hurt. It hurt so bad.

The baby.

Sam's baby.

Gone.

Just like Sam.

"Amy . . ."

She turned her head away from him. She didn't want to talk. She didn't want to think.

She wanted to die.

When Lark arrived at Amy's apartment, a woman she didn't recognize opened the door.

"You must be Lark," the woman said. "I'm Claire Malone, Justin's mother."

They shook hands. Lark immediately liked Claire: her directness, her calm voice, the honesty in her deep blue eyes.

"Where's Amy?" Lark looked around. The place seemed empty except for Claire and the cats.

"Come and sit down. I'm afraid I have more bad news," Claire said.

As Claire explained the events of the night, Lark's heart ached. Pregnant. Amy had been pregnant, and she'd never said a word. And now she'd not only lost Sam, she'd lost his baby. How much should one person be expected to endure? "Where is she?" she said finally.

"At Methodist Hospital."

Within minutes, Lark was on her way. Lunch hour traffic was heavy. It took her more than thirty minutes to get to the Medical Center, ten more minutes to park, ten more to get inside and find Amy's floor.

The door to the room stood slightly ajar. Lark pushed it open gently. The room was dim, the blinds closed. A tall, dark-haired man was sitting next to the bed. He looked up when she entered, then quietly rose and walked toward her. When she was about to speak, he put his finger to his lips and inclined his head toward the hall.

"Hi," he said when they were outside. "I'm Justin." He smiled and held out his hand.

His eyes were the same deep blue as his mother's, and he reflected the same honesty and calm dependability. He wasn't handsome. His face was too angular, his nose too long. Yet he was enormously appealing, Lark thought, with that air of quiet strength. He also had a very nice smile. No wonder Amy had liked him immediately. Lark liked him, too.

"How is she?" Lark asked.

"They gave her something to make her sleep."

"How'd she take the news about the baby?"

Justin shrugged, but the offhand gesture didn't fool Lark. She saw the concern in his eyes. "It's hard to tell," he said. "She wouldn't talk to me."

Lark listened with growing dismay as Justin described Amy's lack of response, the way she'd closed her eyes and refused to look at him or speak to him. It wasn't like Amy to withdraw.

"I'm glad you're here," he said.

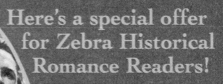

HERE'S A SPECIAL INVITATION TO ENJOY TODAY'S FINEST HISTORICAL ROMANCES— ABSOLUTELY FREE! *(a $19.96 value)*

Now you can enjoy the latest Zebra Lovegram Historical Romances without even leaving your home with our convenient Zebra Home Subscription Service. Zebra Home Subscription Service offers you the following benefits that you don't want to miss:

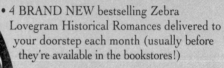

- 4 BRAND NEW bestselling Zebra Lovegram Historical Romances delivered to your doorstep each month (usually before they're available in the bookstores!)

  - 20% off each title or a savings of almost $4.00 each month

  - FREE home delivery

  - A FREE monthly newsletter, *Zebra/Pinnacle Romance News* that features author profiles, contests, special member benefits, book previews and more

- No risks or obligations...in other words you can cancel whenever you wish with no questions asked

So join hundreds of thousands of readers who already belong to Zebra Home Subscription Service and enjoy the very best Historical Romances That Burn With The Fire of History!

And remember....there is no minimum purchase required. After you've enjoyed your initial FREE package of 4 books, you'll begin to receive monthly shipments of new Zebra titles. Each shipment will be yours to examine for 10 days and then if you decide to keep the books, you'll pay the preferred subscriber's price of just $4.00 per title. That's $16 for all 4 books with FREE home delivery! And if you want us to stop sending books, just say the word....it's that simple.

It's a no-lose proposition, so send for your 4 FREE books today!

4 FREE BOOKS

These books worth almost $20, are yours without cost or obligation
when you fill out and mail this certificate.
*(If the certificate is missing below, write to: Zebra Home Subscription Service, Inc.,
120 Brighton Road, P.O. Box 5214, Clifton, New Jersey 07015-5214)*

Complete and mail this card to receive 4 Free books!

YES! Please send me 4 Zebra Lovegram Historical Romances without cost or obligation. I understand that each month thereafter I will be able to preview 4 new Zebra Lovegram Historical Romances FREE for 10 days. Then if I decide to keep them, I will pay the money-saving preferred publisher's price of just $4.00 each...a total of $16. That's almost $4 less than the regular publisher's price, and there is never any additional charge for shipping and handling. I may return any shipment within 10 days and owe nothing, and I may cancel this subscription at any time. The 4 FREE books will be mine to keep in any case.

Name _____

Address_____ Apt._____

City_____ State_____ Zip_____

Telephone ( )_____

Signature _____ LF0996
(If under 18, parent or guardian must sign.)

Terms, offer and prices subject to change without notice. Subscription subject to acceptance by Zebra Home Subscription Service, Inc.. Zebra Home Subscription Service, Inc. reserves the right to reject any order or cancel any subscription.

"Yes."

"Why don't you go on in? I think I'm going to get myself some coffee. Want some?"

Lark nodded. "Black."

She quietly entered the room. Amy lay very still under the white sheets and thin white cotton blanket. Lark stood by the bed and looked at her. Her frailty, her total lack of color, upset Lark, even though she'd thought she was prepared. Her eyes filled with tears she angrily brushed away. Fat lot of good they'd do Amy.

Lark sat in the chair Justin had vacated and waited and watched Amy. At least her breathing was even and untroubled. And sleep was restorative. Maybe, when she awakened, she'd be feeling better. And maybe, with Lark there, she'd finally be able to talk. Get her emotions out in the open. That'd be good for her, too.

She touched Amy's hand. The skin felt cool and dry. *I'm here, Amy. I'm here* . . .

As if she'd spoken the words aloud, Amy stirred. She opened her eyes.

"Amy?"

"Lark?" It was barely more than a whisper.

Within moments, they were holding each other, Amy crying as if her heart would break, and Lark, wishing there were something she could say to make the pain go away, but knowing all she could do was be there.

Fourteen

"I'm so worried about her," Faith said.

Lark nodded. "I know. I am, too."

The two women were having lunch at the River Oaks Deli. Faith had called Lark, saying she needed to talk to her and suggesting lunch. It had been six months since Amy had lost Sam and the baby.

"All she does is stare into space," Faith continued. "Half the time, when you speak to her, she doesn't answer."

"I know."

Faith laid down her fork. "Does she talk to you?"

Lark shook her head. "Not really. She did, that first day at the hospital, but since she's come home? No. Does she talk to you?"

Faith's lower lip trembled. It was one of the few times Lark had ever seen the older woman lose her composure. "No. She . . . she said she knew I didn't like Sam. That . . . I was probably glad he'd died."

"Oh, God . . ." Lark had had no idea. Poor Faith. What a lousy thing to say to her. "When did this happen?"

"Right after we got home."

"She didn't mean it. She was out of her mind with grief then, you know that."

Faith nodded. "I keep telling myself that, but since then . . . she's been so remote. I try to talk to her. I try to get her to go out with me. I invite her over for dinner. Nothing works. It's . . . it's as if all the life has gone out of her. As if, when Sam died, the best part of Amy died, too." She sighed deeply. "I don't know what to do."

"I think you're doing everything you can do," Lark said. She felt an unaccustomed sympathy for Faith, whom Lark had always considered a bit suspect, with her perfect looks and perfect life and perfect behavior. "Maybe all Amy needs right now is more time."

"I hope so."

"After all," Lark pointed out, "the things that have happened to her have been pretty devastating. Not the kinds of things you get over quickly."

Faith nodded and fell silent. She listlessly toyed with her salad and gazed out the window.

Lark picked up her turkey sandwich, looked at it, then put it back on her plate. She'd lost her appetite. "She knows we're there for her. Whether she acknowledges it or not, I think our support is helping her."

Faith turned her troubled eyes back to Lark's. "You know, in retrospect, I think it would have been better if she'd gone back to work."

"Yes, I feel the same way, but she didn't exactly ask for our opinion, did she? I mean, we didn't even know her principal had called and offered to replace her for the remainder of the year until days after it was a fait accompli."

"But I should have known better. I should have talked to her, tried to make her realize it wasn't good for her to stay home."

"Faith . . . quit blaming yourself. You did what

you thought was right at the time. Besides, not only would she not have listened to you, we both know Amy wasn't in any shape to go back. It wouldn't have been fair to the kids in her classes."

"If only we'd insisted she move into the house with us."

Lark had joined Amy's parents in trying to persuade Amy to stay with them once she was released from the hospital, but Amy had refused. And she had gotten angry when Lark wouldn't drop the subject, saying, "Leave me alone, Lark. Just leave me alone, please."

"All she does is stare at that portrait or listen to that music box . . . or sleep." Faith rubbed her forehead. "She must sleep fourteen hours a day."

"Sleep is escape," Lark said. She remembered how, as a teenager, when she was trying to lose weight, she would go to bed so she wouldn't be tempted to eat.

"Lark, I know what you're saying is right. Alan has said all the same things to me. But please, please try to get her out of the house. I—I just can't *bear* to see her this way." Suddenly, Faith's face crumpled and her eyes filled with tears.

Alarmed, Lark reached across the table but Faith shook her head, obviously embarrassed.

"No, I—I'm okay," she said.

Suddenly Lark was ashamed of all the less-than-complimentary things she'd thought about Faith Carpenter over the years. The woman truly cared. There were obviously deep feelings beneath that mask she normally wore.

Who was Lark to judge anyone, anyway? Wasn't she always thumbing her nose at the world? Didn't everyone need *some* kind of armor? Look what happened when you didn't protect yourself. Life dealt you a knockout blow, and you weren't prepared. Amy was a perfect example. "All right," she said at last. "I'll try again."

Amy ran her fingers over the surface of the portrait. The paint had long since dried.

Nothing.

She felt nothing.

What did you think you'd feel? Warmth? Life? This isn't Sam, stupid. This is just a half-finished portrait, and not a very good one, at that . . .

Sam.

The pain that had been so much a part of her life for the past six months throbbed deep within.

"Sam," she whispered.

His unfinished likeness stared back at her. Unfinished. How ironic. A portent, and she hadn't realized it. *I can finish it when he gets home.* She remembered thinking that exact thought. Now they mocked her.

Everything mocked her.

The sun.

The moon.

The stars.

The beautiful April weather.

People—talking, laughing, making love.

The earth still spinning, the clocks still ticking.

How could life go on as if nothing had happened when Sam's life, and their baby's life, were gone? When Amy's hopes and dreams, her future, *her* life, were gone?

"Sam," she whispered again. She hugged herself, cold now, even though it was warm in the apartment. Slowly, as if the effort of putting one foot in front of the other was almost more than she could expend, she walked into her bedroom.

As she had every day, sometimes several times a day, she opened the closet. Some of Sam's clothes hung there. One shirt, a muted print in shades of dusty blue, had been worn and carelessly rehung without laundering. This she buried her face in, imagining she could still smell Sam in the soft cotton.

As she stood there, Delilah and Elvis, ever curious, rubbed up against her legs. Elvis meowed, wanting attention. A few seconds later, Delilah joined him, but Amy ignored both cats. Finally, she lifted her face, let the shirt go and walked out of the closet, the cats on her heels.

A few steps brought her to her bedside. The cloisonné music box sat on her bedside table. She looked down, remembering the look in Sam's eyes as he'd given it to her. She lifted the lid. As the haunting melody filled the air, she lay down on her bed and closed her eyes.

"God damn it, Amy, snap out of it!" Lark said. She had decided to try anger, since patience, gentleness, and sympathy hadn't worked. "You can't spend the rest of your life cooped up in this apartment. Just look at you! I'll bet you haven't been out of that robe for days. Now, go get a shower and get dressed. I'm taking you to a movie, and then we're going out to dinner. And I'm not budging until you agree." She plopped down on the couch, folded her arms across her chest, and gave Amy her best glare.

Amy's wounded eyes stared back at her.

Lark felt like a heel, but she forced herself not to soften her stance. The seconds ticked away.

Amy was the first to drop her gaze. "Please, Lark," she said. Her voice sounded raspy.

No wonder, Lark thought. Amy had not used her voice much in the past months. Like any unused machinery, it had rusted. *Well, it's gonna get oiled today, my friend, whether you like it or not.* "I mean it, Amy. If I have to quit my job and stay here twenty-four hours a day, I will."

After long moments, Amy's shoulders drooped. "All right," she whispered. Her eyes met Lark's again. "But I don't know why you're doing this."

Then she turned and disappeared into the bathroom.

"I'm doing it because I love you, you dope," Lark said.

Amy blinked as the closing credits of *Scent of a Woman* scrolled by. In some surprise, she realized that she had—despite her belief that she wouldn't— lost herself in the movie.

"Great, wasn't it?" Lark said. "Al Pacino was fantastic, wasn't he? God, that tango! I can't believe I waited so long to see it."

"Yes, it was wonderful." Amy felt disoriented. She got up and followed Lark out of the row and up the aisle of the dollar movie house.

"Where do you want to go to eat?" Lark said, as they emerged from the theater into the pleasant spring night.

Amy shrugged. "I don't care."

"How about Chili's? I could really go for one of their margaritas and grilled chicken Caesar salads."

"Okay." Amy didn't really care where they went, but she knew she had to make an effort to behave as if she did. Otherwise Lark might make good on her threat to camp in her apartment.

Later, she was glad Lark had suggested Chili's. The restaurant held no association with Sam. Instead, it reminded Amy of many companionable meals with Lark. It also reminded her that Lark cared about her. That she hadn't wanted to make Amy feel worse by insisting she go out, that she had wanted Amy to feel better. And it was working. Amy did feel better.

"Um, boy, their margaritas are good here," Lark said, after her first swallow of the frosty drink.

Amy nodded and almost managed a smile.

For a while, the two friends sipped at their drinks, and Amy even found herself eating some of the warm chips and *queso* Lark had ordered. The food tasted good, another surprise. Amy hadn't enjoyed food for a long time. She looked at Lark, who was gazing around. She wanted to tell Lark she appreciated everything she'd done in these last, terrible months, but the words stuck in her throat.

Lark reached for a chip, and their eyes met.

Neither woman moved.

And then they both spoke at once.

"Amy, I'm so glad—"

"Lark, thank you for—"

Then they smiled at each other, and Lark reached across the table. Amy met her halfway. When Lark's warm hand closed around hers, Amy knew words were not necessary. Lark understood. She had always understood.

"It worked!"

Lark's voice was jubilant, and Justin smiled. The two of them had fallen into the habit of talking on the phone each evening. At first the calls were concentrated on sharing information about Amy, but after a few weeks, their conversations had expanded to include news of their day and their lives.

It was funny, Justin had reflected more than once, that he had so easily fallen into a comfortable friendship with Lark. She was hardly the kind of woman he would ever have felt comfortable with in the past, and yet he felt as if he'd known her forever. He could talk to her as easily as he talked to Jessie . . . or even Sam. Maybe more easily. And she seemed to feel the same way. In their common concern and love for Amy, they had become friends.

"That's great," he said. "Tell me about it." He listened with growing optimism to Lark's account of the evening out.

"I know this is just a beginning. I mean, I realize she'll have other bad days, but I feel so encouraged, Justin. This is such a positive sign, I think."

"I agree."

"Trouble is, we can't let her backslide. We have to keep up the pressure. Keep making her go out, see people, do things."

"I know."

"Unfortunately, I'm starting a three-day shift tomorrow," Lark said. "Can you fill in the slack?"

"No problem." It was never a problem to spend time with Amy. Sometimes Justin felt guilty about his desire to be with her, but he always managed to shake the guilt off. He had promised Sam he would take care of her. There was nothing to feel guilty about.

"Make her get out. Don't take no for an answer."

"No. I won't." He thought for a minute. Tomorrow was Friday. "Maybe I'll take a vacation day tomorrow. That way the whole time you're gone will be covered." He was thinking aloud now. "I might even go over there early tomorrow morning, make her go out to breakfast with me, then take her for a long drive somewhere."

"That's a wonderful idea. Getting her away from Houston would be the best thing for her."

They talked for a while longer, then Lark said, "Call me and let me know how things go, okay? I've got a new line—sorry, in plain English, a new route—so I'll be in San Francisco."

Justin promised he'd keep her informed, and they hung up. For the first time in weeks, he felt a glimmer of hope. Although he and Lark had assured each other many times that Amy would eventually recover, Justin had had a few doubts. He had been afraid that Amy might be one of those people who love so deeply and completely that she would never get over her loss.

But things looked brighter now. He smiled. Tomorrow was going to be a good day.

Amy awakened feeling better than she'd felt in a long time. And when she looked at her bedside clock, she couldn't believe it. She'd slept for seven straight hours, without dreaming.

It was probably those two margaritas you had . . .

Whatever had caused the uninterrupted sleep, Amy was grateful. She rolled over, hugging her pillow and thinking about getting up. As she did, all three cats stirred. They had taken to spending the night on her bed the way they had before Sam had come into her life. Sheba, always the most skittish, hopped off the bed. Delilah and Elvis, after giving her a why-are-you-bothering-me look, snuggled closer. "Hey, you two lazy things, get up." Amy nudged them, and after a few minutes, they reluctantly moved, Delilah emitting an irritated "Myup" to show her displeasure.

Amy chuckled and got up, too, heading for the kitchen. After filling the coffeemaker and turning it on, she took a shower. An hour later, feeling refreshed and enjoying her second cup of coffee, she actually began to toy with the idea of doing something other than sitting around her apartment today.

The realization amazed her. That emotion was quickly followed by a stab of guilt. Her gaze darted to the half-completed portrait on the easel in the corner, as if Sam would somehow feel her betrayal. Just as the sadness and emptiness that had been temporarily banished began to creep back, the phone rang. She jumped, splashing coffee on her clean jeans.

"Oh, darn. Who could that be?" She didn't pick up the phone, just in case it was a sales type. Instead, she let the recorder answer.

"Amy, it's Justin. Are you awake?"

She reached for the receiver. "Hi, Justin. I'm up."

"Good. Have you had breakfast yet?"

"No . . . just coffee." She refrained from telling him she hadn't been eating breakfast lately. Of course, anyone looking at her would know she'd been skipping meals, because all her clothes were too loose.

"Good," he said again. "I'll be there in thirty minutes. I'm taking you out for breakfast."

"No, Justin, I—" Astonished, she stared at the receiver.

He'd hung up.

* * *

They had breakfast at a little restaurant in Old Town Spring called Mama Jo's. Mama Jo's specialized in old-fashioned country eating and was known for its enormous homemade biscuits that were served with cream gravy or butter and honey or both.

Amy had to admit that the food was worth the drive. She actually managed to down two biscuits, along with scrambled eggs and two pieces of bacon. And throughout, she hadn't once thought about her unhappiness.

"I wonder how many fat grams I've eaten," she said, patting her stomach.

"You don't need to worry about fat grams," Justin said. He motioned to the waitress.

Amy was grateful he hadn't elaborated. She knew how bad she looked.

Once he'd settled their bill, he suggested they might spend some time looking in the various shops. "Or we could go for a long drive, somewhere out in the country. Or Lake Livingston. My brother's got a cabin there, and I've got a key."

"It's sweet of you, Justin, but I'd really rather go back home."

"We're not going home. We'll do whatever you want to do, but going home isn't an option."

Her first reaction to this highhanded statement was a rush of anger. If she wanted to go home, she'd go home. But the anger was quickly replaced with shame. Justin was her friend. He cared about her. He wasn't trying to be high-handed, he was doing what he thought was best for her. What had she ever done to deserve this kind of friendship?

She tried to smile and knew the effort was less than her best. "All right. In that case, I vote for Lake Livingston."

Fifteen

Coming to Lake Livingston had been an inspired idea, Justin decided, looking at Amy's face and seeing the way the lines of strain and unhappiness had gradually ebbed away. The two of them were sitting on the edge of the dock, fishing poles in hand. The late April sun was warm on their backs and shoulders, the breeze silky, the water golden and placid, with only an occasional ripple of bass marring its sun-dappled surface.

Steven's cabin was located off a sheltered inlet on the eastern side of the big lake, which was just northeast of Conroe. In the distance, several fishing boats were visible, and occasionally, the bright flash of a waterskier, but for the most part, Amy and Justin had their tiny piece of the lake to themselves.

Amy sighed—a light, contented sound—and her lips curved into a tiny smile. Her eyes, as she turned to face him, were as peaceful and calm as the water beyond. "Thanks for bringing me here," she said softly.

When she looked at him like that, Justin found it hard to breathe around the knot in his chest. He wondered if she had any idea how he felt about her, how much he wanted to permanently erase the pain from her eyes and her life. "I'm glad you're enjoying it."

"I've always loved the water," she continued, turning her gaze back to the lake. "Even at its angriest, it soothes the soul."

"Yes." Justin remembered the first time he'd seen the Atlantic. The summer he was ten, he'd accompanied his father to Maine to visit a dying aunt who lived in a little town north of Portland. The rocks, the crashing waves, the noisy gulls wheeling overhead, the hot sun and chilly wind—all had made a tremendous impression on him. As young as he was, he had still recognized, on some elemental level, the healing power of the water.

"I used to think," Amy continued, "that I wanted to live by the ocean."

"And you no longer want to?"

She shrugged. "I don't know. Right now, I'm not sure of anything."

Justin hesitated, then reached over and laid his hand on her knee. He squeezed gently. "Things will get better."

She turned to look at him again, her eyes lucent in the brilliant morning light. "Will they?"

"Yes." He could feel the warmth and life beneath her jean-clad leg, and he wanted, more than anything, to put his arms around her. To keep from doing something he knew he shouldn't, he contented himself with squeezing her knee again, then casually removing his hand.

"How can you be so sure?" Now her voice had taken on a ragged edge. "Maybe nothing will ever be better. Maybe this is all there is, all there will ever be."

"I don't believe that."

She was silent for a long time, so long that Justin

began to feel uncomfortable, yet he didn't know what to say.

"Sometimes I hate Sam," she said finally.

Since Sam's disappearance, Justin had felt the same way, many times. "I know."

"Do you?"

"Yes. Sometimes I hate him, too."

"Why do *you* hate him?"

Because of what he did to you. Because the joy is gone from your eyes. Because you never laugh anymore. "Because he left us. Because . . . he hurt you."

She sighed again, but this time there was weariness in the sound. "Can I ask you something, Justin?"

"Sure. Anything."

"You said something a while back, when the Nepalese authorities officially gave up the search, that made me think Sam . . . that he might have been doing something he shouldn't have been doing." Her eyes met his again. "Is . . . is that true?"

Justin could have kicked himself. He remembered his earlier slip of the tongue but had hoped she wouldn't. Well, he wasn't going to lie to her. "Yes, it's true. He'd been warned about climbing down that mountain. The guide told him it was too dangerous, but Sam said he was tired of waiting . . . so he went anyway."

She swallowed. "That . . . that's what I thought. I, oh God . . ." Her voice broke. "He promised me. I specifically asked him not to take foolish chances. And then he did anyway." Her eyes were filled with anguish. "Didn't he love me enough to be careful?"

"Amy . . ." Justin laid down his pole and now he did put his arm around her. At first she held herself stiffly, but after a moment her body relaxed and she leaned against him. Her hair was only inches from his face, and he could smell the fresh sweetness of it as well as the light, flowery fragrance she wore. "He loved you. He loved you more than I've ever seen him love anyone. But being careful . . . that just wasn't Sam's way. Sam lived on the edge; he always had. I think he probably always would have. He tried, but something inside him wouldn't let him hold back. He had to prove he was better, smarter, braver, faster than other people."

When she didn't answer, he tipped her chin up. Tears glistened on her eyelashes, and her bottom lip trembled. A fierce longing gripped him, and reason and caution, which had always been Justin's bywords, flew out of his mind. The next thing he knew, his mouth had settled against hers. At first, she responded, her soft lips yielding and sweet, causing the most exquisite pain, which was a combination of love and need and the desire to protect, to arrow through him. But then, as if she'd suddenly realized what she was doing, she yanked away, putting her hand over her mouth and saying, "I—I'm sorry, I can't, I don't know what . . ." Her expression was a mixture of horror and embarrassment.

It took every bit of self-control and strength Justin possessed to release her, to say in a calm voice, "It's okay. There's nothing to apologize for. It's my fault. You looked so sad. I just wanted to make you feel better."

He should never have given in to his desire, no matter how much he had wanted to comfort her. And now, somehow, he had to make things right. He had to reassure her, show her that what had happened was not important. He smiled, making his voice brisk. "What do you say we go see what we can scrounge up for lunch? I'm starved."

For a moment, he didn't think his ploy would work. She looked uncertain, and he was sure she was going to ask him to take her home. But she nodded and the awkward moment passed.

Together they headed for the cabin, and for the rest of the day, Justin was careful not to do or say anything to make Amy uncomfortable.

May brought a resumption of Amy's parents' traveling. They had postponed or canceled all of Alan's speaking engagements and demonstrations since Sam's disappearance, but now, seeing that Amy was more like her old self, they felt freer to live their own lives.

Amy spent a lot of time with Justin. He was more than a friend. He was a lifeline, her last link to Sam, the person who understood, more than any other, what she'd gone through, because he'd gone through it with her. At first, she'd been uncomfortable with him after that episode at Lake Livingston. Part of her discomfort stemmed from the fact that she had enjoyed being kissed by him. It had felt so good to be in a man's arms again, to have a man's solid body next to hers, to feel the warmth and comfort of a caring embrace. Knowing she'd enjoyed the kiss had confused her and made her feel guilty. What was wrong with her? Sam had only been gone a little over six months, and there she was, kissing someone else and liking it. Then she'd get angry. Why should *she* feel guilty? She wasn't the one who had done something stupid and gotten herself killed.

All these emotions caused a wall to form between her and Justin. But as the weeks went by and nothing else like the kiss happened, she relaxed. Gradu-

ally, she and Justin resumed their comfortable relationship.

One particularly beautiful Saturday in late May,
when the two of them had taken a picnic lunch to
Hermann Park where they spent three pleasant
hours eating and watching the children at play,
Amy said, "I don't know what I would have done
without you the last seven months, Justin."

His eyes looked even bluer than usual as they
met hers. He smiled and continued toying with a
blade of grass. She thought how nice he was, how
reliable and steady and honest. A person could always count on Justin. When he said he was going
to do something, he did it.

She wondered why he hadn't married. He was
thirty-six, attractive, and had a good job and all the
qualities women looked for in a man. What was the
problem? Giving in to an impulse she later questioned, she said, "Can I ask you something?"

"Sure. Go ahead."

"I'm curious. Why are you still single?"

He looked at her for a long moment, then
turned his gaze into the distance. His face was in
profile, so she couldn't see his expression. "Until
last year, I'd never met anyone I wanted to marry."
He turned to meet her eyes. "Unfortunately, she
wasn't available."

Amy's heart beat harder. The look in his eyes
told her this was a subject she should have left
alone. "Oh. I—I'm sorry," she said, because she
had to say something. To give herself something to
do, she started gathering up the remains of their
meal and putting them into the picnic hamper.

"Amy."

Slowly, she looked up.

"You know I love you, don't you?"

She swallowed. Of course she'd known. Somewhere deep inside, the knowledge had been there, even if she'd never acknowledged it.

"I know you still love Sam," he continued quietly. "I know it's too soon, but do you think . . . is there a chance that someday . . . ?"

"I don't know. I—I . . . it *is* too soon . . . I'm sorry." Now she threw things into the hamper. She just wanted to get out of there, to go home, to pretend these words had never been spoken.

"Amy . . ." Justin grabbed her arm and made her stop her frantic movements. "It's okay. Maybe I shouldn't have said anything. I just . . . I wanted you to know how I feel. I wanted you to know that I'll always be there for you. But I'll never pressure you, I promise. If all you want from me is friendship, I can accept that. If you want more, all you have to do is let me know."

For weeks after this episode, nothing more was said, but Amy knew Justin was thinking about it, just as she was. She went over and over her motives for bringing up the subject. Why had she? She didn't know. She only knew she wished she hadn't, because she was so afraid she'd hurt him. But after several times together with no mention of the picnic and his declaration, and with no change in his attitude toward her, Amy once again relaxed and realized he'd meant what he'd said. He would always be her friend, but the future course of their relationship was entirely up to her.

Amy sat by the window, staring at the view beyond. Normally, these clear, bright days of autumn were her favorite time of the year. She loved the gradual turning of the leaves, the frenetic activity of the squirrels, the smell of smoke from fireplaces, and the increased energy level of Houstonians—who were just as glad as she was to see the stunning heat of summer finally go away.

But nothing had been normal this entire year.

Sometimes it amazed Amy that she'd actually gotten through it. God knew there'd been many days she hadn't thought she would.

Tomorrow it would be exactly one year since Sam had disappeared. No trace had ever been found of his body. The search parties had long since ceased to search, especially since a month after Sam's fall, the entire western part of Nepal had been buried under a blizzard and subsequent avalanches. Hundreds of people had been trapped—hikers and tourists among them. Dozens had died.

For a long time, Amy had continued to harbor a secret glimmer of hope, but as winter had worn on, and then spring and summer had come—and with them, the return of Sam's possessions from the trip—even that glimmer had faded away.

Now she knew, finally and irrevocably, that Sam was dead. She sighed, twisting the emerald ring around and around on her finger. She'd had to wind thread around the back of it because she'd lost so much weight. She knew she should remove it, just as she knew she should put the unfinished portrait away, and get rid of his clothes and belongings, but she couldn't seem to make herself do those things, no matter how her mother and Lark urged her to.

It wasn't that she still cried at night or that she felt sad all the time; she didn't. Sometimes hours would go by when she didn't think about Sam at all, especially now that she'd gone back to teaching.

She smiled, remembering her first day back at school. She had been dreading it. Firsts were difficult, and facing her coworkers, seeing their sympathy and curiosity, was sure to reopen many wounds. But it hadn't been nearly as bad as she'd imagined. And that was because of the kids. They were glad to see her. Amy knew, because her principal had told her, that the children had been informed of the cause of Amy's long absence. They didn't know about the baby, of course. Only Amy's family and Lark and Justin knew about the baby. But it was touchingly evident that the news of Sam's death had made an impact. The children were on their best behavior that day, and almost all of them brought her some sort of welcome-back gift.

The gifts and the unspoken sympathy of the children brought tears to Amy's eyes more than once. One student, in particular, affected Amy more than any other. The girl, a fourth-grader named Michelle, had been battling leukemia for several years. She was in remission right now, but her prognosis was iffy. She was a bright, articulate child with better-than-average artistic talent, and she was a favorite of Amy's.

Michelle waited until after school that first day, and once the others were gone from the classroom, she came forward and gravely presented Amy with a beautifully wrapped leatherbound volume of Elizabeth Barrett Browning's poems. "Oh," Amy said. "Michelle! What a wonderful gift. Thank you."

"You're welcome, Miss Carpenter." The girl's dark eyes shone softly. "I—I missed you while you were gone."

"I missed you, too," Amy said, and knew it was true.

"You've been sad, haven't you?"

Amy nodded.

Michelle reached over to touch Amy's hand. "Don't be sad," she whispered. "My dad says when good people die they go to a better place where they never feel pain or any bad things. M-maybe when you feel sad, you could remember that."

Amy had managed to smile at the child. "Thank you," she murmured. "I won't forget."

She also wouldn't forget the little girl's courage and generosity. There she was, facing her own death on a daily basis, living with pain and fear and the prospect of not ever making it to her adult years, and she was comforting Amy.

After that, things got easier. Each day, Amy thought less and less of her own problems and more and more about the children and theirs. She spent long hours at night planning lessons, poring over books of art projects to find ones she thought would particularly interest and stimulate the children's creativity.

And now, eight weeks later, she was once again facing a difficult first. But when tomorrow was past, there would be no more firsts. They would all be behind her, and maybe; just maybe, she would start looking forward to the future.

Again, getting through a milestone turned out to be easier than Amy had anticipated. But that was because of Justin. Obviously, he had been thinking about the date, too, because he called her early that morning—while she was getting ready for school.

"Hey," he said.

"Hey, yourself. What are you doing, calling me so early?" She was proud of herself. She actually sounded happy.

"I wanted to be sure to catch you before you left

for school," he said. "I was hoping you'd go to dinner with me tonight."

"Justin, that's sweet of you, and I appreciate it, but you don't have to babysit me. I'll be okay."

"I know you'll be okay. That's not why I asked you. I asked you because I want to be with you. You know that."

Amy fiddled with the telephone cord. "Well, when you put it that way . . . okay. Great. I accept, but only if we go dutch."

"We're not going dutch. I'm inviting you to be my guest," he said.

He took her to Pappasito's, and Amy knew the choice of the noisy Mexican restaurant was a carefully chosen one. His understanding and thoughtfulness touched her deeply. There were so many people there, talking, laughing, eating, and drinking, that she couldn't possibly feel sad.

Justin plied her with margaritas and kept urging her to eat more, and by the time the evening was over, Amy felt sated and amazingly at peace. When he took her home, he kissed her cheek and said, "Sleep well."

"Thank you, Justin. I will."

And miraculously, she did.

Even the holidays were not so difficult as they might have been, with their reminders of the agony of the previous year. Amy allowed herself to be persuaded to go with her parents to Steamboat Springs over Thanksgiving, where Alan's sister, Marian, and her daughter, Hannah, joined them.

The change of scenery, the skiing, the company of her cousin, who Amy had always wished to know better—all served to keep her mind and body occupied and away from any sad thoughts.

Christmas, too, turned out to be far more pleasant

than Amy had feared. Her parents held their annual
Christmas Eve open house, which was lovely. They
invited half a dozen friends—including Lark—to
join the family for Christmas dinner. They were
overly generous with Christmas gifts for Amy, but
she understood their motives and appreciated the
kindness and love behind the Mizrahi sweater set,
the Mikimoto pearls, and the St. John knit dress.
And if, when she fingered the soft wool of the
sweater, she thought fleetingly that if things had
been different, she might have been fingering a re-
ceiving blanket, she managed to banish the emotions quickly.

Christmas night, Justin came over, and he and
Lark and Amy spent the evening in her apartment
playing Monopoly and drinking eggnog and listening to Christmas music on the radio.

And anytime Amy started to think about Sam and
what this Christmas might have been like if he'd
lived and they'd gotten married and had their baby,
either Lark or Justin seemed instinctively to know
which way her thoughts were turning, and they'd
say something silly or ask her a question so she'd
have to respond, and the bad moment would pass.
At midnight, when by unspoken agreement they
both rose to leave, Amy hugged each in turn and
whispered her thanks.

Later, after she'd turned out the tree lights and
cleaned up the kitchen and gotten ready for bed,
she walked out into the moonlit living room and
stood in front of the unfinished portrait of Sam.

She kissed the tips of her fingers, then placed
them against his mouth. And then she picked up
the canvas, carried it over to the cupboard where
she stored her art supplies, and placed it inside.

Sixteen

The day after Christmas, Lark slept late. At 11 A.M., in the middle of her third cup of coffee, Justin called.

"Last night was fun, wasn't it?" he said, after they'd disposed of the hellos.

Lark smiled. "Yes, it was."

"And I thought Amy did really well, considering."

"Me, too. I think she's finally starting to mend."

After a little more chitchat, Justin said, "Do you have plans for New Year's Eve?"

For one moment, Lark thought he was asking her out on a date, and her heart took a crazy hop. "Well, um, my mother always has an open house. It's a tradition, and I'm expected to be there. But I don't usually stay long."

"Well, my brother always has a party, and I thought if you didn't have plans, maybe you'd like to come. I plan to ask Amy, and I thought she'd be more likely to say yes if you were coming, too."

Amy. Of course. Lark should have known.

"That's a good idea, Justin," she said evenly, swallowing her disappointment.

"Great. I'm taking her to lunch tomorrow, and I'll ask her then."

After they'd hung up, Lark stared at the phone for a long moment. Her reaction when she'd thought Justin was going to ask her out disturbed her. When had this happened? When had he become more to her than just a friend?

Lark, old girl, this is trouble. It's obvious to anyone with eyes how he feels about Amy . . .

"Oh, fuck," she muttered. Of all the stupid things to do, she'd gone and fallen for a guy who—in terms of romance—didn't know she was alive.

Giving way to the temper she normally succeeded in controlling, she kicked at her couch, forgetting she was barefoot.

"Ouch! God damn it!" She hobbled to the front of the couch and sat down.

She didn't know whether to laugh or cry.

Lark talked Amy into going to her mother's open house with her, and then on to Steven Malone's party. The two friends arrived at the lavish, pseudo-Spanish, Memorial-area home of Isabel Markham DeWitt Reiner Cardosa at eight. There were already a dozen or more cars parked in the driveway and along the meandering street that paralleled Buffalo Bayou.

"Oh, God," Lark moaned. "I detest this."

Amy gave her a sympathetic smile. "I know. That's why I let you talk me into coming . . . to give you moral support." Lord knew Lark had given her endless support over the past year.

"Lark, darling, *there* you are!" Isabel said, rushing to greet them. She wrapped thin, tanned, gym-toned arms around her daughter's neck and they exchanged air-kisses. "And Amy, poor love, I'm so glad to see you."

Amy suffered through Isabel's hug and her gushing concern. Lark's mother was hard to take. Most of the time you couldn't be sure if her interest was real or faked, although Amy usually gave her the benefit of the doubt. She looked beautiful tonight. Her wheat-colored hair and blue eyes were perfectly complemented by her topaz satin cocktail dress and diamond teardrop earrings.

"Come. I don't believe you've ever met Armand," Isabel said, referring to her current husband.

Armand Cardosa was at least fifteen years younger than his wife, who was pushing sixty. He might even be twenty years younger, Amy thought, as she studied him. Slickly handsome, with brilliant dark eyes, he reminded Amy of the smoldering actors found in silent movies.

"So young, so innocent," he murmured, "so beautiful." He raised Amy's hand to his lips and kissed it, letting his lips linger a tad too long.

Lark bit back a grin as she saw how her mother's eyes hardened and how she slipped her arm possessively through her husband's arm.

"Let's let the youngsters amuse themselves with people their own age," she purred.

Armand took the not-so-subtle rebuke well, letting his wife lead him off. Amy and Lark were left to their own devices.

"C'mon, let's hit the buffet table," Lark said. "That's one thing about Mommy Dearest's parties—you sure can't fault the food."

"Lead the way," Amy said.

Amy selected stuffed mushrooms, fried calamari, and grilled shrimp.

"How much longer do you think Armand will last?" Lark said, spearing several slices of rare roast beef and adding it to the other items on her plate.

"I mean, he's now making eyes at other women in front of my mother. Can you imagine what he does when she's not around?"

Amy shrugged. "Some men are just like that. You know—they flirt, but they don't mean anything by it."

Lark snorted. "Yeah, sure."

A few minutes later, after they'd found a place to sit and eat, Lark said, "What is wrong with women like my mother? Why does she always have to have a man? Does she feel she has no value unless she's got a lapdog?"

"Not everyone is as sure of themselves as you are, Lark."

"Me? I'm as full of self-doubts as anyone. It's just that I . . ." She broke off. "Aw, hell, forget it. My mother is my mother, and she's never going to change. I don't know why I let her get to me."

And even though they started talking about something else, Amy continued to think about Lark's question. Later, as they were driving to Steven Malone's house, Amy said, "Lark?"

"Hmm?" Lark flipped on her right turn signal in preparation for exiting the Katy Freeway.

"You know, that thing you said about your mother needing a man to feel complete?"

"Yeah?"

"Well, in some ways, I understand. I . . . without Sam, I feel . . . disconnected . . . as if part of me is gone. I—I know I'm not explaining it very well."

"The two situations are not the same, Amy."

Amy nodded.

"I mean, my mother goes from man to man. She cannot be alone. You were alone for a long time. You weren't willing to settle for just *any* man, like my mother is."

"You're hard on her, Lark."

"Yeah, maybe."

By now they'd reached Briar Forest Drive and the entrance to Stonehenge, an upscale West Side complex of patio homes and townhouses. It took only a few minutes to find Steven's house. Lark had to park the Amigo a few doors down, and the two women walked slowly back to the festively decorated house.

The door was opened by a fresh-faced girl of about nineteen. "Hi," she said. "I'm Katie."

Amy smiled. She should have known. Katie had the Malone eyes. "Hi. I'm Amy Carpenter. And this is Lark DeWitt."

Katie's smile faded, and her big eyes got bigger. "Amy! Oh, I'm so glad to finally meet you. I've heard so much about you. I've been wanting to tell you . . . I'm so sorry about Sam. We all loved him so much."

Her sweetness touched Amy. She could see why Sam had liked her. "Thank you."

Belatedly, Katy turned to Lark. "And Lark . . . hi. I'm glad y'all could make it. I'll go get Justin."

But Justin had already seen them and was headed in their direction. "Hey," he said. "You made it."

His smile included them both, but Lark couldn't help but notice how his eyes lingered on Amy.

"C'mon," he said, "I'll introduce you to everybody."

For the next twenty minutes, they met dozens of Malones and their friends. Lark liked all of Justin's siblings, but his mother and Katie were her favorites, she decided later. All in all, they were one terrific family. She wondered what it would have been like to grow up the way they had, surrounded by brothers and sisters, all of whom seemed to really like one another, and with a mother you could count on to be there when you needed her. Lark had always had to count on herself.

She thought about her earlier conversation with Amy. How Amy, in saying that Lark didn't have self-doubts, was really suggesting that Lark was strong enough that she didn't need to lean on other people. Maybe that was true. Okay, it *was* true, but the reason Lark was strong was that she'd *had* to be. And maybe, once in a while, she'd *like* to lean on someone else . . .

She sipped at a glass of chardonnay and watched as Justin, with a protective hand at Amy's waist, introduced her to a latecomer.

Something painful squeezed at Lark's heart. Someone would always want to take care of Amy.

"Are you having a good time?"

Lark nearly spilled her drink.

"Oh, I'm sorry," Claire Malone said, "I startled you."

Lark gave a forced chuckle. "No, it's my fault. I was daydreaming."

Claire nodded, her gaze moving to Justin and Amy, then back to Lark. "Amy seems to be doing better."

"Yes, I think she is." Lark still felt a bit rattled. Claire was altogether too astute.

"Justin tells me she's gone back to work this year."

"Yes."

"That's good. There's nothing like work to keep the mind occupied. I know after Sean died, my job kept me sane. Of course, I had all the kids, too." Then she laughed. "But half the time they drove me *insane.*"

Lark chuckled. "I can imagine. That must have been hard. Raising all those kids alone."

"It was, but when I look back now, I realize I was awfully lucky. I had Sean for fourteen years, and he gave me five wonderful children." Her gaze returned to Amy. "She only had Sam a few months, and she lost her child."

"Yes." Guilt nudged at Lark, because for a moment there, watching Justin and Amy, she'd felt the long, green arm of envy.

They fell silent. The party noises surrounded them: people talking and laughing, Eric Clapton and his band coming from the CD player, dishes clinking from the kitchen.

"Justin's in love with her," Claire said.

Lark was proud of herself. She didn't flinch. And she didn't allow any inner emotion to color her voice. "Yes, I can see that."

"I wonder if she can."

Lark shrugged. "I don't know. She's never said anything." And Lark had certainly never encouraged the subject. Today, she had finally realized why. "I think, though, for the past year, she's been so wrapped up in her own emotions, it's been hard for her to see anyone else's."

"I'm afraid he'll get hurt."

"It's possible."

Claire sighed. "Well, there's nothing much I can do about it if he does. I learned a long time ago that as much as I love my children, I can't protect them from hard knocks."

Lark nodded.

"And no one can help who they fall in love with, either."

How true, Lark thought. How sadly true. Suddenly, she wished she hadn't come tonight. It was too hard to be there. Too hard to see Justin's wonderful family and talk to his terrific mother and see, so plainly, just exactly what it was she might have had if circumstances had been different.

She wondered if there was any way she could leave. She thought about it for a few minutes, then decided, why not? She would tell Amy she had cramps. It wouldn't be much of a lie, because Lark figured she'd have them tomorrow. Yes, that's what she'd do. If Amy wanted to stay at the party, Justin would probably jump at the chance to see her home.

Once Claire had drifted away, Lark moved in Amy's direction.

Justin said he would be happy to take Amy home.

"But Lark, it's not even midnight yet," Amy said.

"I know." Lark looked at Justin. "Do you mind, Justin? This is girl talk."

He grinned, then leaned over to kiss Lark's cheek. "I'm going. Happy New Year, Lark."

"Happy New Year, Justin."

Amy watched, thinking how at one time she'd fantasized about maybe getting Lark and Justin together. But that was another lifetime ago. *Before Justin told me he was in love with me.* The thought disturbed Amy. Normally she managed to keep that knowledge at a distance. She wondered if Justin still felt that way. Since that day in May, he had been true to his word and had not brought up the subject again. Tonight, for some reason, this disturbed her.

After Justin walked off, Lark said, "Listen, Amy, I'm sorry. I know it's not midnight yet, but you know how I am when I start getting cramps. Nothing is going to help except Motrin and my bed."

Amy studied Lark's face and wondered why she

didn't believe her. Yet why would Lark lie? If she was having an awful time, she'd say so. "Well, if you're going, I'll go, too."

"No, you stay. You're having fun. I can tell."

Amy *was* having fun. She liked Justin's family. And it felt good to be dressed up and out among people who weren't constantly watching what they said. Sure, Justin's brother and his sisters all knew about Sam, but the rest of the people here didn't. The conversation wheeled freely, and for once, Amy didn't feel like a roadblock. "I hate for you to have to drive home alone, though."

"For God's sake, I'm twenty-eight years old. I travel all over the country alone. Besides, I've got my car phone and Mr. Rescue. I'll be just fine."

"Well, okay. But call me tomorrow. Maybe we can go see a movie. If you're feeling better, that is."

"It's a date."

They hugged and wished each other a happy new year, and then Lark was gone.

Amy sipped her champagne and was just about to walk over and talk to Justin's mother when his sister Jessie approached her.

"You having a good time?" Jessie said.

"Yes, surprisingly so," Amy said. Then she laughed. "I didn't mean that the way it sounded. I meant I've been out of circulation for so long—"

"You don't have to explain. I understand."

For a few moments, they stood silently. Then Jessie said, "I've been curious about you for a long time."

Not quite sure what to answer, Amy said nothing.

"I knew if Sam had fallen in love with you, you had to be someone special," Jessie continued.

"What a nice thing to say."

Jessie's smile was bittersweet. "Well, Sam was a pretty special guy."

Suddenly, without knowing how, Amy knew that Jessie had been in love with Sam. The realization made her feel a kinship with Justin's sister. "Yes, he was."

"I wanted to call you several times and . . . tell you how sorry I was, but I felt kind of funny about it, since I didn't know you."

"Well, we know each other now," Amy said gently.

Their eyes met, and slowly, Jessie smiled. "We do, don't we?"

Smiling back, Amy said, "I hope we can be friends."

"I'd like that."

Just then, Justin walked up, and then several others did, too, and Amy had no more chance to talk to Jessie alone, but she kept thinking about her as the evening progressed. What must it have been like for Jessie, loving Sam and having to see him fall in love and get engaged to someone else? And then to lose him without ever having had him? At least Amy'd had Sam's love and now had so many wonderful memories. And maybe, one of these days, she'd be able to remember those happy times without feeling sad.

"Is something the matter?" Justin said. "You seem preoccupied, all of a sudden."

"Oh, no," Amy said, shaking off her thoughts. "I'm fine. I guess I was just daydreaming."

"Well, it's almost midnight. And I see Lisa and Susan passing out hats and noisemakers. Let's go get ours."

Soon the house was filled with noise and laughter, and someone turned on the TV set so they could watch the countdown to midnight. And then it was more noise and everyone kissing everyone else and yelling "Happy New Year."

Amy good-naturedly joined in the merrymaking, kissing people indiscriminately. Mostly the kisses were friendly pecks. And then Justin said, "My turn," and put his arms around her. "Happy New Year, Amy," he said.

Amy smiled up into his eyes. "Happy New Year, Justin."

And then he kissed her. This kiss was more than friendly. This kiss said everything that had been unsaid between them for all these long months. This kiss told Amy that he did indeed still love her and that he wasn't going to change his mind.

She was a bit breathless when they finally broke apart, and her pulse was beating harder. She was very glad for the commotion around them and the fact that Justin's brother Steven claimed her next, because she wasn't certain where to look or what to say. She also wasn't sure exactly what it was she was feeling.

After all the kissing, more champagne was poured and everyone toasted everyone else. Someone put more music on the CD player and the awkward moments were past.

Shortly after midnight, Katie made the rounds and said her goodbyes. She and a bunch of her friends were leaving to go to another party.

"It was *great* to meet you, Amy," she said.

"You, too, Katie."

"Bring her to dinner some Sunday," Katie said to Justin.

He smiled, meeting Amy's gaze. "I will." Then he turned back to his sister. "Now, you be careful. There'll be a lot of crazies out there tonight."

Katie's expression was indulgent. "I will, I will, don't worry."

It wasn't long after Katie left that Justin said, "Anytime you're ready to leave, just say so."

"Actually, I'm ready now," Amy said.

So they said their goodbyes, and shortly after 1 o'clock, they reached Amy's.

"Your folks home?" Justin said, looking over at the house, which had lights in several windows.

"I doubt it. They went to a party at the country club."

By now they'd walked over to the steps leading up to her apartment.

"I'll walk you up," he said.

"All right."

Moonlight silvered the yard, casting ghostly shadows over the winter-bare trees and lawn. The night air was cold, and Amy's breath puffed out in front of her. She could smell woodsmoke and hear firecrackers popping in the distance. The charcoal sky glittered with stars.

When they reached the top of the stairs, she turned. Although no words were spoken, Justin seemed to sense that something had changed. He reached out, and she let herself be drawn into his arms.

And when he kissed her, she kissed him back. It felt good to be in a man's arms again. And if the kiss didn't send her skyrocketing, it made her feel safe and warm and as close to happy as she'd been in a long, long time. As they slowly drew apart, she looked up, and he looked down.

They stood that way for perhaps five seconds, but it seemed longer to Amy. She could feel her heart beating, and something else—a yearning, deep inside.

Wordlessly, she took Justin's hand, and together they walked inside.

Seventeen

Faith and Alan left the New Year's Eve party shortly before 2 A.M.; five minutes later, they were home. The first thing Faith saw when they entered the driveway was Justin's Toyota.

She glanced up at Amy's apartment. It was dark.

"Look's like Justin's here," Alan remarked, as he pulled the Cadillac into the garage.

"Yes."

Was Justin spending the night? Faith had harbored a secret hope that something might develop between him and Amy, ever since she'd realized Justin was in love with her daughter. From the looks of things, maybe her wish had come true.

She mentally crossed her fingers. If only this worked out! Justin was perfect for Amy, the kind of man Faith had always *hoped* her daughter would choose. But most important, if Amy was involved with Justin, there'd no longer be any need to worry that another Sam might come along.

As Alan unlocked the back door, Faith glanced up at the apartment again. She couldn't suppress a tiny, satisfied smile. If she got any opportunity at all, she'd do everything she could to further Justin's cause.

* * *

Justin lay awake long after Amy had fallen asleep. When the night had begun, he hadn't dreamed Amy would allow him to kiss her, let alone make love to her. He had thought about this, hoped for it, so many times in the past few months, and now it had happened.

His arms tightened around her. Making love to Amy had been incredible, everything he'd imagined it would be and more. Just thinking about their lovemaking caused a wellspring of happiness and a deep sense of contentment.

He refused to feel guilty on Sam's account. He wasn't the one who'd gone off and left Amy. He wasn't the one who'd been stupid enough to go climbing down a cliff thousands of feet over a gorge. He wasn't the one who'd had to prove he was more daring than everyone else.

It was Sam's own damn fault he'd died. His own damn fault Amy was now alone . . . and lonely.

I love her, and Sam is gone. Besides, Sam wouldn't have wanted Amy to spend the rest of her life alone. Sam was nothing if not realistic. He'd never wasted time lamenting the way things were. He'd simply moved on. If situations had been reversed, if it had been Amy who'd died, Sam would have grieved, but eventually he'd have moved on. And if the situations had been reversed in another way, if it had been Justin engaged to Amy and Justin who had died, he certainly wouldn't have wanted her to mourn and be lonely the rest of her life. He'd have been glad to know Sam was taking care of her and loving her.

But I'll never leave her . . .

It was his last thought before he fell asleep.

* * *

The next morning, when Amy awakened to find herself cradled in warm arms, her first reaction was guilt as memories of the night before flooded her. Then she thought, *Wait a minute, why should I feel guilty? I'm free, I'm an adult. What did I do that was so wrong?*

Fully awake, she thought about everything that had happened, from the moment she'd stepped through the door at Steven's town house until the moment she'd gone to sleep in Justin's arms.

Examining her feelings, she decided she didn't regret anything, although this morning might be awkward, because she wasn't sure what Justin would expect now. She wasn't sure what it was *she* wanted, either.

But last night?

No.

Making love with Justin had been surprisingly satisfying. Maybe not wild and intense, as it had been with Sam, but comforting, and tender, and deeply stirring. From the moment she'd indicated her willingness, Justin had taken charge. He hadn't been rough, but he'd been masterful. She had felt loved and protected and . . . *cherished.* Yes, cherished was exactly the word to describe the way he'd made her feel. And because the experience with Justin was so different from her experiences with Sam, she had not, as she'd first feared, imagined herself to be with Sam or tried to project Sam's image in place of Justin's or made comparisons. No, all through their lovemaking last night, she had known exactly who it was kissing her and touching her . . . and she had not felt sad or unhappy or the least bit regretful.

She looked at Justin. He was a great guy. Such

a rock. His dark hair tumbled over his forehead, his face was peaceful and trouble free. Resisting the urge to smooth his hair away—she didn't want to wake him—she wondered if he'd felt any guilt last night. She hoped not. There was no reason for either of them to feel guilty—not on Sam's account, anyway. If Sam were still here, none of this would be happening. And it was Sam's choice to leave, she thought, with a trace of bitterness.

In fact, she wouldn't feel any regret at all if she had only been able to give Justin her whole heart, the way she'd given him her whole body.

And that inability was the reason for her uncertainty now. Moving carefully, she slid out from under Justin's arm. As she pulled on her robe and slid her feet into slippers, she decided that the best thing to do would be to confront the situation immediately. When he woke up, she would tell him how she felt and ask him how he felt. And then they would take it from there.

The coffee had just begun to drip into the pot and she was pouring fresh cat food into the cats' bowl when Justin, barefoot and bare chested, walked into the kitchen.

Amy had sternly told herself not to be coy or shy. Yet shyness attacked her, and it was hard to meet his eyes. "Good morning," she said, hoping her smile didn't look as forced as it felt.

"Good morning."

She recapped the plastic container of cat food, still not meeting his gaze directly. "Coffee's almost ready."

"Great." He walked closer.

Amy swallowed.

"Amy . . ." He reached over to still her restless hands.

She slowly looked up, her heart beating too fast.

For a long moment, they simply looked at each other. Then, firmly, he drew her into his arms.

She sighed, closing her eyes as their lips met. The kiss was long and sweet, but there was an undercurrent of desire there, too. It would be so easy to succumb to it, so easy just to climb back into bed with him, something he clearly wanted. Summoning all her willpower, Amy gently pushed him away. "Justin, wait . . . I . . . I think we have to talk first."

Something flamed in his eyes. Denial? Anger? Fear? Amy wasn't sure.

"Okay."

Oh, God. Was she really ready for this? "Um, would you like to shower first? I'll make breakfast, then when you're done, we can eat and talk." Again, she avoided his eyes. What a coward she was!

"Amy . . ."

His voice compelled her to look at him.

"You're stalling."

She laughed uncertainly. "I know."

Suddenly, he laughed, too, and some of the awkwardness and tension dissipated. Still chuckling, he bent and kissed the tip of her nose. "All right. I'll go get a shower and let you gather your thoughts, but when I'm done . . ."

His tone left no doubt in her mind. He was not going to be put off any longer. He had told her once he would never pressure her, that the next move was up to her. Well, now he was clearly telling her she'd made that move, and they could never go back to their old relationship. It was time for a decision, and he wasn't going to let her off the hook until she made it.

Twenty minutes later, showered and shaved and

neatly dressed in the clothes he'd worn last night, he joined her at the table.

She poured him a cup of coffee. "I made corn muffins. They'll be ready in about ten minutes."

He smiled, his eyes very blue as they met hers. "A beautiful woman who cooks. What more could a man ask for?"

Amy kept her voice just as light as his. "Yep, I slaved all of three minutes opening that box of mix and adding water and eggs."

Justin was scared, but he was determined not to show it. He wanted her, yes, and for a while, he'd even believed he'd take her any way he could get her. But this morning, he'd realized he didn't want her out of pity. So he wouldn't let her see his fear, even as he desperately hoped she wouldn't say last night had been a mistake.

He heard her behind him, heard the clank of the baking tray as she removed the muffins from the oven, the clink of dishes, the rattle of silverware—all the ordinary sounds of getting breakfast ready. A painful lump formed in his chest.

A few minutes later, plate of muffins in hand, she settled across from him.

Their eyes met.

"Amy . . ."

"Justin . . ."

They both laughed self-consciously.

She thought about how much she cared for him and how she didn't want to hurt him and how good it had felt to be with him last night.

He thought about how much he loved her and how beautiful she looked and how much he wanted to see her across the breakfast table from him every morning.

"This is hard for me to say," she began, "but I

feel as if I have to say it. Last night . . ." She took
a deep breath. "Last night was . . . really wonderful . . . but I want to be sure . . . I . . . oh, God
. . . this is *really* hard."

Justin thought, what the hell. What would happen, would happen, so why not make it easier for
both of them? "Amy, let's not play games. I'm a big
boy. If you're sorry about last night, just say so."

"No! No, I'm *not* sorry. I just . . . well . . . I'm
not in love with you the way . . ."

She broke off, and Justin knew she'd been about
to say, *The way I was with Sam*. He told himself not
to be hurt. It was too soon, that was all.

"The way a woman should be when she . . . be-
gins an intimate relationship with a man," Amy continued doggedly. She *had* to make him understand.
Unless everything was clear between them, she
wouldn't be able to go to bed with him again, ever,
without feeling guilty, and she wasn't sure she could
live with those feelings. "I love you. I love you a lot.
But I'm not *in love* with you. And I don't think it's
fair to you to go on unless you know that."

Relief and happiness were all mixed up together
as Justin reached across the table to touch her
hand. "But you love me, and that's a start. The
other doesn't matter, Amy. I can wait for that."

"But Justin, I . . . I might not ever be in love
with you."

He looked into her troubled eyes. They were so
beautiful, just as everything about her was beautiful, from the inside out. She was trying so hard to
be honest and fair. He loved her more at this moment than he'd ever loved her before. "Even that
doesn't matter . . . as long as we're together . . .
and as long as you want me. *Do* you want me?"

Her smile was like the sunlight appearing on a

dark, gray day. "Yes," she said, "I want you. I want you very much."

Justin left at noon with the promise that he'd be back that evening. He was taking her to dinner at Ciro's.

At 12:30, just as Amy was getting out of the shower, her phone rang. Hastily wrapping a towel around her head and another around her body, she raced into the bedroom.

"Hello?"

"Hi." It was Lark.

Amy smiled. "Hi. You feeling better today?"

"Oh, you know, same old, same old. But yeah, I guess I'm feeling better."

"Good."

"I was wondering . . . you still want to try to catch a movie today?"

"Um, sure, if, um, we can go early enough for me to be back by seven. Justin's taking me to dinner tonight."

"Oh." There was a brief moment of silence, then, "Well, if you'd rather just forget it, that's okay."

Amy frowned. Lark sounded funny. Maybe she had figured the two of them would go out for dinner after the movie. Sure. That must be it. "No, I'd love to go to a movie with you. In fact, why don't you plan on going out to dinner with Justin and me?"

"Oh, no. Two's company, remember?"

"Lark, don't be silly. Justin's as much your friend as he is mine, and I know he'd love to have you come with us." As soon as the words were out of her mouth, Amy knew they weren't quite true. She and Justin were more than friends now. They were lovers. But that didn't matter. The sentiment was true.

"I don't think—"

"That's right. Don't think," Amy said, laughing. "You're going with us, and that's that."

After they hung up, Amy wondered if she should tell Lark about what had happened the previous evening. The fact that she was wondering disturbed her. Always, in the past, she'd told Lark everything. What she was feeling as well as the things that had happened to her. What was different about this?

She wasn't sure. She only knew something was, and until she figured out why she felt reluctant, she would say nothing to Lark.

It didn't take Lark ten minutes in Amy's and Justin's company to realize that something had changed and to know exactly what that something was. There was a not-so-subtle possessiveness in Justin's attitude toward Amy, in the way he contrived to touch her . . . and in the way he looked at her. And a couple of times, Amy gave him one of those soft, gooey looks, too.

Oh, shit! They were sleeping together. Lark knew it as surely as she knew her own name. Last night, after he'd taken Amy home, Justin had stayed on, and they had made love. The knowledge cut deep, hurting more than she would have believed possible. Oh God, why? Why had she fallen in love with a man who loved her best friend? It was going to be a long and difficult evening, and she would have to call on every bit of acting talent she possessed to get through it.

Somehow, she did.

Somehow, she managed to make it through two

and a half hours of food and wine and conversation and having to watch Justin look at Amy with his heart and soul in his eyes.

When they were finally finished and on their way home, Lark was so relieved she could have cried.

Later, she did cry—hopeless tears that left her feeling spent and miserable. When she finally stopped, she vowed that this was the last time she would ever cry over Justin. Or any man.

Still, she had a hard time sleeping, because she couldn't help worrying about the future. Despite the looks she'd given him tonight, Amy wasn't in love with Justin. She couldn't be. She was still mourning Sam.

Just like Amy's involvement with Sam, this situation had all the potential for disaster. But this time, Lark was afraid Justin was the one who was going to get hurt.

After thinking about it most of the day Tuesday, she finally called and left a message on Amy's answering machine saying she'd like to come over and see her that night.

A little past 4:30, Amy called back. "Sure. Come on over. You feel like Chinese takeout? I'll order some."

"Sounds good."

At 6 o'clock Lark pulled into Amy's driveway. She had thought hard about what she should say and had decided to be completely honest.

"I'm glad you came over," Amy said, hugging her. "We really didn't get a chance to talk last night."

Deciding they would wait a while before ordering their food, Amy poured them each a glass of wine and they walked out to the living area. She curled up on one corner of the couch, and Lark sat on the other.

Lark sipped at her wine. "Amy—I, um, *noticed* something last night."

"Oh?"

Was it Lark's imagination, or did Amy's expression become just a little bit wary? "Something has changed between you and Justin, hasn't it?"

Amy's cheeks turned pink and she fiddled with a loose thread in her sweater. "Is . . . is it that obvious?"

"Maybe not to others, but I know you."

"Oh, God, Lark, do you think I'm terrible?" she asked.

"Why would I think you're terrible?"

Looking down into her glass, she murmured, "I don't know."

"No, I don't think you're terrible. I *am* a bit concerned, though."

"About me?"

"No. About Justin."

Amy slowly lifted her eyes to meet Lark's gaze.

"You're not in love with him," Lark said.

"No." The word came out as little more than a whisper.

"And you know he's in love with you."

"Yes."

"Then why, Amy? Don't you think letting him make love to you is unfair? Look, I know you're still hurting. I know how much you've lost. But Justin has been a terrific friend to you. You don't want to hurt him, do you?"

"No, of course not!"

"But you will if you're not careful."

"I know all that, Lark. I do. But you don't understand. And I'm not sure I can explain it. Besides, he knows how I feel, and he's okay with it."

"He's *okay* with it?"

"Yes. He knows I'm not in love with him, but he says that doesn't matter."

"Oh, Amy, for God's sake! Of course it matters!" It was on the tip of Lark's tongue to say, *Don't you think you're being selfish?* when she stopped herself. Who was she to criticize or tell Amy what to do? And would she even feel this way if she wasn't in love with Justin herself? Wasn't she being hard on Amy? After all, it wasn't Amy's fault that Justin had fallen in love with her.

"I *do* love him, Lark," Amy said, her eyes troubled. "He's a wonderful person."

"I know."

Amy looked away. When she spoke again, her voice was bleak. "Sam is gone. I've accepted that." She looked up again. "I don't want to be alone the rest of my life. And Justin makes me happy." This was said almost defiantly. "Is that so wrong?"

"No, not wrong, but—"

"But what?"

"What will you do if he asks you to marry him?"

Amy sighed deeply. "I don't know."

"You'd better think about it, because he will."

Amy nodded.

"If you don't think you can go through with it . . . marry him, that is . . . then it would be kinder to tell him the score now."

"I know."

"Because the longer you allow this . . . *situation* to continue," Lark went on relentlessly, "the harder it will be for him in the end. The harder it will be for *both* of you."

"I know," Amy said again.

"Besides, Amy, if, in your heart, you know you'll never marry him, what you're doing now is *using* him."

Eighteen

"Justin spent the evening with Amy again last night," Faith said on Saturday morning. She eyed the margarine regretfully and poured a small amount of lite syrup on her pancakes. She had been on a low-fat diet for months, ever since her doctor had told her her cholesterol was too high, and she wasn't enjoying it.

"Hmm?" Alan said, not looking up from the sports page.

"Alan, are you listening to me?"

He finally lowered the paper. "I'm sorry, darling. What did you say?"

Faith repeated her observation, then added, "I see this as a good sign, don't you?"

"What? Amy's friendship with Justin?"

"Yes. He's in love with her, obviously."

"Is he?"

Faith rolled her eyes. "Honestly, you men can be so dense. Yes, of course he's in love with her. Why, you'd have to be *blind* not to see it. When they're together, he can't keep his eyes off her."

Alan helped himself to a couple more pancakes and liberally spread margarine over them. "He's a nice young man."

"Yes, he is. This would be a good thing for Amy. I only wish she and I could talk the way we used to. I'd encourage the relationship."

Alan's expression was sympathetic, although Faith knew he had disapproved of her attempt to dissuade Amy from marrying Sam. Alan believed Amy's choices were hers to make, and if they ended up being bad choices, so be it. "She has to make her own mistakes," he'd said more times than Faith could count.

"Best to keep your nose out of this," he said now in a mild tone.

Faith nodded. Yes, she'd certainly learned her lesson. Amy's coolness to her since Sam's disappearance had abated somewhat, but they had a long way to go before they'd recapture the closeness they'd once shared. "What I was hoping was that *you'd* talk to Amy."

"Me?" Alan said, incredulous.

"Yes, you. She'd listen to you."

"Faith, you know perfectly well how I feel about this kind of thing. It's Amy life. If she wants to be with Justin, that's her decision—not ours."

"Oh, Alan, for heaven's sake! Can't you bend those rules of yours once in a while? After all, you're her *father.* Don't you *care*?"

"Of course I care. But I don't think this is any of our business."

"Fine," Faith said, trying to stifle her exasperation. "Perhaps I'll talk to Lark, then . . . see how she feels about all of this."

"Faith," Alan said in a warning voice.

She sighed. "Oh, all right, Alan, all right. I won't say a word. But I can hope, can't I? Because I think Justin would make Amy a wonderful husband."

In answer, Alan just gave her an amused look and began reading the sports page again.

By March, Amy knew that if and when Justin asked her to marry him, she'd say yes. She felt safe with him, and quietly happy. So what if she didn't feel the same kind of giddy joy she'd felt with Sam? Perhaps happiness was like candy. A little bit of it went a long way.

She knew she could trust Justin. He'd always be there for her. He'd never let her down.

And that was the bottom line.

They had fallen into a comfortable routine since New Year's Eve. He generally spent a couple of weekday evenings with her and they always spent their weekends together. They'd go out to dinner on Friday night and come back to her apartment, and he would stay there until Monday morning.

Gradually, he began leaving clothes and personal articles at her place. Occasionally, she'd spend the night at his townhouse, but she didn't like leaving her cats alone.

For Amy's twenty-ninth birthday, the third week of March—which, happily, coincided with spring break—Justin suggested a three-day trip to Las Vegas.

"Oh, I'd *love* to go. I've never been there," Amy said.

He grinned. "Great. I'll make the arrangements."

When Amy told her mother she'd be away for a few days and where she was going, her mother seemed equally pleased. "You'll have a good time. Las Vegas is fun."

"Do you mind feeding the cats for me?"

"I don't mind at all."

Amy couldn't help comparing her mother's reaction to this trip to Faith's much less positive reaction to her New Orleans trip with Sam. She wasn't surprised, though. Justin was much more mainstream, much more reliable than Sam. Of course he'd appeal to her mother.

So? Isn't that reliability, that safety factor, one of the things about him that appeals to you?

Amy was taken aback by the realization that she and her mother might be closer in their ideas than she thought.

"Have a wonderful time, darling," Faith said.

Amy did have a wonderful time. She loved everything about Las Vegas—the flash, the noise, the people, the carnival-like atmosphere, even the garishness. She didn't care that so much of the city was horribly trashy and sinfully excessive, because it was also wickedly fun.

She and Justin stayed at one of the newest and biggest casinos, in an opulent suite that might have belonged in an expensive bordello, with its red velvet and gold-trimmed faux French furniture and dripping crystal chandelier. The round bed tickled her fancy, the satin sheets and mirror on the ceiling made her feel decadent and totally unlike herself. Because the environment was so different, their lovemaking was different, too—much more uninhibited and passionate.

"Maybe I should buy a round bed," Justin said, after a particularly energetic session.

"It's the mirror that does it," Amy replied, giggling.

Amy discovered she loved slot machines. She played the quarter machines at Caesar's Palace for such a long time, her right arm became sore. "Now

I understand how a person could become a compulsive gambler," she told Justin.

He shook his head in mock disapproval. "And you look so wholesome and prim."

"Prim! I'll give you prim!" She pretended to punch him. "I'm definitely not prim."

No, he thought, she was definitely not prim. And if he'd ever thought so, last night in bed would have changed his mind forever. He still couldn't believe how aggressive she'd been. It was the first time, in the months since they'd first become lovers, that she had acted as if she couldn't wait for them to be together. Thinking about the way she'd touched him and the way she'd moaned when he'd touched her, he could feel himself wanting her again.

He bent closer, nuzzling her neck as she pulled the arm of the slot machine. She turned, her eyes only inches from his. Oblivious to the people around them, Justin slipped his arm around her waist and gently squeezed. "Let's go back to the room," he muttered, his voice thick with the desire that had become a hot flame.

Their lovemaking was swift and urgent, and this time, when Justin plunged into her and she cried out, he was absolutely certain—as he'd never been before—that he was the only man she was thinking about.

The entire time Amy and Justin were in Las Vegas, Lark could think of nothing else. It infuriated her, this inability to put them out of her mind.

Always before, when Lark had wanted to forget about a man, she had had no trouble. Of course, she'd never really been in love before.

She alternated between hating herself and hating

them. Finally, she decided she'd just hate everyone and everything and be done with it.

On the day they were scheduled to arrive home, she called Amy's and left a falsely cheerful message. *"Hey, kiddo, did you have fun in Sin City? Call and fill me in on all the details. Tell Justin I said 'hi' and hope he won the jackpot."*

She laughed bitterly after hanging up the phone. Oh, Justin had won the jackpot, all right. He had Amy. And that's all the jackpot he'd ever want or need.

The day after their return from Las Vegas, Amy removed the emerald ring from her finger and put it in her jewelry box. The dark green stone sparkled in the lamplight. An aching sadness gripped her as she stared at its beautiful surface and remembered the happiness she'd felt when Sam had given it to her. Her hand felt empty without it. For a moment, she almost grabbed it up again.

Resolutely, she closed the lid of the jewelry box. No. She had made her decision. It wasn't fair to Justin to continue wearing it.

The ring belonged to the past.

Sam belonged to the past.

He would always have a part of her heart, but for her own happiness and wellbeing, she had to do her best to move forward . . . into the future . . . with Justin.

The first thing Justin noticed when he went to Amy's a few nights later was the absence of the ring. His heart leaped. *Yes! Finally!* He wanted to say something, but he didn't, not right away. He waited until they'd finished the pizza he'd brought and were sitting on the couch listening to a Pavarotti CD.

Then he took her hand in his, gently rubbing the ring finger. "You put away your ring."

She turned to look at him. "Yes."

If she was feeling sad, she was disguising it well. Encouraged, he smiled and said, "How would you feel about another ring?"

She hesitated, and Justin immediately wanted to kick himself. It was too soon. Why hadn't he waited? He wished he could take the words back, but it was too late.

But then she smiled and said sweetly, "Could we wait a while before we discuss this? I—I'm not quite ready," and everything was all right again.

In May, Amy was asked to chaperone the sixth-graders' class trip to Washington, D.C. She would be gone five days.

"What am I going to do with myself Friday and Saturday night?" Justin complained, putting on a sad face. "You'll be having fun in Washington, and I'll be all by myself."

"Oh, sure, I'll be overseeing twenty-two eleven-year-olds. Some fun." But Amy was looking forward to it. She loved the kids and knew they'd all have a great time in Washington. "Anyway, if you're lonesome, call Lark and take her out to dinner."

Although Amy had offhandedly tossed off the suggestion, Justin thought it was a good idea, so a couple of days later, he did call Lark.

"Well," she said when she heard his voice. "This is a surprise. What's up?"

Justin felt a bit guilty, because even though Lark had not criticized him, he knew he had neglected their friendship in the past months. And he really liked Lark and had missed their conversations. He resolved not to neglect her again. "You know Amy's going to Washington tomorrow."

"Yeah, she told me."

"I was hoping, if you don't have plans, you'd keep me company Friday night. Let me take you to dinner."

"Well, actually, I *do* have plans."

"Oh." He knew he had no right to feel disappointed, but somehow, he did. "What about Saturday night?"

She was silent for so long, Justin began to think she might not have heard him. Finally, though, she said, "Sure. Why not?"

They decided he would pick her up at 6:30 and that they would go to Las Alamedas.

After they'd hung up, Justin thought about that long silence before Lark had said okay to Saturday night. Something about it, something about the entire conversation, bothered him. He wondered if there was anything wrong. He'd seen so little of Lark in the past couple of months that he had no idea what was going on in her life.

Well, Saturday night, he'd make it his business to ask. Now that he'd made the first move to recapturing the friendship they'd built since Sam's death, he didn't want to lose it again.

Lark was disgusted with herself. She'd tried on at least six different outfits before finally deciding she'd wear her favorite Carole Little pants and long tunic top in a muted wine-colored print and be damned with the whole thing. Who cared what she wore, anyway? Certainly Justin wouldn't. Hell, no.

She wasn't kidding herself he wanted to take her to dinner because he missed her company or anything. He just wanted, in Amy's absence, to be able to talk about her to someone who would listen.

Lark felt like throwing something. Why had she said she'd go tonight? Why was she letting herself in for this misery? She could see the entire scenario now. All night Justin would go on about Amy, and Lark would have to listen and smile and say appropriate gushy things back.

Well, she'd be *damned* if she would. If he started in about how wonderful everything was, Lark might just say a few choice things, like he was a god-damned fool if he thought Amy really loved him the way a woman should love a man and that she would *never* love him that way.

Lark continued to mutter and curse even as she picked up her bottle of Shalimar and gave herself four good squirts and put extra mascara on her eyelashes and brushed her cheekbones with a darker blush than she normally used and defiantly made up her lips in a dark lipstick that matched her outfit.

Then she glared at herself in the mirror.

Starkly unhappy eyes looked back at her.

"I hate him," she said. "I don't know why I'm going tonight. I'm crazy."

Seconds later, the doorbell rang.

When she saw him standing on her doorstep—dark hair slicked back, blue eyes depthless and filled with warmth, smiling down at her—she knew exactly why she'd said she'd go. Because being with him, having his smile and his eyes and his warmth all to herself, even if only for a few hours, was worth all the pain and unhappiness she would feel when the hours were over.

He gave a low whistle. "Wow. You look nice."

"Well, gee," she said, "don't act so surprised. I really do clean up well."

He laughed and bent down to kiss her cheek. "I've missed you, smart mouth."

"And whose fault is that?"

"Mine. I know."

"Good. Now that we've got the apology for your shameful neglect out of the way, let's go eat. I'm starving."

The evening turned out to be both easier and harder than Lark had expected. It was easier in that Justin didn't talk about Amy much, except to say he hoped she had a good time in Washington. It was harder in that Lark realized all over again just what it was about Justin that had made her fall in love with him in the first place.

He was so damned *nice.*

Why couldn't he be a horse's ass, like so many of the men she met? Why couldn't he be selfish and thoughtless and totally wrapped up in himself? Why did he have to be so honest and sincere and really sweet?

He actually cared what she said.

He asked her questions, and he listened to the answers, and his eyes didn't stray the way a person's did when they weren't really hearing you but thinking about what they were going to say next.

And he laughed at her jokes. When she made one of her smart remarks, he grinned, and she knew he was amused and entertained, and that he liked being with her.

And, oh, God, she loved being with him.

As the evening drew to a close, and they ate their flan and drank their coffee, she pretended that they were a couple. That when they left to go home, he would come inside, and they would go into her bedroom, and he would slowly undress her, and she would slowly undress him, and then they would make love.

She knew it was stupid. She knew she was only hurting herself, but she couldn't seem to help it. The wanting and needing were too strong. Suddenly, she could no longer stand her feelings and the terrible emptiness in her heart. "I . . . I'll be back," she said, standing. "I'm going to the ladies'."

He smiled. "Okay."

Once inside the restroom, Lark put her hands over her feverish face. She was shaking, as close to tears as she'd ever been. She knew she had to get herself under control before she went back out there. The last thing in the world she wanted to do was let Justin see how she felt about him.

She managed to get herself calmed down. She splashed cold water on her face and repaired her makeup. Then she took several deep breaths.

It had been a mistake to come tonight. She couldn't handle it. She couldn't handle being with him. Her emotions were too raw.

But she'd learned her lesson.

From now on, she would stay as far away from Justin as she could get.

Nineteen

The dream came and went.

It was always the same. He was in a maze, and he kept walking and walking, but he could never find the way out. He knew it was there, probably just around the corner, but it always eluded him. Just as his name and where he'd come from and what had happened to him eluded him. Somehow the two were tied together, and he knew, if he ever found the way out of the maze, he'd also find himself.

He fingered the plastic-enclosed picture of the beautiful girl with the laughing eyes. The picture and the clothes he'd worn when the villagers had found him were all he had of his former life.

He knew the girl was important to him. Sometimes, when he looked into her green eyes, he felt as if he were almost there. Something, some tiny memory buried deep in his subconscious, would tug at the corners of his mind. He'd strain, trying to reach it, but it would drift away.

At times like these, his head would hurt unbearably, and he would moan. Within moments, Reena would come, with her sympathetic dark eyes and soothing, cool hands and gentle words of comfort. She would stroke his forehead and give him water and sit with him until his headache went away. Sometimes she would sing, and he would fall asleep.

He had figured out early in his sojourn that Reena was the matriarchal head of the village. The other women looked up to her and deferred to her opinions.

He knew he was lucky, because Reena had obviously adopted him. It was clear she considered him a son of sorts, because she mothered him and fussed over him.

In the first days after they'd found him, when he'd been nearly delirious with pain, she had directed the men to move him into her *ghar,* and she'd nursed him day and night. She'd fed him endless cups of tea, which she called *chiyaa* and a type of gruel made of potatoes called *aalu,* and then, when he got stronger, *maasu* mixed with cooked *banda kobi*—meat and cabbage.

"Ramro, ramro," she would say, when he finished his food. She would give him a wide smile, and eventually, he figured out she was praising him, that the word *ramro* meant "good."

During that first winter, when the blizzards, followed by the terrible avalanches, cut the village off completely, she had tended him gently and lovingly.

Gradually, he had healed. Not completely. Not the way he imagined he had been before, but enough so that by spring, he could walk with the aid of handmade crutches. Now the only help he needed was a cane.

At times he wondered why the villagers had not sought help for him, had not tried to take him to one of the bigger cities, where surely someone would know who he was. But eventually he had realized that the villagers were simply wary of outsiders, although they did not seem at all wary of him.

In fact, he was treated as if he were an honored guest. At first, he couldn't understand why. Later, he realized his status had nothing to do with him but everything to do with Reena and her position in the village.

During the long summer that followed, as he learned to communicate more easily, he became friendly with a young boy who seemed to be an orphan and was watched out for by several of the male villagers.

The boy, whose name was Jamuna, spent long hours sitting at his feet and teaching him words from the Nepalese language. Patiently, Jamuna would point, then say the word, and he would repeat it until he knew what it meant. In this way, he learned that he was an American and that the villagers revered Americans and considered them all to be rich and powerful.

After he'd healed to the point where he could walk with the cane, he wondered if he should try to find his way back to some kind of civilization, but each time he considered going, he became frightened.

This village, these people, and especially Reena, were the only people he knew. Here he was safe. Outside, who knew? When he'd been hurt and lost his memory, maybe he had been involved in something illegal. He had no idea. Maybe, if he left the village, he would be arrested and thrown in jail . . . or worse.

If only he knew.

If only he could make his way out of the maze and recapture the lost pieces of his life.

Then, maybe, he could go home.

Twenty

"Amy?"

"Hmm?" She stirred from her comfortable niche in Justin's arms and twisted so she could see his face.

"Remember what we talked about after we got back from Las Vegas?"

"Yes." She'd been wondering when he would re-introduce the subject. Lately, she'd felt deeply contented and more than ready to move on to the next phase of their relationship.

He bent his head and kissed her, a lingering kiss that spoke not so much of desire as of love. "I love you so much," he whispered against her mouth. "You know that, don't you?"

"Yes."

"You've been happy with me, haven't you?"

She smiled. "Yes."

His gaze clung to hers for a long moment. "Amy, I want you to be my wife. Will you marry me?"

She tried not to think about the last time someone had asked her to marry him. She tried not to remember her soaring happiness and the eagerness with which she'd given her answer. It wasn't fair to Justin to compare him with Sam or to compare this situation with the other. They were nothing alike, and she was nothing like the girl she'd been two years ago, either.

Sam had been the love of her heart. She would never again feel the same way about anyone.

Justin was her friend and her lover, someone she cared for deeply, someone who would always be there for her.

She caressed his cheek. "Yes," she said. "Yes, I'll marry you."

His smile nearly broke her heart, it was so filled with joy. She wished she could tell him, without reservation, that she loved him the way he loved her, but she couldn't, and she wouldn't pretend.

"What do you think about October?" he said, after another lingering kiss.

"October? But October's only three months away, and I don't get any time off in October." *And Sam died in October.*

"I thought we could postpone a wedding trip until your Christmas break."

Amy involuntarily stiffened. She knew he hadn't realized the significance of a wedding trip over the Christmas break. "Justin," she said slowly, "I really want everything about . . . about our wedding to be different."

"Different?" For a moment, he seemed confused, then realization dawned. "Oh." He grimaced. "That was pretty stupid of me, wasn't it?"

She shrugged.

"Well, then, why don't we get married over Thanksgiving and just go somewhere for a three-day weekend?"

Four months.

Was she ready to get married in four months? It

seemed so soon. Then again, why not? She wanted to marry Justin, didn't she?

There really wasn't any reason to wait.

"Please be happy for me, Lark. I know you don't approve. I know you don't think I love Justin the way I should, but I do love him. And I think I can make him happy."

Lark tried to ignore the pain that had come so swiftly and with such intensity. She had thought she was ready for this announcement, but obviously she wasn't. "I am happy for you, Amy. My only concern in all this is that Justin deserves one hundred percent."

"And I'll *give* him one hundred percent."

Lark looked at Amy's eyes—at the honesty and sincerity she saw there. Amy really believed she would do what she said, and maybe she would. Lark hoped so. Taking a deep breath, she gave Amy her best smile. "Congratulations, then."

Amy rushed forward, and they hugged.

"You'll be my maid of honor, won't you?" Amy said, as they broke apart.

"I'd be hurt if you hadn't asked me."

They smiled at each other.

"Have you told your parents yet?" Lark asked.

"Not yet, but we're planning to tomorrow night."

"Your mother will be happy."

"I know."

"Justin's mother will be happy, too," Lark said, remembering Claire's concern for Justin.

"I hope so. I really like her." Amy hesitated. "Sam thought the world of her, too."

"I never told you, but at the New Year's Eve party, she talked to me about you and Justin."

"Really? What did she say?"

"Not that much. Just that she was worried because she knew Justin was in love with you and she was afraid he might get hurt."

"Why didn't you tell me?" There was no criticism in the question, only curiosity.

Lark shrugged. "What was the point? By the time I saw you again, your relationship with him had obviously changed. I figured I'd laid enough on you with my worries. You sure didn't need to feel guilty about Justin's mother."

"Now that my life is settling down, we've got to work on yours," Amy said. "There's *got* to be a guy out there for you."

"Oh, no! Forget that. I told you once before—no more fixed up dates for me. I'm perfectly happy the way I am."

Later, as Lark drove home, she wondered if the day would ever come when she could be completely honest with Amy again.

She certainly hoped so.

Because when that happened, she would no longer feel this pain.

"Amy, darling, I'm so happy for you!" Faith exclaimed. "And Justin . . . this is wonderful." She gave him her warmest smile.

"Thank you, Mrs. Carpenter. I'll do my best to make Amy happy."

"I know you will," Faith said.

"Congratulations," Alan said, shaking Justin's hand.

Faith hoped Justin didn't sense Alan's reserve, which was so obvious to her. Well, Alan was very like Amy—a complete romantic, whereas Faith was more realistic. Yes, she and Alan had seemed destined to be together, but if something had happened to keep them apart, Faith had no doubt she would have eventually met someone else with whom she could have been happy.

Justin would make Amy a wonderful husband. And one of these days, Alan would be just as enthusiastic as Faith was. She looked at Amy. "So— have you picked a date?"

"Yes. We thought we'd get married on Wednesday night, the day before Thanksgiving."

"Perfect," Faith said, glad they weren't waiting too long.

Later, after Amy and Justin had gone, Alan said, "Well, you got your wish."

Faith smiled. "Yes, thank goodness."

Alan nodded, but his eyes were concerned.

"Alan, darling, don't worry. This is the best thing that could have happened to Amy."

It was a while before he answered. "No, it isn't. The best thing that could have happened would be for Sam not to have died."

Faith held her tongue. She still firmly felt that Sam would eventually have made Amy unhappy. Justin was a much better choice for her, much more settled and mature, and certainly more dependable. But why argue? Sam was dead, and Justin was alive.

And nothing Alan believed or wished would change those facts.

That Sunday, Justin brought Amy to his mother's for dinner. Amy wore on her left hand the square-cut diamond he'd given her. He was so proud of her. And she looked so beautiful today, in a green flowered dress made out of some kind of silky material that floated when she moved. He couldn't wait to see his family's reaction when they made their announcement.

They didn't disappoint him.

His mother was obviously thrilled. "I couldn't be happier," she said, hugging Amy.

"Thank you, Mrs. Malone."

"Please, call me Claire," his mother said. " 'Mrs. Malone' makes me feel old."

Amy laughed. "You sound like my mother."

When his mother turned to him, there were tears in her eyes. She laughingly brushed them away. "Don't mind me. I'm being silly."

"No, you're not," he said, putting his arm around her. He felt a bit choked up himself.

Jessie hugged Justin hard. "Good for you," she said.

Katie laughed happily. "This is great!" She threw her arms around Justin. "Sam would've liked this, too, don't you think?"

Her words caused a twinge of uneasiness, and Justin quickly looked at Amy to see if she'd heard his sister's remark, but she was laughing and talking to Susan and Lisa. Then he got mad at himself for falling into that old guilt trap again. There was no reason for him to feel the least bit guilty. He hadn't stolen Amy from Sam. Sam was dead, and Amy and Justin were alive.

He looked at Amy again. She fit in with his family perfectly. And they all loved her, just as he'd known they would.

He thought about everything he and Amy had been through together. All the pain, all the sadness. But that was all behind them.

From now on, things would only get better.

And in November, when Amy was finally his wife, life would be perfect.

PART THREE

AMY

Twenty-one

It was a stupid accident.

One minute he was walking along the path to the stream where he did his daily bathing. His leg was feeling good; he was hardly limping at all, so he was barely using his cane. The next minute he had tripped over a protruding root of a larch tree. He fell hard, hitting his head on a rock, and he lay sprawled on his stomach. Pain stabbed at his temples, and for a moment, he was afraid he was going to pass out. He called out weakly.

Several of the villagers heard him and came running, Reena among them. *"Sahib,"* she murmured, *"sahib."*

As the villagers helped him up, his head spun. Gently, they led him to Reena's hut and laid him on his pallet. Reena wet a cloth and cleaned his forehead. He moaned. Still murmuring comforting words, she filled a small bowl with *dhal,* the lentil soup that was a mainstay of the villagers' diet. In the combination of Nepalese, bits of English, and sign language that had become their mode of communication, she urged him to eat.

Sam couldn't help smiling. Food. The universal cure-all for what ailed you.

Suddenly, in the process of lifting a spoonful of

the hearty soup to his lips, he stopped. Shock radiated through him.

Sam.

His name was Sam! *Sam Robbins.*

Slowly, over the next few hours, in bits and pieces, everything came back to him. The reason he was in Nepal. What he'd been doing when he'd fallen. The magazine. The snow leopards. And Amy.

Amy.

Excitement caused his hands to tremble. Reena, who had been watching him closely since his fall, looked at him wide-eyed. He knew she was frightened.

He grinned. "Reena," he said, pointing to her. *"Naam."*

Nodding, she echoed him. "Reena, *naam."*

He pointed to his chest. "Sam. *Mero naam . . . ho Sam." My name is Sam.*

"Sam," she repeated wonderingly. A sweet smile spread across her face. "Sam."

He lifted the picture of Amy that he always wore. "Amy," he said. He did not know how to say she was his fiancée, so he said the word for friend. *"Saathi."*

Reena's smile became coy and knowing, and she giggled. "Ah, *saathi, saathi . . ."*

Sam's heart swelled with happiness. *Amy.* He couldn't wait to see her, to hold her in his arms again. He closed his eyes, remembering every detail of her face, her body. Remembering that last night together. "Amy," he whispered. He knew that no matter how hard it was to leave the village or how long a trek it would prove to be to reach a place where he could make arrangements to fly home, the thought of Amy would carry him through.

What would she think? How would she react? He

had been gone a long time. What if she thought he was dead? He pushed the thought away. He knew Amy. She would never believe he was dead.

The following day, his few possessions packed in a type of knapsack, Sam stood ready to leave the village. Pemba, one of the youngest and strongest of the male villagers, would accompany him, taking him to the nearest city with a telephone. From there, Sam would go to Kathmandu, where he would board a plane for home.

Home.

He could hardly believe it.

In just a few days, he would be with Amy.

And Justin.

He smiled just thinking about Justin. Hell, he hoped he wouldn't cause poor Justin to have a heart attack.

As Sam and Pemba prepared to leave, Sam looked around the village. A pang of regret pierced him. He had grown to love these reclusive and primitive people. They had been good to him. If not for them, he probably would have died.

He would especially miss Reena. His gaze met hers and he saw the sadness underlying her happiness for the return of his memory. Slowly, he said his farewells, leaving hers for last.

They embraced. "I'll come back to see you," he promised, hoping she understood. "Thank you for everything."

"Namaste," she murmured. *I salute the God in you.* A sentiment given in greeting and in goodbyes. Sam's eyes stung as he gave her a final hug.

The last thing he saw before turning to walk away was a lonely tear slipping down her cheek.

* * *

Justin always listened to the radio when he worked on Saturdays. Lately, he'd been tuning in to 94.5—the oldies station. He especially liked the songs from the fifties and sixties. Selections like Chubby Checker's "Twist and Shout," Elvis's "In the Ghetto," and Peter, Paul and Mary's "I Dig Rock-and-Roll Music" were particular favorites.

This morning he was working on the third-quarter financial report. It was a beautiful autumn day—bright and clear—and he wished he could be outside, enjoying it, but the report was important. Anyway, he was almost finished. Another twenty minutes or so and he could leave.

He smiled, thinking about the afternoon and evening he had planned. He and Amy were going out to lunch and then on to a movie. Justin wasn't crazy about movies in the same way she was, but he didn't mind going, if that was what made her happy. He didn't mind doing anything that made her happy. And she *was* happy.

Sometimes he still couldn't believe how good things were between them. For so long, he'd worried that she was still thinking about Sam. The worry had been like a cancer, eating away at him, no matter how many times he reminded himself that she had chosen to be with him, that he had not coerced her or in any way forced her. He knew it was stupid to keep doubting her feelings, but he couldn't seem to help himself, because occasionally she would stare off into space, and when he'd ask her what she was thinking about, she'd give herself a little shake and say, "Hmmm?" distractedly. She'd always laugh then, and say, "Oh, I was just daydreaming."

During these episodes, he told himself it was normal that she should occasionally think about Sam. After all, she had loved him very deeply. But no matter how many times he reassured himself, he knew there'd always be a tiny, niggling fear at the back of his mind. And it wouldn't go away completely until she was his wife.

Well, she soon would be. In just a little over six weeks, they would be married. Almost all the arrangements had been made. He grinned, thinking about the wedding, and how he and Amy had prevailed against her mother.

That mother of hers was really something. Justin liked Faith because he knew she was on his side and very much in favor of him marrying Amy, but he wasn't blind to her faults. She was a strong-willed woman, used to getting her own way and formidable when she was crossed. She had wanted them to have a big, splashy wedding, but in this, he and Amy were in perfect accord. And they'd held their ground. Eventually, Amy's mother had capitulated on almost everything.

The wedding was going to be small, with only a few of their closest friends and members of their families invited, and the reception afterward would take place at the Carpenter home. Amy was wearing her mother's wedding dress. Lark would be her maid of honor, and Steven was going to be Justin's best man.

That night, Amy and Justin would stay at the Houstonian, and early on Thanksgiving morning, they would fly to San Francisco for three nights. Justin had booked the bridal suite at the St. Francis Drake Hotel on Union Square. Both he and Amy were excited about the trip. Neither one had ever been to San Francisco.

Amy'd laughed about that. "I've been to Rome and Paris and London. I've even been to Moscow. But I've never been to San Francisco."

Still thinking about the good days ahead of them, Justin finished his report, cleared off his desk, turned off the radio, and headed for Amy's.

Amy hummed as she worked. She felt completely happy today, with none of the doubts and fears that still occasionally plagued her.

She was doing the right thing in marrying Justin, and she knew it. She appreciated him more and more as the days went by. They would build a good marriage. What they had together was different from what she and Sam had had, but it wasn't inferior. It was solid and stable, something that would give them a firm foundation when it came to making a home for the children they both wanted. And most important, she would never have to worry about Justin leaving her. Her welfare, their children's welfare, would always be first in his heart.

All these thoughts drifted through her mind as she dusted the furniture in the living area. The October sunlight streamed through the windows, catching her diamond ring and firing it with light.

Amy sighed. The ring was beautiful, but—and she'd never have admitted this to *anyone;* she could hardly admit it to herself—it didn't mean as much to her as the emerald ring Sam had given her. It hurt her to think this. It hurt her that she felt this way. And if Justin knew! God, she couldn't imagine how he would feel.

Well, he would never know. Never. She was stupid even to feel this way. Still, her thoughts strayed to the emerald. It still sat in her jewelry box. Every time she opened the lid of the box, she saw it. She knew she should put it away somewhere, completely out of sight. She knew Justin had caught sight of the ring and wondered what he thought about it. Several times, she had wanted to ask him, but had then stopped herself.

They never talked about Sam. Sam was a forbidden subject, and that hurt her, too. Why couldn't they talk about him? Would they ever be able to?

Perhaps one day, after she and Justin were married, and he was finally secure about her and her feelings for him, they would be able to openly love Sam again, because Amy knew Justin *did* love Sam, and it saddened her that she was the cause of that love being denied. Wouldn't it be sweet, she fantasized, if some day they had a little girl and named her Samantha? Amy could save the ring for her to wear when she grew up. That would be lovely.

She finished her dusting and was just about to walk out onto the deck to shake out the dust cloth when she heard the sound of a car on the driveway below.

It must be Justin, coming a little earlier than she'd expected him. She looked in the corner where Major lay sleeping in a patch of sunlight. The dog spent most of his time at Amy's now, since Justin was rarely at home. As she watched, Major opened his eyes and his ears perked up. He'd heard the car, too.

Now she heard a *thunk*. A few seconds later, slow footsteps started up the stairs.

Funny how different Justin's footsteps sounded from Sam's. Sam had always bounded up the stairs, taking them two at a time. Justin was slower, more methodical.

Major stood up. He listened for a moment. Then, bewildering Amy, he raced for the door and pawed it frantically, whimpering the whole time.

What had gotten into the dog? He never acted this way when Justin came home.

Suddenly, a clear whistle floated in the air. *Our song . . .*

Goosebumps broke out on Amy's arms. She moved, trancelike, to the door.

The moment she opened it, Major bounded out and down the stairs, barking joyously. Amy felt as if time had been suspended, as if the earth had stopped moving. Dazed, she walked out onto the deck. Looked down. Blinked to clear her eyes. This couldn't be happening. *This can't be real. I'm dreaming.*

But the barking was no dream. The whistle was no dream. And the lean, tanned man standing halfway up the stairway was no dream. Her heart beat wildly as she stared, hardly able to believe her eyes. His hair was lighter than she remembered it, and longer, tied back in a ponytail. His skin was much darker, as if he'd been outdoors for a long time. But his eyes hadn't changed. They were still golden-brown, still intense, still filled with that wonderful light.

"Sam!" Tears filled her eyes, even as she rushed forward. "Sam, Sam!"

By now he'd reached the top, and she catapulted herself into his arms. Sam! Sam was alive! His arms closed around her the way they had so many times before, crushing her against his chest.

And then they were kissing and laughing and crying and Major was running in circles around them, barking at the top of his lungs. Amy said Sam's name over and over again, touching his face, still hardly grasping the miraculous fact of his return . . . alive and warm and breathing.

"Amy, Amy . . ." Sam said. His heart was a battering ram against his chest as he drank her in. She looked so beautiful. So clean and fresh and beautiful. Her eyes were filled with tears, but her smile was blinding.

"Oh, Sam. You're alive. You're alive," she cried. The tears rolled down her cheeks.

They kissed again and again. The only thought in Amy's head was that Sam had come back to her. Her love was alive, and he had come home.

"I thought about this moment the whole way home. I could just picture you here, on the steps, waiting for me," he said, as they finally stopped kissing long enough to look at each other. He touched her face, her eyes, her cheek, running his hands over her silky skin. He would never get enough of her. The love he felt for her threatened to burst his heart. She looked even more beautiful than he remembered.

"Oh, Sam, we thought you were dead! Where have you been? What happened? Oh, God, I can't believe you're here!" *Sam . . . Sam . . . Sam,* her heart sang.

"Whoa," he said, laughing. "One question at a time. Let's sit down. My leg . . . it bothers me to stand too long."

"Oh, I'm sorry!"

"No, no, don't worry. It's all right. It'll just be better for me to sit."

So they sat on the top step and there, with the sun warm on their faces, the soft breeze caressing their skin, and the song of the birds filling the air around them, he told her everything. How elusive the snow leopards had been. How tired he had felt. How Morgenstern had gotten sick. And how, that last day, he had seen his chance to get his pictures and go home to her. "That's what I was thinking about, Amy," he said. "How much I wanted to go home. It's the first time I'd ever resented being

away, ever wanted a job to just be over. And that's
because of you."

"Oh, Sam . . ."

He told her how he'd decided to climb down to
the cave, how the Sherpa guide had warned him
not to, how he hadn't listened. "I was stupid," he
said. "Stupid. Jesus, I wouldn't blame you if you
never forgave me." His arm tightened around her
shoulders as his eyes implored her to understand.

She forgave him. She would forgive him anything, now that he was home again.

He told her about the thoughts that raced through
his brain as he fell. "In those seconds," he said, his
voice rough with emotion, "all I could think about
was you."

She swallowed, then remembered what it was like
to hear about his accident. To be told he was dead.
"It was awful," she whispered. "When they told me,
I didn't want to believe it." Then she remembered
something else, something she would have to tell
him, something they would cry over together, but
not now . . . later . . . there would be time to talk
about their little lost baby later. . . .

He told her about waking up and finding himself
in a remote village in western Nepal. "I had no
memory," he said slowly. "I didn't know who I was
or where I'd come from. I was delirious and in
terrible pain. Both my legs were broken, and I had
all kinds of injuries. It's a miracle I was alive. The
villagers, especially one kind older woman, nursed
me back to health."

He told her about the big blizzard and the avalanches that followed. He told her about gradually
being able to walk again, about the crutches one
of the village men had fashioned for him, about

how he'd eventually been able to get around with only the aid of a cane.

He told her about Reena and how good she'd been to him. A sadness clouded his eyes when he talked about her, and Amy squeezed his hand. "She was wonderful," he said softly. "I want you to meet her some day."

He told her how his memory had come back to him. And how he'd made his way home.

"But Sam," she said when he'd finished, "I don't understand why, after the winter was over, the villagers didn't get help for you."

"You'd have to know what a closed kind of society they live in to understand. They are mistrustful of outsiders, especially outsiders in their own land. It's a lucky thing for me that so many Americans have visited Nepal and been so forthcoming with their money. Now even the people in the most remote areas have kindly feelings toward Americans. But the most important thing was, Reena had kind of adopted me. From what I've been able to figure out, I don't think she was able to have children, and she made me her son. So the villagers wouldn't have wanted to take me away unless she sanctioned it." His eyes softened. "I'm sure she didn't want me to leave, but once I'd indicated that I wanted to, she wouldn't try to hold me."

"But why didn't you leave when you were able to? I mean, I know you had no memory, but didn't you want to find out who you were?"

He shrugged. "It's hard to explain, but I was afraid. The village was the only security I had. Everything else was unknown . . . and frightening."

"Well, why didn't you call me once you had your memory back?" Amy demanded.

"All I could think about was coming home. I didn't want to talk on the telephone. I didn't want to try to explain long distance. I wanted to see your face. God, I love you."

"Oh, Sam—I love you, too." Tears filled her eyes again, tumbling down her face. She paid no attention to them. "I've never stopped loving you."

He drew her closer. The kiss he gave her was filled with a fierce hunger and it drove any remaining questions completely out of her mind.

"Let's go inside," he muttered.

"Yes."

They barely made it through the door before he was kissing her again, kissing her and touching her. "Amy, Amy, I've been thinking about this for days . . . wanting you so much . . ." His voice was rough as his hands grazed her breasts and his mouth dropped to her neck.

It was only then, as Amy's head fell back to give him better access, that her gaze fell on the book Justin had been reading last night, which lay open on the coffee table.

Her heart slammed against her chest. *Oh, my God. Justin!* How could she have forgotten him? Now her heart pounded in fear. What was she going to do? Justin would be home soon. Panicked, she said, "Sam, I—I have to tell you about—"

"No, no. Let's not talk," he muttered. "Not now." He sought her mouth, even as she tried to turn her face away, his hands moving down to cup her buttocks and press her close.

Amy could hardly think. His mouth captured hers again, open and hungry. His tongue, his hands, the way they were caressing and stroking her, brought a torrent of emotion and sensation and a reawakening of the wild passion he had always been able to ignite. She clung to him, forgetting everything else. Her body trembled with desire, she felt as if her insides were on fire, and only he could put the fire out.

He pushed her sweater up, buried his face in the hollow between her breasts. "Amy, Amy," he muttered, his voice ragged. His thumbs rubbed against her nipples. She moaned as pain and pleasure arched through her, and wove her fingers through his hair.

Then, as if through a dense fog, she heard the unmistakable sound of a car in the driveway. A car door slammed. Slow footsteps sounded on the stairs.

"Sam . . . stop. *Stop!*" She pushed him away, managed to get her sweater back down.

"Amy," Sam said, "what's wrong?"

The footsteps were louder now, climbing, crossing the porch.

Amy could hardly breathe.

The door opened.

Over Sam's shoulder, she saw Justin's face. His happy smile. His mouth open to greet her. And then, like a slow-motion movie, his eyes widening, the smile fading.

Sam turned around.

Amy's heart was beating so fast and so hard, she thought she might faint. Her stomach rolled. She didn't know what to do, what to say . . .

The three of them stood there, frozen.

As understanding swept over him, Justin's face blanched, shock and disbelief pummeling him. Sam! Sam was alive! He stared at Sam's face, at his arm around Amy, at her swollen lips and disheveled hair and the guilty look on her face. He realized what they'd been doing when he'd come in. A sick feeling washed through him.

Sam's face spread into a wide grin, then he gave a whoop of joy. "Justin!" he shouted, releasing Amy and moving as fast as his still-stiff right leg would let him. He grasped Justin in a bear hug. "Oh, man, it's good to see you!"

It was only as Sam felt the rigidness in Justin's body and the lack of enthusiasm in his return embrace that he realized something was wrong.

He dropped his arms and backed away so he could see Justin's face. It looked frozen, the blue eyes filled with some emotion Sam couldn't identify. "Justin?" he said.

"Hello, Sam," Justin said stiffly. "You're alive, I see." Then his gaze swung to Amy.

Completely bewildered, Sam turned to look at Amy, too. Her expression was stricken as her eyes moved from Justin to him and back to Justin again.

"What's wrong?" Sam said.

No one answered.

"Would someone please tell me what the hell is going on here?"

"Are you going to tell him, or should I?" Justin said, voice still strained and tight.

"Tell me what?"

When Amy, who seemed incapable of speech, didn't answer, Justin brushed past Sam to her side. He put his arm around her possessively, and the look he gave Sam was challenging. "Amy and I love each other," he said. "We're engaged to be married."

Twenty-two

The words fell like stones into the suddenly silent room, broken only by the *thump, thump* of Major's tail.

Justin took Amy's left hand and raised it.

Sam stared. The diamond on her finger blazed in the sunlight. He swallowed, raised his eyes to Amy's face. "Amy?" He wanted to say he didn't believe Justin, but the ring on Amy's finger was all too real. His mind spun. This couldn't be true. It couldn't. Amy loved *him*. She was engaged to *him*.

"Oh, Sam, I . . ." Her voice trailed off as she looked from one man to the other.

"It's true," Justin said, tightening his arm around Amy. He was frightened, terribly frightened, but determined not to show it. How can Sam be alive? he kept asking himself. How can he just walk in, as if nothing happened, as if the past two years were nothing, and take over again? His mind reeled as anger, fear, and guilt churned chaotically. He didn't want to feel any guilt, didn't want to see the confusion and torment on Sam's face, didn't want to remember that this man had been his best friend for years . . . was *still* his best friend. The guilt made him even angrier.

"Sam . . ." Amy said helplessly, practically wringing her hands. "I—I'm sorry." Her heart filled with pity. She knew this was a terrible shock for Sam, yet there was nothing she could have done to prevent it. "It's been two years. We . . . we thought you were dead."

Sam stared at her. "So it's true? You . . . and Justin?"

"I—I'm sorry," she whispered again. *Why? Why?* she thought. Why did this have to happen?

"But you're engaged to me. I said I'd be back. You knew I'd be back."

"How could I know?" she whispered.

"Get real, Sam," Justin said. "You've been missing for two years. Two years! The authorities said you were dead. Amy had to believe it whether she wanted to or not. We all did."

Sam just kept staring at Amy. He heard the words, but his brain wasn't willing to accept them. He kept waiting for her to deny Justin's statement. She couldn't be engaged to Justin. She didn't love Justin. She loved *him.* Slowly, as he waited and as the silence lengthened, a hard knot of pain replaced the bewilderment, followed by an anger so strong, he wanted to hit something.

Amy and Justin. The woman he loved more than anything or anyone in the world . . . and his best friend . . . the man he trusted above all others. Together all this time. All the time he was hurt and sick. All the time he was looking at Amy's picture and straining to remember. All the time he was struggling to return and picturing the happiness on her face. He wanted to shut his eyes to blot out the images that flashed through his mind.

Bitterness overwhelmed him as he remembered the way he'd teased Justin about Amy, how he'd thought it was harmless and flattering the way Justin had been so taken with her. "What a friend," he said, unable to stop the bitterness and pain from overflowing. "You couldn't wait to move in on me, could you? My good old buddy. *I'll look after Amy, don't worry.* And I believed you. Just how long did it take before you were in her bed, *old buddy?*"

Amy felt as if someone had stuck a knife into her heart and twisted it. She couldn't stand this. Couldn't stand the way they were looking at each other and talking to each other. She didn't know what to do. Part of her wanted to rush to Sam's side, to erase the look of pain and betrayal from his eyes, to shout *it's all a mistake!* But how could she? How could she hurt Justin that way? What had he done except be here . . . and love her?

Justin tightened his arm around Amy. Of all his emotions, the fear had won out, and it hardened his voice, because he knew he was fighting for his life. "If you're trying to make us feel guilty, forget it. You made your choice. You could have stayed here with Amy. You could have been married to her for nearly two years now. But you just had to go off and have your great adventure, didn't you? What happened is your own damned fault. You'll never change. You're the same old Sam—taking all kinds of risks, proving what a big man you are, not thinking or caring about anyone but yourself.

"What did you expect Amy to do?" he went on relentlessly. "Wait around forever? Grow up. We were told you were dead. And I'm the one who was here to pick up the pieces. I'm the one who was here when she lost your baby."

Each word was like a poisoned dart aimed straight for Sam's chest. "My *baby?*" he said. "You . . . you were carrying my *baby?*" His mind reeled under the weight of this new disclosure. Pregnant. When he'd left, she'd been pregnant with his baby. The most unbelievable pain, worse than any he'd yet experienced, grabbed his heart and squeezed it. He could do nothing but stare at her. Her tortured eyes confirmed everything Justin had said.

"I—I . . ." He couldn't think. His baby. Amy had been pregnant with his baby. And she'd lost it.

Amy's eyes filled with tears. She couldn't stand to see the pain in Sam's eyes. It brought back all her own feelings of pain and loss. She wanted so badly to go to him, to throw her arms around him. He should never have been told about the baby this way. Justin had had no right to tell him, no right at all. Yet even through her own pain, she understood why he had. He was scared, and her miscarriage was one of the few weapons he had against the accusations Sam had hurled.

She didn't know what to do. She knew she had to say something . . . do something. But where did her loyalty lie? With Sam, who had promised her the world, and then left her? Or with Justin, who had helped her survive the past two years?

She loved them both. She didn't want to hurt either one. It killed her that they were saying such awful things to one another, even though she understood the reasons on both sides. Justin was terrified of losing her. And Sam. She tried to imagine how Sam must feel—coming home with such joy and hope—and finding out the two people he loved and trusted most had—in his eyes, anyway—betrayed him.

Please, God, help me. Help me.

Sam's tormented eyes met hers again. He seemed to have gotten himself under some semblance of control. "Amy, I'm sorry. I can't tell you how sorry

I am. And if there was any way I could erase the
past couple of years, I would, but I can't." He ran
his hands through his hair the way he always had
when he was upset. "I—I think I understand how
this all happened." He was obviously struggling,
trying to be fair. His gaze slowly moved to Justin.
"I shouldn't have said what I did. I—I'm sorry. I'm
grateful for everything you've done for Amy, don't
think I'm not, but I'm home now. And Amy and I
. . . we belong together."

"I don't want your gratitude," Justin said. "I love
Amy, that's why I did what I did."

Amy's heart felt as if it were splintering into
thousands of pieces. "She could feel the tremor in
Justin's body, but his voice was calm as he continued.

"I'm glad you're alive," Justin continued, "but it
doesn't change anything."

Sam thought about the way Amy had kissed him.
The way she had acted before Justin came. He
looked at her. "Is that true, Amy?"

"You think all you have to do is crook your little
finger, and she'll come running back, don't you?"
Justin said, desperation goading him on. "That's
the way it's been your entire life! Anything Sam
wants, Sam gets. Well, you're wrong this time. Amy
loves me. We love each other. We're going to be
married November twenty-fourth. Last week, we
even mailed the invitations. Tell him, Amy. Tell him
you don't belong to him anymore. You belong to
me."

"Well?" Sam said tightly. "We're both waiting."

Amy couldn't believe this. It was like a bad
movie. The two of them were squared off like box-
ers in a ring, each one looking for the knockout
punch.

"Why don't you just go away?" Justin said through clenched teeth. "You will eventually, anyway. Why not save everyone a lot of trouble and go now?"

"How about it, Amy?" Sam said, ignoring Justin's taunts even though he felt like punching him in the nose. "Do you want me to go away, too? I've heard what Justin has to say, but now I want to hear *you* say it."

Suddenly, Amy was furious with both of them. What did they *want* from her? Blood? Did they want her to cut herself in two so each one could have a piece? "I don't *belong* to anyone," she said, her voice trembling with the force of her anger. "I belong to myself. I can't believe the way you two are behaving. You're supposed to be best friends. You're supposed to love each other. You both say you love me. Well, prove it, then. And stop trying to tear me apart!"

Then she yanked herself from Justin's grasp, whirled around, and raced into the bathroom, slamming the door shut behind her.

"Happy now?" Justin ground out.

"What happened isn't my fault," Sam said. *"I'm* not the one trying to hold her against her will."

"I'm *not* trying to hold her against her will. I've never tried to hold her against her will."

"Sure you are. You were laying guilt on her with every word you spoke." He ran his hands through his hair. "I admit, I was angry when I realized what's been going on between you two, but I can understand it as far as Amy's concerned. She was going through a bad time. She was vulnerable. It's *you* I blame. Hell, you saw your chance, and you didn't give a damn about me or anyone else, did you? You just stepped right up and took advantage of her."

"Took advantage of her? *You bastard!*" It was all Justin could do to keep from smashing that cocky face. "She wanted to die after she lost the baby. It wasn't just a *bad time,* as you put it. It was pure hell. I would have done anything to help her, because, unlike you, her welfare is more important to me than anything else."

They glared at each other, bodies taut, shoulders squared, fists clenched. Neither knew what to do. Sam was exhausted—the strain of the long airline flight and the emotional confrontation taking its toll. His right leg had begun to throb, and he knew he needed to sit down soon or he would collapse. But he couldn't show any weakness in front of Justin.

Trying not to limp, Sam walked over to the bathroom door. He rapped softly. He couldn't hear any sound from inside. "Amy?" He rapped again. "Amy."

"What?" she said in a muffled voice.

He lowered his voice. "Please open the door, Amy. I—I'm leaving, and I wanted to say goodbye."

Behind him, Justin was afraid to hope. It wasn't like Sam to give up so easily.

There was a long silence. Then the door opened. Sam's heart twisted. Her tearstained, puffy-eyed face looked up at him. He wanted to draw her into his arms, kiss away the tears, hold her gently and tell her how much he loved her. He kept thinking about the baby they'd lost. He wanted to ask her about it, share the pain with her. But he could do none of those things with Justin there.

If only she'd tell him to stay.

If only she'd tell Justin to leave.

"W-where are you going?" she asked, her voice husky with the tears she'd shed.

He shrugged. "I don't know. I don't suppose my apartment is still around, is it?"

"Owen terminated your apartment lease over a year ago," Justin said. "He put your stuff in storage."

Sam didn't turn around. "I'll get a room in a hotel, then." He felt sick and drained. He had to get away, sort out his thoughts, try to figure out what to do.

"Okay," she murmured. She looked completely drained, too.

"I'll call you later," he said softly. "Let you know where I am."

She nodded, her eyes meeting his again. Something flickered in their depths, and suddenly, the need to take her in his arms, to put his stamp on her, to show them all whose woman she was, was too strong to deny. The kiss he gave her was quick and hard, and when it was over, he swung around, gave Justin a defiant glare, and trying his best not to limp, walked out.

Justin swiftly moved to Amy's side. He put his arm around her and kissed the side of her forehead. "You okay?"

She nodded, but she wasn't okay. She could hardly think, let alone talk. Sam's kiss was still imprinted on her lips.

"Let's sit down," he said gently. "You've had a shock."

"Justin . . ." Her voice didn't sound like her own. "I—I'm really sorry, but I want you to leave, too."

He stiffened, momentarily tightening his grip on her shoulders. "Amy—"

"Please, Justin. You're right. I have had a shock. And I want . . . I *need* to be alone right now."

She knew it wasn't fair to ask him to go, but she just couldn't face talking about this right now. She thought he was going to protest, but after a few seconds, he said, "All right. I understand; I'll go. But I'll be back later."

"Tomorrow . . . we'll talk tomorrow."

He was terrified, but he knew he wouldn't be helping his cause if he pushed her. "All right," he agreed. "Tomorrow."

She lifted her face and he kissed her, but there was no real enthusiasm in her response. He tried not to let this lack hurt him, telling himself it was just the shock and not any change in her feelings toward him. "Try to get some rest," he said, as he gently released her. "I'll call you in the morning."

Once Justin was gone, Amy sank onto the couch and stared into space. The cats, sensing her distress, butted up against her legs, then settled around her in a kind of protective circle.

The events of the day seemed unreal. She couldn't believe how, in just hours, everything had changed. This morning she was happy and comfortable with her decision to marry Justin. She had been looking forward to the future. Now her entire world lay in a shambles. And she had no idea how to go about putting it back together.

Lark had just gotten home from a three-day trip, and she was exhausted. God, she *had* to find another job. She just wasn't up for all this traveling anymore. She walked into her apartment and im-

mediately began shedding clothes, letting them stay
wherever they landed. The apartment felt stuffy
from being closed up for three days, so she turned
on the air conditioning.

She was in her bedroom, pulling on jeans and a
T-shirt, when the doorbell rang. She hastily zipped
up the jeans and walked barefoot out to the living
room.

Her heart jumped when she opened the door to
find Justin standing on her stoop. He gave her a
little half-smile and said, "Hey."

"Hey." She smiled, trying not to reveal how rattled she felt by his unexpected presence. "What
are you doing here?"

"What kind of welcome is that?" he countered,
his tone light, even though he looked tired and
unhappy, with lines of strain around his mouth and
eyes. It was obvious something was wrong.

"I'm sorry. C'mon in." Her heart had finally begun to slow down. "God, this place is a mess." She
picked her navy blue uniform jacket and pumps
up from the floor. "Sit down. Do you want a beer?"

"Yeah, make it a triple."

She raised her eyebrows. "That sounds omi-
nous."

He nodded wearily. "You don't know the half of
it."

"I'll be right back," she said. *What can be the matter?* she wondered, as she walked into the tiny
kitchen and took two cans of beer out of the refrigerator. She'd talked to Amy before leaving on
this latest assignment, and everything had seemed
to be rosy with her and Justin—so rosy it was hard
for Lark to hear about it without feeling an ache
of emptiness. Distractedly, she dumped the uniform
jacket and pumps on the kitchen counter, then

headed back to the living room. He was still standing, but at least he'd taken off his jacket. Lark
couldn't help smiling to see that, unlike her, he'd
draped it neatly over a chair.

She handed him a beer.

"Has Amy called you?" he asked.

"No. At least I don't think she has. But I haven't
checked my answering machine yet. Why? Has
something happened?"

"I guess you could say that." He took a swallow
of beer.

"What?" she said softly. Had they broken up?
She hated herself for the spark of hope that leaped
to life.

He laughed, the sound so filled with bitterness
and pain, it tore at her heart. "Sam's back, that's
what."

Lark stared at him, sure she'd misheard. "Sam's
back?" she repeated incredulously. "You . . . you
mean he's *alive?*"

His mouth twisted. "Yep. Alive and kicking."

For once in her life, Lark was speechless. Sam
was alive! "Oh, my God," she said, finally finding
her voice. "Does Amy know?"

"Oh, yeah, she knows."

"I—I hardly know what to say. Have you seen
him or talked to him?"

"Hell, I walked in on them," he said, his eyes
very blue as they met hers. "She was in his arms."

He didn't have to say anything more. She understood, could just imagine the scene. Could just
imagine how Justin had felt. "Oh, Justin . . ." She
set her beer down on the coffee table, then put
her arms around his waist and hugged him. After
a second, his arms closed around her, too. They
stood that way for a little while—Lark closing her

eyes and simply absorbing the wonderful feel of him.

When they finally drew apart, he smiled crookedly. "Thanks. I needed that."

"Why don't we sit down?" she said gently.

Once they were settled on the couch, she said, "Tell me about it."

For the next twenty minutes he described the scene between him and Amy and Sam. "I don't know what Amy's going to do," he said finally. "She said she needed time to think." His voice was bleak.

Lark chose her words carefully. "That's understandable, don't you think? I'm sure she's an emotional mess right now. After all, Justin, this was a terrible shock for her, too."

"Do you think she'll go back to him?"

Lark shrugged. "I don't know." She looked at him, hurting for him, knowing exactly how he felt, because she lived with this kind of pain. "But I'll tell you something, Justin. If she has any sense, any sense at *all*, she'll eventually realize that you're ten times the man Sam is, and she'll tell him to go take a flying leap."

And then she took his hand and squeezed it.

After a moment, he laughed softly. "You're one in a million, you know that?"

She made herself grin, made herself answer as lightly as he had. "Yeah, sure, I'll bet you say that to all the girls."

He laughed again, and Lark thought about friendship and love and loyalty and how totally fucked up the world was.

* * *

The moment Justin left, Lark grabbed a jacket and her purse and practically flew out the door.

She got to Amy's in ten minutes flat.

One look at Amy's face told Lark Amy was in just as much pain as Justin. "You look like hell," she said, hugging her.

"Thanks," Amy said sarcastically. "You want some coffee? I was just about to make a pot."

"I think a good shot of whiskey might be a better choice."

"I'm in enough of a daze. I'm sticking with coffee."

"Okay, sure. Coffee it is." Lark sat on a bar stool.

Amy walked around the bar to the kitchen and began to fill the coffeepot. "I wasn't sure if you got my message, but I guess you did."

"No," Lark said slowly, "Justin came to see me."

Amy stared at her. "Justin came to see you?"

Lark nodded.

"Is . . . is he okay?"

"As okay as anyone can be under the circumstances. I think he's still in shock."

"Imagine how *I* feel," Amy said with an attempt at a smile. "One minute I was happily cleaning house and waiting for Justin. The next, Sam arrived, and I nearly had a heart attack."

"He just came? No warning? Nothing?"

"Nope. He just walked in." Amy sighed heavily as she flipped on the coffee maker. Her eyes met Lark's. "It's a fine mess, isn't it?"

"Yes, it is. What are you going to do?"

"I don't know." Her eyes were just as bleak as Justin's had been. "I—I love them both, Lark, and I don't want to hurt either of them."

But someone was going to be hurt, Lark thought, whether Amy wanted to face it or not.

"There's no way everyone's going to come out of this happy," she pointed out gently.

Amy nodded glumly.

Lark sighed. "Well, we're not going to solve that problem tonight. So tell me about Sam. Where's he been? What happened to him?"

As Amy talked, gradually forgetting her own turmoil in the telling of Sam's ordeal, her voice softened and her eyes shone, and Lark could see the underlying joy she felt at finding out Sam was alive.

Lark's heart sank. Amy was still in love with Sam, whether she wanted to acknowledge it or not. And Lark was terribly afraid that in the end, Justin wouldn't stand a chance.

Twenty-three

Everyone wanted a piece of him. Someone from NBC called on Monday, then in rapid succession on Tuesday, he heard from ABC, CNN, and CBS.

The switchboard at the magazine was bombarded. *People Magazine* wanted to interview him. *Inside Edition* called about doing a story. AP and UPI both sent reporters. And *Time* magazine called.

In addition, friends and colleagues from around the country were thrilled he was alive and called to say so.

Sam talked to as many of them as he could, but when the commotion got to be too much, when his head and leg started to ache, he'd go back to his rooms at Embassy Suites, pop three or four Advils, and crash.

He called Amy several times, but she asked him not to come over for a couple of days.

"I've asked Justin to stay away, too," she said. "I'm sorry, but I need to have some time to think."

He didn't want to, but he knew he'd better respect her request. For the first time in his adult life, he was really frightened. She sounded so remote and detached, as if she were talking to a stranger. He knew she'd been pushed too hard and that if he tried to push harder, he might lose her altogether.

On Wednesday, Sam stayed away from the office entirely. Instead, he got a haircut, went shopping for clothes, consulted with his banker—finding out that whatever else he might have lost in the past two years, he'd gained a substantial amount of money because the magazine had continued to pay him for a year after his disappearance—and ate lunch at Serafina's. The whole time he was there he kept remembering that first dinner with Amy.

Suddenly, he could no longer stand being away from her. "I don't give a damn whether she wants to see me or not, I'm going over there!" he muttered. He climbed into his 'Vette, which Owen had been driving in his absence, and roared down the street.

When he arrived at Amy's, she wasn't home. He'd forgotten she would still be at school. It was only 2:30. He glanced over at the big house. Why not? He might as well see what the lay of the land was. Who knew? He might have a bigger battle to fight than he imagined, if Amy's parents were against him, too.

He walked around to the front of the house—scaring a few squirrels in the process—and rang the doorbell. A few minutes later, the door opened, and Amy's mother stood there. She looked just as cool and elegant as ever in a forest-green suit.

"Well, hello, Sam. Welcome home." Her smile seemed genuine enough. "I was wondering when we'd get to see you."

"Hello, Mrs. Carpenter." They clasped hands, and he bent to kiss her cheek.

"Come in," she said. "I have an appointment at four, but I've got some time before I have to leave."

He followed her into the living room and took

the indicated seat on one of the yellow silk wing chairs, while she sat across from him in the other. "Would you like some coffee . . . or perhaps a beer?"

"No, thanks. I just ate lunch."

"We were all very glad to hear of your survival."

He wondered. He knew Amy's father really liked him, but he'd never felt Faith was sold on him. Still, she seemed sincere. "Thanks."

"It was a shock to Amy, of course."

"I know."

She sighed, sitting back and crossing her legs. Her eyes were enigmatic as they met his. "It's a terribly awkward situation, isn't it?"

He shrugged. "I guess it is."

"Amy's very confused right now."

"Is she?" He wanted to say Amy's reaction to his reappearance hadn't seem confused at all. She had been overjoyed to see him. He couldn't have asked for a warmer or more passionate welcome. It was only when Justin had appeared on the scene that she had gotten upset. But he was sure Faith had guessed as much. Besides, he wasn't here to tell Faith anything. He was here to see how she felt. Whether she'd be an ally or an opponent.

"You know how tender-hearted Amy is. She never likes to hurt anyone."

Sam looked at her steadily.

"She especially doesn't want to hurt you," Faith continued. "After all, you've been through so much already."

Sam stiffened. "Did she say that?"

She smoothed her palm over the arm of the chair before answering. "Not in so many words . . . no . . . but I know Amy."

"I know Amy, too."

Faith's green eyes, so like Amy's in some ways, so unlike them in others, met his. Her words were measured, as if she were choosing them carefully. "Justin and Amy have been together nearly ten months now. They've forged a very strong bond. And they are extremely well suited to one another."

Sam clenched his jaw. She'd made her point. She approved of Justin in a way she'd never approved of Sam. "You think she should stay with him."

"Yes, I do." Her voice softened, and her eyes were sympathetic. "I have nothing against you, Sam. You're a fine young man, but I don't think you'll make Amy a good husband. I never have."

Sam abruptly stood. He didn't want sympathy from her—or from anyone. "It's a good thing you're not making the choice for her, then, isn't it?"

She stood, too, although more slowly. "Oh, dear. You're angry."

"Damn right, I'm angry."

"I guess I can't blame you. I had hoped, though, that you might care enough for Amy to do what's best for her."

Sam stared at her. At the perfect face and the perfect clothes and the perfect voice. "Who made you God, Mrs. Carpenter?" The only indication that his words had made an impact was the barest movement of her facial muscles. "Amy's an adult. I think she can decide what's best for her without your help."

"Well, of course, I can understand how you might feel that way, but I think—"

"I intend to marry Amy," he said, not caring that he was interrupting her, not caring about anything right now except making sure she understood. "Whether *you* like it or not."

Later, he wondered what reply she would have made, but at that moment, Amy's father entered the room, saying, "Sam! Welcome home!" and seconds later, Sam was enveloped in a warm hug, followed by a big smile.

"I was out golfing," Alan said, "and just got home. I thought I heard your voice. It's good to see you."

"Thank you, sir."

"You look good. Amy said you were having some trouble with your right leg, though?"

"Yes. I broke it when I fell, and it didn't heal right. I guess I'll always walk with a limp."

"Physical therapy could probably help you. If you want the name of someone, I'd be glad to refer you."

Sam smiled. "My doctor said the same thing."

They all sat down again, and for a while, they talked about Sam's ordeal and his life in the village. Faith was silent throughout the conversation, and Sam wondered what she was thinking. He also wondered if Amy's father had heard what they'd been saying right before he'd walked into the room. Alan didn't act as if anything was amiss, but that didn't mean anything.

After about thirty minutes, Faith stood up. "I'm sorry, but I have to leave now." She looked at her husband. "There's a meeting of the Heart Association benefit committee at Georgette Schiffer's this afternoon. I should be back before seven, though, and I thought we might go out to dinner tonight."

Alan smiled up at her. "All right, darling. See you then."

"Goodbye, Sam." Faith's gaze swung his way. Once again, her smile seemed natural. An outsider would never have known there had been any conflict between them.

Sam stood, too. He extended his hand. "It was good to see you again, Mrs. Carpenter. I hope to be seeing you much more often." He looked her squarely in the eye.

"It was good to see you, too."

After she'd gone, Alan said, "You planning to stick around until Amy gets home?"

"I thought I would."

"Good. Let's go back to the kitchen and see if we can find something to drink. You can keep me company while you're waiting."

He tossed his arm around Sam's shoulders as they walked out of the room. Then, making Sam feel better than he'd felt in three days, he said, "Don't worry about Amy, Sam. She loves you, and it won't take her long to figure out the two of you belong together. Just give her a little time." He squeezed Sam's shoulder. "And remember, I'm on your side."

Amy's heart gave an excited little hop when she pulled into the driveway and saw Sam's Corvette. Even though she'd told him not to come, she couldn't help being happy he had.

After parking her car in the garage, she walked out and looked around. She wondered where he was.

A moment later, the back door of her parents' house opened, and Sam, followed by her father, walked out.

Her heart began to race as she looked him over hungrily. He looked ten times better than he had the other day. Rested, well fed, well-groomed, and oh, so handsome. His eyes, which she'd always loved so much, were clear as they met hers. A few weeks at home, and he'd probably gain back all the weight he'd lost, too.

She smiled, her stomach fluttering with nerves. "Hi."

"Hi," he said.

"Hi, Sunshine," her father said. "Sam's been keeping me company while he waited for you to get home."

They chatted about nothing for a few minutes— Amy feeling oddly shy—and then her father said, "Well, you two kids go on. I'm going in and take a shower. 'Bye, Sam. Good to see you. And remember what I said."

"Thank you, sir. I will."

"What was that all about?" Amy asked, as they climbed the stairs to her apartment.

"Your father said he's on my side."

"Meaning?"

"Come on, Amy. You know what he meant."

Yes, she did know what he meant. Her father had always liked Sam. It didn't surprise her that he wanted the two of them to get back together. She didn't answer, and he didn't say anything else, for which she was grateful.

She unlocked the apartment door, acutely conscious of him behind her. They walked inside, and no sooner was the door shut behind him than he reached for her, drawing her into his arms.

Amy's heart raced. She knew she should pull away, but she couldn't make herself.

"Amy . . ."

She swallowed.

"God, Amy, I've missed you the past couple of days."

He lowered his head, and she raised her face to meet him. When his mouth slanted over hers, she sighed deeply, melting into him. The world around them faded away as the need and love between them became the only reality.

Afterward, Amy wondered how long they would have stood there and where the kisses might have led if the telephone hadn't rung, forcing her to pull away from Sam to answer it.

"H-hello," she said, trying to control her breathing. She avoided Sam's eyes.

"Hi."

It was Justin. Amy's heart knocked against her rib cage, and a guilty flush stained her cheeks. "Hi," she managed to say without stammering.

"Just get home?'"

"Yes. About five minutes ago." Out of the corner of her eye, she saw Sam walk over to the window sill to pet Delilah, who sat sunning herself. Sheba, who had also been sitting on the sill, hopped off lightly and walked away, her tail in the air and a haughty expression on her face.

"I think it's time to talk, don't you?" Justin said.

Amy wet her lips. She had been putting off talking to Justin, just as she had Sam. She glanced at Sam, who was watching her steadily. Remembering the way she'd kissed him only moments ago, her face heated. "Yes," she said quickly, trying to rid her mind of the images it had conjured. "I think so, too."

"Good. You want to go out to dinner?" He sounded happy.

Oh, Justin, she thought. *I'm sorry.* "Why don't you come here instead?" Why was she so weak? Why was it that all Sam had to do was touch her, and she forgot everything else?

"All right. What time?"

"How about six-thirty?" That would give her some time to talk to Sam first.

"Okay, great. I'll see you then. And Amy?"

"Yes?"

"I love you."

"I—I know." Try as she might, she simply couldn't say the words she knew he wanted to hear in response. Not with Sam standing there, looking at her. An aching sadness crept through her as she replaced the receiver in its cradle.

"That was Justin," she said.

"I figured."

"He's coming over at six-thirty."

He nodded. "Do you want me to leave?"

"No. I want to talk to you, and then I—I hoped the three of us could sit down and talk. Calmly. Like adults."

"He doesn't know I'm here, right?"

"No. He doesn't."

Sam's smile was cynical. "If he did, he'd probably race over here right now."

The bitterness in his face wounded her. "Please, Sam. Won't you at least *try*? I so want you and Justin to be friends again."

He snorted. "Dream on. That's never going to happen, because we both want you. And only one of us is going to get you. He knows that as well as I do."

"I hate it when you talk that way. Don't you see what that does to me?"

Suddenly, Sam was ashamed of himself. He knew what kind of person Amy was. Her sweetness and the way she never wanted to hurt anyone was one of her most endearing qualities. Yet somehow he had to make her face facts. "I'm sorry. I don't want to argue about Justin or anything else. That's not why I came here."

Her eyes met his. "Why *did* you come?"

"I told you. I missed you. And I . . . I wanted to talk about the baby."

She swallowed and looked away. Her face in profile looked unbearably sad.

He walked closer and touched her shoulder.

She looked up. Tears glistened on her eyelashes. "When they told me you were dead, I thought the pain was the worst I could ever feel . . . but I was wrong. Losing the baby . . . that was agony. I—I wanted to die, too."

His throat constricted and he felt the loss as keenly as he imagined she had felt it. She should never have had to go through something so terrible alone. *Alone? She wasn't alone. Justin was with her.* Suddenly, sickeningly, he realized the enormity of his mistakes and exactly what it was he was up against. And with this realization came another: it wasn't Justin's fault he was here when Amy needed him and Sam wasn't. It was Sam's.

But in spite of everything, he knew Amy still loved him. And somehow, he would make things up to her.

Slowly he drew her into his arms. "I should have been here," he said. She trembled, the tears sliding down her face. Sam held her and stroked her hair, fighting his own demons as he waited for the storm to pass.

For the first time in the past four days, Justin felt hopeful. He hurriedly finished his work for the day and left the office. On the way over to Amy's, he stopped at a roadside flower stand and bought her a big bouquet of daisies and carnations. He was whistling as he entered the already opened gates. The whistle died on his lips when he saw Sam's Corvette.

He hit the steering wheel. God damn it to hell, what was *he* doing here? Had he been here when Justin talked to Amy? Justin parked alongside Sam's car and started up the stairs. It took all his willpower to keep his steps even and not race to the top.

He tried not to peer into the windows as he knocked on the door. He'd never give Sam the satisfaction of thinking he was worried. The door opened almost immediately. Amy, looking pale and subdued in a long red skirt, oversized white sweater, and black boots, smiled up at him. It was a valiant effort but lacked her usual sparkle.

"Oh, how sweet," she said, when he handed her the flowers. She reached up to kiss his cheek, effectively circumventing any attempt he might have made to give her another kind of kiss. As she moved aside so he could enter, his eyes met Sam's, who was sitting on a bar stool facing the living room. He had a can of Budweiser in his hand.

"Hello, Justin," he said.

"Hello, Sam."

Neither of them smiled.

"Well," Amy said with false cheerfulness, "I think I'll find a vase and put these in water. Would you like a beer, Justin?"

"Sure." Justin eyed Sam in his chinos and black turtleneck and wished he'd had time to go home and change out of his suit and tie. He'd always envied Sam his natural ease in clothes, the way anything he put on immediately became just the right thing to be wearing, whether it was faded jeans, designer slacks, or black tie, which Justin had actually seen Sam wear once to an awards banquet. The memory of that night caused a lonely stab of regret for happier, less complicated times.

After Amy brought him his beer, she sat in her bentwood rocker. She'd poured herself a glass of wine and drank some. "Please sit down, Justin," she said, eyes begging him to cooperate.

Justin walked around and sat on the couch. He took a slug of his beer. No one said anything.

Elvis, Amy's big male cat, padded up to him and rubbed against his leg. Justin winced inwardly, knowing he'd have a pant leg full of cat hairs, but he gave the cat a head rub, grateful for something to do to fill the uneasy silence.

Amy cleared her throat. "I thought the three of us needed to talk." She looked at Sam, then at Justin.

Fine, Justin thought. *Let Sam talk.*

Sam stared down at his beer and said nothing.

The silence lengthened.

Amy sighed. "Neither one of you is going to make it easy, are you?"

Justin's gaze flicked to Sam. As their eyes met, he almost felt a return of their old camaraderie. He and Sam both understood the reality of the situation, whereas Amy wanted a happy ending for everyone.

"Look," she said softly, "we can't go on like this. I—I love both of you, and I want you to be friends again."

Sam gave a strangled laugh.

Justin shook his head.

"Sam . . ." Amy said, a plea in her voice. "Justin. Please . . . talk to each other."

"I have nothing to say to him," Justin said.

"You heard the man," Sam said.

Now Amy's sigh was exasperated. "If this is the way you two are going to act, then I have nothing to say, either, so you both might as well leave."

No one moved.

"I mean it," Amy said.

Justin looked at her. Her chin was set at a stubborn angle. "Amy, what you're asking for is impossible. We can't go back."

"I told you before he came that this wouldn't work," Sam said. His earlier fear had disappeared. Because in spite of everything that had happened, he knew she still had the same feelings for him she'd always had. Her reaction when he'd kissed her, the way she'd talked to Justin on the phone, even the way she'd greeted him a few minutes ago, told Sam everything he needed to know. She just needed time to work it all out in her mind.

And when she did, she would come back to him . . . where she belonged.

Twenty-four

"What were you and Sam talking about when I came home today?" Alan asked.

Faith took her time chewing the forkful of soft-shell crab before answering. "Oh, this and that."

"Faith . . ." Alan's voice carried a slightly reproachful note. "It's not like you to be evasive. Not with me."

Sighing, she laid her fork down and picked up her water glass. The two of them were having dinner at Don's, a favorite seafood restaurant. "All right. We were talking about Amy."

Alan nodded and ate some of his cole slaw.

Deciding she might as well put her cards on the table, she said, "I was telling him that I felt Amy and Justin were much better suited to one another than he and Amy."

Alan shook his head, his expression saying more than words ever could.

"I know you don't approve, darling, but that's the way I feel." She refused to allow him to make her feel guilty. She had done nothing except state the truth as she saw it.

"You know I love you," Alan said, his eyes meeting hers, "but sometimes you really do make me angry."

Faith could feel herself flushing.

He reached across the table to touch her hand. She would have liked to snatch it away, but she didn't, although she was very hurt by his criticism. "How would you have liked it if someone had said something like that to you when you and I wanted to be married?" he asked gently.

"The two situations are entirely different," she said stiffly.

"How are they different?"

"Oh, Alan, you *know* how!" Now she did pull her hand away under the guise of lifting her wineglass and taking a sip. "You and I were from the same background, had the same kinds of interests—"

"I don't want to hear all that crap again," Alan said, his eyes narrowing. "The only question here is, which one of these young men is Amy in love with? And I think we both know the answer to that."

Faith pressed her lips together angrily.

"I want you to promise me you'll stay out of this," Alan forged on. "I don't want you pressuring Amy and making it even harder for her to make a decision."

"I'm her mother, Alan. I have a right, a *duty*, to steer her in the proper direction. I'm sorry you don't approve, but I can't make that kind of promise."

They stared at each other, at an impasse for one of the few times in their married life.

"Then," Alan said, "I guess I'll have to do everything in *my* power to make sure she knows I'll support her no matter what she decides."

They ate the rest of their meal in a strained silence, and that night, in bed, for the first time

Faith could ever remember, Alan went to sleep without kissing her goodnight.

Amy lay awake long into the night, thinking, thinking. What was she going to do? How could she choose between Sam and Justin?

She alternated between despair and fury. The despair was caused by the terrible rift between the two men, for the death of a wonderful friendship, and for the knowledge that she was the cause of it. She finally admitted to herself that Justin was right. They couldn't go back to what they had been. The fury was caused by their stubborn refusal to even try to come to some kind of compromise or understanding. Didn't they understand what they were *doing* to her?

She thought about the way she'd felt when Sam had come this afternoon. The way she'd felt when he'd kissed her. The way she'd felt when she looked into his eyes. And especially the way she'd felt when they talked about the baby. She loved him so much. How could she say goodbye to him?

She thought about all the days and nights Justin had spent with her. The way he'd taken care of her. The way he'd been there whenever she'd needed him. She thought about how happy he'd made her. He was such a good man. She loved him, too. How could she push him away?

But no matter how many times she asked herself the same questions, the answer was always the same: she couldn't choose.

Sam didn't sleep well that night. His leg ached, and his heart ached. He kept remembering days gone by. He remembered the first time he'd ever seen Justin. It had been November, his second November since moving to Houston. He'd had Major for six months and had had to put the dog in a kennel four times. Major had spent more time in the kennel than he'd spent with Sam.

Sam had just gotten a new assignment. He was scheduled to leave for Kwajalein the following week for a story on the Marshall Islands. He had finally realized it was unfair to Major to try to keep him, and so, reluctantly, he'd put an ad on the bulletin board at the office.

He'd been sitting at his desk in the photography department, and his phone had rung.

"Robbins," he said.

"You the guy who put the ad on the bulletin board about the dog?" said a male voice.

Sam sat up straighter. "Yes, I am."

"I might be interested. Can I see the dog?"

"Sure. Do you work here at the magazine?"

"Oh, sorry." He laughed. "My name's Justin Malone, and I'm in the business department. You're a photographer, right?"

"Yeah, right."

"Well? Could I see the dog tonight?"

"Sure. No problem. I don't live very far from here. We could go after work."

"Sounds good."

They'd met by the elevators. Sam had immediately liked Justin with his no-nonsense eyes and his no-nonsense manner. They shook hands and smiled at each other and there was a kind of instant rapport between them.

In his own car, Justin followed Sam to his apartment. After Sam showed him Major and Justin decided he liked the dog and wanted to take him, the two men had fallen into easy conversation, ending with Sam asking Justin if he wanted to go get something to eat.

"I'll bring Major over to your place tomorrow," he'd said. "Give you a chance to get things ready for him."

They'd spent the evening together, eating Mexican food and drinking a pitcher of margaritas and shooting the bull. Sam hadn't talked so much in years. Justin admitted he hadn't, either. By the time the evening was over, Sam felt as if they'd been friends forever.

And in the years since, that friendship had only grown stronger. They'd weathered bad times and good. Justin had been more than a friend. He'd been like the brother Sam had never had. His family had taken Sam into their hearts, too, giving him warmth and a feeling of belonging, including him in their holiday celebrations and their personal triumphs and tragedies.

Remembering all this, then remembering the look of almost-hate in Justin's eyes today, made Sam feel half sick. Amy was right, he thought as he fell into an uneasy sleep. He had to at least try to salvage something out of this mess.

The following morning, he debated whether or not to call Justin and see if he wanted to go to lunch. While he was still thinking about the possibility, the phone rang. Hoping it wasn't another reporter, he picked it up and said, "Robbins."

"Um, hello, is this Sam Robbins?"

It was a young, unrecognizable female voice. "Yes," Sam said.

There was silence for a moment, then the woman said, "I—I rehearsed what I was going to say, but now I—"

"Who *is* this?" he said irritably. He was tired of being hounded by these press types.

There was an audible sigh from the other end. Then, softly, she said, "This is Holly, Sam."

For perhaps three seconds, Sam sat there, uncomprehending. And then, in a blinding flash, realization hit. Holly! His heart made a crazy loop. *Holly!* His sister!

"Sam?" Her voice was uncertain. "Are you there?"

"Holly? Is . . . is it really you?"

Her laugh rang out joyously. "Yes. It's really me. I—I was afraid you might have forgotten me."

Sam's eyes stung, and his chest felt tight. "Forgotten you?" he said softly. "I could never forget you." As if it were yesterday, he was assaulted with memories. Holly, on the day she was born, a little wizened creature with a red face and tufts of bright hair and a lusty wail. At four months—fat and pink-cheeked, laughing up at him when he waved a rattle over her crib. Holly, with eyes the color of a stormy sea—a legacy from their mother. Holly, crying as if her heart would break when she and Sam were separated.

They talked for a long time. She told him all about her new parents and her life and how she'd only found out about him a few days earlier. "Mom and Dad said they'd always intended to tell me about you when I got older, but somehow they kept putting it off. At first, I was really mad at them, but now, I guess I understand . . . see, they didn't know where you were or what kind of person you might be until you disappeared two years ago and they saw a story about you on the news. And then . . . well, I guess they didn't want to upset me. I mean, if you were dead, why tell me and make me sad?" And then she laughed. "But you're not dead! I have a real, live brother!"

"I can't believe I'm really talking to you," Sam said, still dazed.

She told him she'd just graduated from college. "I studied broadcast journalism at UCLA. I haven't had much luck finding a job, though. That's why I'm still at home."

"Do your parents live in San Diego?"

"No, La Jolla."

Her parents must be well off if they could afford to live in La Jolla.

"Sam? I'm dying to see you. I've . . ." Her voice trembled slightly. "I've always wanted a brother."

Sam's voice was gruff as he answered. "Well, you've got one now."

Two days later, Sam left LAX in a rental car and headed south on the San Diego Freeway. The drive was one he hadn't made in a long time, and he'd almost forgotten how stark the landscape was. People who had never visited southern California always thought of it as lush and green and filled with flowers and palm trees. That's the way it was in the cities, where the citizens planted and watered and tended, but the countryside from LA to San Diego was mostly ocher mountains and barren, sun-scorched valleys.

The drive to La Jolla took only a couple of hours, and it was still daylight when Sam parked in front of the small, Spanish style home a few blocks from downtown. In the near distance, church bells rang the Angelus as he got out of the car. The air smelled crisp and salt-tangy in this pampered enclave tucked into its sheltering cove and framed by the brilliant blue ocean beyond.

The Etheridge home was surrounded by a high wall. Scarlet and deep magenta bougainvillea spilled over the tops and sides.

A beautiful place to grow up, Sam thought, as he opened the wrought-iron gate and entered the small front courtyard where hibiscus and oleander, jasmine and passion flowers vied for dominance.

Holly had been watching for him, because the heavy, carved door opened before he'd had a chance to ring the doorbell.

"Sam!"

He would have known her anywhere, because she was the image of their mother. She had the same heart-shaped face, the same big gray eyes, the same delicately arched eyebrows. Even her hair was the same color—brown streaked with gold—although Holly's was fashionably cut and styled and gleamed with health, whereas Sally's had too often been lank and dull. The other difference was height and body shape. Holly was tall: Sam guessed about five feet seven inches—and slender. Their mother had been shorter and rounder. His sister was dressed like a typical, twenty-something Californian in Guess jeans, T-shirt, and sneakers.

He managed a smile over the lump in his throat and opened his arms.

Without hesitation, she came into them. They held each other for a long time. He could feel her heart beating against his and smell the light, lemony scent of her hair, and all he could think was, *this is my baby sister.* Some of the heartache and disappointment that had surrounded his homecoming and the discovery about Amy and Justin eased away.

"Oh, Sam," Holly said in a muffled voice, "I'm so glad you're here."

When she looked up, he could see that her eyes were bright with unshed tears.

"Me, too," he said. "Me, too."

They went inside where he met her adoptive parents—Jack and Sandi Etheridge. Sandi was a short, slightly plump fifty-something matron with kind hazel eyes and a sweet smile, and Jack was a big, bearish sort of man with intelligent dark eyes, thick salt-and-pepper hair, and a cautious, more reserved manner than his wife's. They were nice people; Sam could see that immediately. And they loved Holly; that was another thing he saw immediately. They were also thoughtful. After about fifteen minutes of conversation, Sandi turned to Holly and said, "Your father and I thought we'd go into town for dinner. I know you and Sam have a lot to talk about."

Holly smiled gratefully and hugged her mother and father in turn.

Once they were gone, she said, "Are you hungry? We could order a pizza, or I could make us some sandwiches."

"Maybe later. Right now, I'd just like something cold to drink."

She got them each a beer, then suggested they sit out on the back patio. "It's my favorite place."

Sam could see why. This, too, was a courtyard, but a much bigger one than in the front. It was mostly paved with terracotta tiles, with a three-foot-wide border of shrubs and flowers. A bird feeder in the corner had attracted several swallows and goldfinch, who noisily flew away when he and Holly walked outside.

They sat in comfortable cushioned redwood chairs.

Sam breathed deeply, enjoying the absence of the heavy humidity of Houston. He gazed around with pleasure. "Have you lived in this house long?"

"Ever since I was adopted."

Sam nodded. He couldn't help comparing his growing-up years to hers, but he felt no bitterness or envy. He was happy for Holly, glad to know she'd been surrounded by such beauty and comfort and love. He turned to look at her and found her eyes on him. They were filled with sadness. "What's wrong?" he asked softly.

She shrugged. "I—I just wish I could remember you, from before."

"You were only a year old when we were separated. How could you?"

"I know. But it's sad, don't you think? All those lost years?"

He reached for her hand. It felt good in his. "Don't be sad. We've found each other. That's what matters."

Her smile was slow and sweet. "You're right, of course. That's what matters."

They talked for a long time. She wanted to know everything he could remember about their mother, and Sam obliged, although he filtered out or glossed over the more unsavory details.

"I'm proud of you, Sam," she said much later. "You've made something of yourself without anyone else's help."

"No, that's not true. I had a lot of help." He told her about Gus and Peggy and Owen Church.

"Tell me about your life in Houston. Do you have a girlfriend?"

Sam found himself talking about Amy, and then about Justin and the whole dilemma.

"Oh, that's *awful*," she said. "How could they do that to you?"

Even though this was exactly how Sam had felt when he'd first found out about Amy and Justin, he now found himself in the strange position of defending them. "To be fair," he said, "I understand how it happened."

"What are you going to do about it?"

"There's not much I can do except wait."

"Well, I wouldn't worry about it if I were you," she said loyally. "It shouldn't take her long to come to her senses. I'll bet the two of you will be back together in no time at all."

Twenty-five

"I haven't seen Sam around lately," Faith said. "Does that mean what I think it means?"

"He's in California, Mother," Amy said. It was Friday night, and she'd just gotten home from school. Her mother must have been watching for her, because Amy had no sooner turned off her ignition than the back door opened and Faith emerged to waylay her.

"Oh? On a new assignment already? I would have thought the magazine would have given him some time to recuperate."

"They did. He's not on an assignment. Because of all the publicity surrounding his return, he got a call from his sister—the one who was adopted as a baby. He flew out to California to see her." Remembering Sam's happiness when he'd called to tell her what happened, Amy smiled. Although, in her fantasies about Sam eventually finding his sister, she had always thought she'd be right there with him, she was genuinely thrilled for him and eager to hear all about the reunion when he returned to Houston. He'd been gone almost a week now, but he was supposed to get back sometime tomorrow afternoon.

"How nice for Sam," her mother said. She pulled her cardigan sweater closer as the wind picked up.

Amy shivered herself. "If you want to talk, let's go up to my apartment. It's too cold out here." A front had blown in during the night, turning the late October day into an unseasonably chilly one. The gunmetal sky looked like rain, too. It would be a nice night to curl up under the afghan with a good book. *Or snuggle up to a lover* . . . Amy pushed the unwelcome thought away as she climbed the stairs. There'd been no snuggling for her in the two weeks since Sam's return. She had determinedly resisted all Justin's efforts to get her into bed and fought her own reawakened desire for Sam. Until she came to a decision about the future, she had to keep a clear head. Sex would only fog the issue.

Once inside her apartment, Amy dumped her satchel and purse and bent to pet the cats, who one by one came to greet her. "I'm going to fix some tea," she called over her shoulder, as she headed for the kitchen. "Want some?"

"All right." Her mother walked around the living area, fingering things as she went.

Amy stifled the irritation that had lately become the norm when she was with her mother. What was Faith doing, anyway? Amy nearly bit her tongue to keep from calling out, *Put that down!* when Faith lifted Amy's sketchbook and began leafing through it. She knew exactly when her mother saw the sketches of Sam, because Faith's shoulders stiffened and her mouth got that set look.

Maybe it was time to move. Funny how, before meeting Sam, Amy had been perfectly contented to live so close to her parents. She'd never felt smothered, never felt as if they intruded on her

privacy, never felt in any way inhibited or controlled. Now, though, she felt all those things. Not
from her father . . . her father was the same as
he'd always been. No, it was the difference in her
mother and the way she treated Amy that caused
the feelings of resentment and anger.

But old habits die hard. Amy had been raised to
be polite, to honor her parents, to deal with nega-
tive feelings calmly and rationally, and above all—
to think before she spoke. So she didn't give voice
to the annoyance flooding her. Instead, she decided to confront the issue of Sam head-on. After
all, that topic was obviously what her mother
wanted to discuss. "He looks different than he
looked before, don't you think?"

Faith looked up. "Who?"

Amy smiled sardonically as she loaded the tea
things onto a tray. "Oh, come on, Mother, you
know who. *Sam.*"

Green eyes met green eyes.

"Well," Faith said, "it's no wonder. He went
through quite an ordeal."

Amy carried the tray into the living area and set
it on the coffee table. "Yes, he did."

"He put you through a worse ordeal, though."

"It's not like he did it on purpose, Mother," Amy
said, keeping her voice mild. Losing her temper
would solve nothing. In fact, knowing how her
mother viewed people who couldn't control their
tempers, Amy would have cut off her hand before
she'd lash out at Faith.

"Perhaps not, but he didn't exercise good judgment, did he?"

Amy shrugged, although this was still a sore point
with her.

"Nor did he give much thought to you when he chose to do something dangerous and foolhardy."

"We all make mistakes," Amy pointed out. "And he certainly paid for his." It was ironic that her mother was only giving voice to thoughts Amy had had dozens of times, yet now Amy found herself defending Sam's actions.

Faith poured herself a cup of tea, saying, "That's true, but I think even you have to agree that Sam doesn't exhibit the traits of dependability or maturity."

Unsaid was the qualifier: *these are two traits essential in a husband.* Even though they were unsaid, the words throbbed in the air between them.

Amy sighed. "Look, I know how you feel about Sam. I've always known how you felt." She began to pour herself a cup of tea. "But I have to make my own decision about this."

Her mother sighed. "What's happened between us, Amy? We used to be able to talk about anything, and we almost always agreed with each other."

Amy's answer came slowly. "You mean I always agreed with you."

Faith stared at her. "No. That's not what I said, and it's not what I meant. I meant we had the same ideas about life."

"Maybe that's because I never cared enough about anything or anyone to disagree with you."

For a long moment, the silence between them was so profound Amy could hear the ticking of the wall clock and the high whine of a leaf-blowing machine somewhere outside.

"You're going to go back with Sam, aren't you?" her mother finally said.

"I don't know."

"You don't know . . . or you won't say?"

For the second time, Amy had to bite her

tongue. *Don't get mad,* she told herself. "I honestly don't know."

Faith nodded. "All right. But will you promise me something, Amy? Will you promise me to at least think about what I've said?"

"Yes, I'll think about it," Amy said slowly, "but in turn, I want you to promise *me* something."

"What?"

"I want you to promise me you'll support whatever decision I finally make."

It took Faith a few minutes, but she finally sighed in resignation. "I promise."

Justin called later that evening. They talked for a while, then he said, "I miss you."

She swallowed. "I know. I—I miss you, too." And it was true. She did. She missed the camaraderie, the comfortable conversation, and the way he'd always understood her. As long as she was being completely honest with herself, she also missed the undemanding love he'd always given her.

"Come for dinner tomorrow night," she said impulsively. It wasn't right of her to shut him out. He had done nothing wrong. And he was still her fiancé. She hadn't called off the wedding. How could she have forgotten that?

After they said goodbye, she stood there for a long moment. She had to make some kind of decision . . . and soon. This waffling wasn't fair to anyone.

Sam took an earlier flight home than he'd intended, landing at Intercontinental Airport a little after 1 o'clock on Saturday.

He couldn't wait to see Amy. She'd sounded almost as excited about Holly calling as he'd been himself, and he was eager to tell her all about the visit. He decided he'd go straight to her apartment.

He arrived at 2:30. He'd been half afraid he might see Justin's car in the driveway, but the driveway was empty. He peered into Amy's part of the garage, grinning when he saw her Miata. Good. She was home.

He whistled their song as he walked up the stairs, something he hadn't done since that first day back. Before he'd gotten halfway up, the door opened, and she smiled and waved.

His heart lifted, and he thought how pretty she looked today in black tights and a long pink sweater that made her look younger and more carefree than she'd seemed in weeks.

"You're back early," she said, when he'd reached the top. Her eyes told him she was glad he'd come.

He nodded. He wanted badly to kiss her, but decided he would wait. He contented himself with giving her a shoulder hug and kissing her cheek.

They went inside, and she cleared some papers from the couch. "Sit down. Want something to drink?"

"Got any Coke?"

"Uh-huh. I'll get you some."

A few minutes later, two glasses in hand, she walked back to the living room. She handed him one, then sat on the couch, too, carefully keeping one pillow length between them. Suddenly, he was filled with memories of the first time he'd ever come to this apartment. He wondered if she ever thought about that night . . . and all the ones that had followed. He was gripped with sadness for everything they'd had and lost. Could they recapture that happiness?

"Tell me about Holly," she said.

He smiled. "She's really something. You'll love her."

Something flickered in the backs of Amy's eyes. "I'm sure I would."

He noticed how she'd said *would* instead of *will* but decided to ignore it for now. "She looks so much like our mother," he began, and then he talked and talked and talked.

Amy listened, watching his face and thinking how glad she was for him. She had always felt bad that he didn't have any family, and now he did. *If I marry Justin, at least he won't be completely alone . . .* The thought made her feel unbearably sad.

"I might try to help her find a job here," he said, winding up his recital of the past week's events.

"Really? That would be great." She was ridiculously afraid she was going to cry. She put down her glass and stood, walking over to the windows and looking out. She fought to get her emotions under control. She was a pathetic mess.

"Amy?"

She hadn't heard him walk up behind her. She shivered as he touched her neck, then slowly turned her to face him. His eyes searched hers. "What's wrong?" he said softly.

She shook her head. Oh, God. She *was* going to cry.

"Ah, Amy . . . don't cry." Her tears were his undoing. He couldn't stand seeing her so unhappy. He put his arms around her and kissed her cheeks, her eyes, her nose, all the while telling her not to cry.

She finally stopped, but he kept kissing her, his lips eventually seeking hers. She sighed as his mouth slanted across hers, and she twined her arms around him. They kissed hungrily—kisses that became more and more heated, urgent, and frantic. Kisses that said everything they hadn't been able to say in words. Kisses that spoke of unfulfilled desires and longings that could no longer be denied.

Sam hurt, he wanted her so much. He had been without her for two long years, and he couldn't wait another day, another hour, another minute. It seemed the most natural thing in the world to stop kissing her long enough to pick her up and carry her into the bedroom.

"Amy, Amy," he groaned, laying her on the bed and climbing on top of her. He pushed her sweater up, filling his hands with her breasts, then bending to draw first one, then the other nipple into his mouth. Her indrawn breath, followed by a low groan, fueled his desire for her. His control was very near to the breaking point. Almost crying from his need, he managed to pull her tights down, and within seconds, his hands had found her.

Amy's body bloomed under his touch. She had forgotten this, forgotten how he could make her feel, forgotten the intensity of the pleasure they had always brought to each other. She moaned as he touched her, threw her head from side to side as his fingers gently slipped inside. All sanity, all reason, was gone.

And then, like a burst of icy water, reality, in the form of sunlight glancing off her diamond and causing brilliant prisms of color to dart across the ceiling, doused her. What in God's name was she doing?

"No," she cried, pushing at Sam. "No. Stop. Stop!" At first Sam didn't seem to hear her, but then, eyes bewildered, he pushed himself up and rolled off her. She couldn't meet his gaze as she pulled her pants up and her sweater down. Her face was on fire. "I—I'm sorry," she stammered. "I just can't do this. It's not right."

"It's the only thing in this whole crazy mess that is right," he said, still breathing hard, "and you know it."

Amy really felt like crying now. She was sick with shame, sick with the knowledge that she had almost done something irrevocable and despicable. "I can't betray Justin like this."

Sam stood. He carefully and deliberately rearranged his clothing. "You'll betray him even more if you marry him without loving him," he said quietly.

"I—I do love him." God, how many times had she said that? She buried her face in her hands.

"Amy."

She was too embarrassed to look at him again.

"Amy," he said, his voice softening, "Look at me. I love you, and I know you love me. We belong together. We always have."

Sam . . . Sam . . .

"Why don't we just pack a few clothes," he said urgently, sitting down next to her on the bed and gently pulling her hands away from her face. "We can fly to Vegas or Mexico and get married. Justin will get over it."

She shook her head. "No, no. I can't. I can't hurt him that way. I love him."

"You love me." He tipped her chin up and kissed her lips tenderly.

She shuddered and closed her eyes again.

"See?" he whispered. "You're in love with *me*. And I love you."

Shocking herself, she wrenched away from him, jumping up and glaring at him. "Then why did you break your promise to me?" she cried. "You said you wouldn't take any chances. And you did! If you really loved me, you wouldn't have, and if you hadn't, none of this would ever have happened."

Sam stared at her. "Now the truth comes out. You're angry. You're totally pissed-off." He stood, too, standing too close to her.

She wanted to back away, but she didn't.

"Why don't you just take a swing at me and be done with it?" he said. "Maybe then we can finally settle this."

Furious tears threatened to overflow. She raised her hand, drew it back, stared at him. Later, she wondered if she really would have slapped him. He never gave her the chance. He grabbed her wrist and yanked her toward him. And then he kissed her again, grinding his mouth against hers. At first, she struggled, but then, with a guttural cry, she wound her arms around him and kissed him back desperately.

He released her so suddenly, she almost fell. When he spoke, his voice and eyes were very angry. "I'm tired of screwing around, Amy. The last two years haven't been a picnic for me, either. How long are you going to keep punishing me for my mistakes?"

She slumped back against the bed. "That's not what I'm doing."

"What *are* you doing?"

"Just trying to be fair. Just trying to do what's right."

"Yeah, well, maybe that's what you *think* you've been doing, but you sure as hell have been sending mixed signals."

Amy felt battered. Sam refused to understand. She couldn't just run out on Justin. It was wrong. How could she be happy hurting someone she loved?

"Make up your mind," he continued relentlessly. "Justin . . . or me. But if you decide you want me, don't wait too long, because if you do, I might be gone."

asco, he'd probably walk out, too. And she wouldn't blame him. It would be just what she deserved.

Sam drove too fast as he left Amy's, and he narrowly missed hitting some old geezer driving a big Lincoln town car at the intersection of River Oaks Boulevard and San Felipe. Sam laid on the horn and gave the old guy the finger, then was immediately ashamed of himself. He was also ashamed of the way he'd lashed out at Amy. He knew she hadn't been teasing him, the way he'd insinuated. She wanted him, but her conscience wouldn't let her do something she felt was wrong. She might be misguided, but she wasn't cruel or selfish.

The trouble was, he was miserable—emotionally and physically. And he knew he couldn't go on like this much longer. If Amy was going to marry Justin, Sam needed to know—*now*. No matter how much it hurt. Because this limbo was killing him.

For the first time, he seriously considered what he would do if that was her decision. He sure as hell wouldn't stay in Houston. No way. He wondered how Owen would feel if he wanted to make his base somewhere else, maybe only work for the magazine part-time. It was not unheard of. Sam remembered another photographer who had worked out a similar arrangement a few years before. He could also do freelance photography and be his own boss. He had the credentials now. He knew he'd have no trouble finding work.

Maybe instead of trying to find Holly a job in Houston, he'd move out to California and see what he could do for her out there. He had connections. He could probably help her come up with something.

He decided he would drive over to Owen's right

now—see if he was home, and talk to him about the future. Determinedly keeping his mind away from Amy and the unfulfilled need still burning away inside, he made a U-turn at the next light and headed west.

She was still wearing his ring.

Nowadays, that was the first thing Justin looked for. But something was wrong. He hadn't been there five minutes before he realized she wasn't herself. When he asked her, she quickly smiled and shook her head. "I'm just tired. Maybe I'm coming down with a cold," she said.

He nodded, but he wasn't convinced.

At 9:30, after they'd cleaned up the kitchen together, he slipped his arms around her and said, "Amy, I know something's happened. Tell me what it is."

She laid her head against his chest and put her arms around his waist. Then, sighing, she gently extricated herself from the embrace. "Let's go sit on the couch."

"Sam came by today," she said when they were seated.

Justin stiffened. A sick feeling of dread settled into his stomach.

"I realize now how terribly unfair I've been . . . to both of you."

Justin didn't breathe.

"I . . ." She took a deep breath and met his gaze squarely. "I think we should call off the wedding."

He stared at her. He'd expected this from the moment he'd known Sam was alive, so why did it come as such a shock? And why did it hurt so damned much?

She touched his hand, her eyes telling him how sorry she was, but he'd suddenly had enough. He stood. "Fine," he said tightly, determined he wouldn't show her how mortally she'd wounded him. He might have lost her, but he hadn't lost his pride. In that moment, he realized he'd forgotten something important the past couple of weeks. He would never have been able to build any kind of happiness with her if she'd come to him because she felt she owed him something. "Tell Sam I said congratulations." The words nearly choked him.

She jumped up. "No, Justin, you don't understand. I haven't decided I want to marry Sam. That's not it."

"What? Then why . . . ?"

"I know you're probably thoroughly disgusted with me, and I don't blame you. In fact, I wouldn't blame you if you walked out tonight and never came back." She looked at him in consternation, wishing she could express her feelings better.

"Amy," he said, exasperated, "would you please explain what the hell you're talking about?"

"I just think it's not fair to keep you dangling like this. Maybe *call off the wedding* isn't the right thing to have said. What I mean is, I think we should postpone it until we can—"

"Let me get this straight," he interrupted, his blue eyes glinting dangerously. "Instead of making a decision, you want to *postpone* the wedding and *postpone* your decision indefinitely. Is that it?"

"When you say it that way, I know it sounds . . ." She broke off. "Oh, God, I knew I'd make a mess of this. I've made a mess of everything else today."

Her words reinforced his belief that something had happened between her and Sam today, something she wasn't ready to admit. And as much as

Justin loved her, as much as he wanted her, he knew he couldn't allow her to do this, even if it meant she was lost to him forever. "No, Amy," he said, calm now. "I won't agree to postponing the wedding. If we don't get married November twenty-fourth, the way we planned, we won't get married at all." He forced himself to go on. "If you want Sam, say so."

It was so quiet in the apartment, Amy fancied she could hear her heart beating.

"You're right," she said finally. "Sam feels the same way. He's tired of waiting, too."

She looked so miserable, Justin felt sorry for her, but he knew they couldn't go on like this, so he hardened his heart. "Amy," he said, "decide. We continue with our wedding plans, or you call off the wedding permanently. Either way, I want your decision by the end of the week."

Later that night, as Sam lay in his hotel room, trying to sleep, he decided he wouldn't call Amy or try to see her again. No matter how much he loved her or wanted her, he'd meant what he'd said. He wouldn't wait around forever. The ball was in her court.

Justin lay awake a long time. He felt almost resigned, now that he knew he wouldn't have to wait much longer. Just before he fell asleep, he decided he wouldn't call Amy again. He'd let her have the week unpressured, and whatever she decided, he would learn to live with it.

* * *

Amy didn't fall asleep until after 3. She thought and thought and thought. She went over all the reasons why Justin would make her a better husband and all the reasons why Sam would make her a better husband. Unfortunately for Sam, Justin's list was a lot longer. If she were choosing with her head, Justin would be the clear winner.

But what about her heart?

At one point, she turned on her bedside lamp and opened her jewelry box, removing the emerald ring. Picking up Justin's ring, which she always removed at night and put on the dresser, she laid both rings on the bed and looked at them.

How like the men who had given them to her they were. The emerald ring was gorgeous, eye-catching, and special, but almost too beautiful and too large to wear every day. The diamond was beautiful, too, but smaller and much more practical and sensible.

She fell asleep still thinking . . . and still undecided.

Sam had a doctor's appointment Monday morning, so he didn't get into the office until after 11. When he arrived, he found a message on the desk in his cubicle. Marked "urgent," it came from someone named Bill Castleman at a 212 area code.

Sam frowned. Who was Bill Castleman, and why was someone he didn't know at a Manhattan area code calling him?

"Did this guy say what he wanted?" he asked Marianne, the clerical assistant who had taken the call.

"Nope," she said, cracking her gum.

Sam didn't return the call immediately, figuring Castleman was probably just another news hound, and he wasn't in the mood for that right now.

At 12:10, his phone rang.

"Robbins," he said.

"Mr. Robbins, this is Bill Castleman, from the Castleman Literary Agency in New York."

"Oh?" Sam said warily.

"I've got a proposition for you. You don't already have an agent, do you?"

"No." Why would he need an agent?

"Good, because I've got a publisher interested in a book about your experiences in Nepal and I'd like to represent you."

Sam listened, at first astounded, then, as the validity of Castleman's offer sank in, increasingly flattered and excited.

They talked a long time, then Castleman, who was by now calling him Sam, said, "I'll fax you one of our agency contracts today, and if we're lucky, we'll have a concrete deal by the end of the week."

After hanging up, Sam swiveled his chair around so he could look out the window. If Castleman could put this deal together, it would mean Sam could go back to Nepal and do something for the villagers who had done so much for him.

For the first time since his return, Sam admitted to himself that he was restless, that even the thought of a new assignment in the near future hadn't mitigated that feeling. He wondered now if, because he'd fallen for Amy so hard, he had lied to himself, thinking he could change and become the kind of man she so obviously wanted. He seriously examined the possibility that he would never be contented with the kind of life he had imagined before the accident that had so changed things—not only between him and Amy—but inside himself.

Maybe Amy's mother and Lark and Justin and everyone else who had raised their eyebrows at the thought of Sam Robbins settling down to a normal, nine-to-five, picket-fence existence had been right. Maybe he was all wrong for her. Maybe he could never make her happy.

Maybe she *would* be better off with Justin.

Rumors travel fast in offices, which are very like small towns. On Wednesday, Justin heard through the grapevine that Sam Robbins was getting ready to sign a book deal with a New York publisher.

"I heard he's going back to that village," Justin's secretary said, "to take pictures and everything, then go stay in Minneapolis where the woman who's actually going to do the *writing* of the book lives. Gee, isn't that exciting?" she gushed. "He'll probably end up rich and famous and get asked to go on *Oprah.*"

What did this mean? Justin wondered. Did Amy know?

His heart felt heavy the rest of the day. How could he possibly compete with Sam? Everything Sam did was romantic, and everything Justin did was mundane and boring.

Maybe Justin had been kidding himself, telling himself what he wanted to believe and not what was true. Maybe Amy *would* be happier with Sam.

By Wednesday, Amy had faced some hard truths. The first was that she could not give Sam up again.

The second was that she would have to hurt Justin, like it or not, and she would probably lose his friendship in the bargain.

Too bad, she thought wryly, she couldn't combine the two men. Take Sam's charm and sex appeal and the magic she felt when she was with him and add Justin's dependability and thoughtfulness and the feeling of safety he engendered. *In other words, Amy, you want to have your cake and eat it, too.*

She called Lark that evening. "You doing anything tonight?"

"Nope," Lark said. "The most ambitious thing on my agenda is calling Domino's for pizza."

"Want to make it a large one and feed me, too?" Amy said.

"If you'll agree to extra cheese and extra mushrooms, you've got yourself a deal."

"I'll see you in thirty minutes."

Later, over the remains of the pizza, Lark said, "So what's on your mind?"

Amy smiled. "You know me too well."

Lark sat back in her chair and waited.

"I've finally made a decision."

Lark tensed, girding herself.

"I'm going to marry Sam."

Although Lark had been expecting this, she still felt stunned that anyone could give up a man like Justin for a man like Sam.

"Well, say something," Amy said.

"What? You want my blessing?"

Amy flinched, and Lark was immediately ashamed of herself.

"No," Amy said slowly. "I don't need anyone's blessing. I guess I was just hoping you'd say good luck and you knew it must have been hard to make the decision and you'd support me, no matter what."

"Ah, shit, Amy, I'm sorry. Fine friend I am. I can't remember you *ever* sitting in judgment on me, even when I've done really stupid things—things I knew you didn't approve of at all—yet here I am . . . thinking I know better than you what's right for you to do." She reached across the table to clasp Amy's hand. "I *do* wish you good luck, and I *do* know it was a hard decision, and I *do* support you, no matter what."

"Thanks, Lark." Amy's smile looked a little watery, and Lark felt a bit misty-eyed herself.

"The only thing . . ." Lark said.

Amy laughed. "I figured there'd be a qualifier."

"I'm sorry. I just feel like I have to say this. Sam let you down once."

"I know. Don't think I haven't thought of that. But he's changed, Lark. He's changed a lot. I think he learned his lesson. I think he's really ready to settle down, and I think we can build a good life together."

Lark bit back the words she wanted to say, because she'd already said them. Things like, people don't change, and some men can't be caged, and you're still seeing things the way you want them to be and not the way they really are.

"When will you tell Justin?" she said instead.

"Friday night."

Lark decided she would find someone to take her route Friday night, just in case.

The book became a done deal Friday morning. The first thing Sam did was go talk to Owen. "I've thought about this for a few days now," he said, after describing what the publisher wanted and how he felt he could best deliver it. "And I think the fair thing to do is give you my resignation instead of taking a leave of absence. That way, you can fill my slot with someone else."

"I'll miss you," Owen said. "But in the best interests of the magazine, I think you're right."

Sam had thought he'd feel sad; instead, he felt free.

"When you're finished with the book, maybe we can work out freelance assignments," Owen said.

"I'd like that."

The two men shook hands, then, in one of his rare shows of affection, Owen hugged Sam. "Congratulations, son. And good luck."

The next thing Sam did was call Amy. She was at school, but he left a message on her answering machine telling her he had to see her that night. "It's important," he said. "I have some news."

That day Amy felt better than she'd felt in weeks, maybe years. Now that she'd made her decision, she understood what people meant when they said they felt as if a load had been taken off their backs.

When she got home that afternoon, the first thing she did after greeting her cats and looking at her mail was head for the answering machine.

Sam's voice startled her: *"Amy, this is Sam. I have to see you tonight. It's important. I have some news."*

News? What news? Was he leaving for another assignment? Already? But he was still under a doctor's care. Her mind churned as she hastily dialed the magazine's number and asked for him.

"I got your message," she said a little breathlessly, because hearing his voice after not hearing it for a while always affected her this way.

"Can I come over now?"

He sounded funny. Tense, or maybe excited. It was hard to tell without seeing his face. Her stomach clenched. "Sure."

The thirty minutes she had to wait for him to arrive were agony. What was so important it couldn't wait? Had something happened?

When he arrived, some of her anxiety drained away, because he didn't look upset. His eyes were bright and his smile was the old Sam smile—the kind that made her heart turn over.

She listened, dazed, as he told her about the book. "Are . . . are you planning to take the offer?" she finally said.

"Yes."

But where did that leave her? Where did that leave them?

He took her hand, his voice filled with intensity as he tried to explain. "I know this is a shock to you. But Amy, this offer has clarified everything in my mind. It's shown me that I've been kidding myself . . . and you . . . for a long time."

She could do nothing but stare at him, while her heart beat too fast, and her entire being was filled with fear.

"I can't be the kind of man you want me to be. I wish I could, but I can't. I'm who I am, Amy, and even though I love you and want you, I can't make myself into someone different. I've resigned my position at *World of Nature*," he continued. "I'm going to Minneapolis on Tuesday, to meet Cheryl—Cheryl Gerhardt—she'll be the collaborator on this project . . . do the actual writing, that is . . . then I'll come back here and make all the arrangements for my return to Nepal. Hopefully, I can head out before winter sets in, because I don't want to wait until spring. Then, when I'm finished in the village, I'll go back to Minneapolis and stay until the book is finished."

Amy felt stunned. She couldn't believe this. It was so ironic. Only two days ago she'd told Lark that Sam had changed. That he would never again let her down. That he had learned his lesson. That he was ready for marriage and all that it meant.

And now . . . he was showing her so plainly that nothing had changed. Sam would always be off chasing rainbows. Leaving her behind to cope and wait. She would never be first in his life.

For a long moment, neither spoke.

"You could come with me, Amy."

"Come with you?" she said dully.

"Yes," he said eagerly. "I know it's not what we planned, but it could still be a good life. Who knows? You might even find you like it."

"Sam . . . I—I have a job. A contract. I can't just walk out in the middle of the term. And . . . how would we live? Wh-what about my things?" She looked around, her gaze settling on Delilah, who was delicately giving herself a bath. "What about my cats? What about . . . having a home and . . . children?"

The eagerness slowly faded from his eyes. "Of course, you're right." His smile was self-deprecating, his voice gentle. "I knew it was a long shot, but hell, can't blame a guy for trying." He squeezed her hand. "I'm sorry for the way I've hurt you. I never meant to. And you're right, I know you are. Justin's better for you than I am. He can give you all the things I can't. He'll make you a good husband."

And then, he took her in his arms and kissed her goodbye, holding her close for long moments before whispering, "Be happy, Amy."

Five minutes later, he was gone.

Justin had done nothing but think for two days. And he'd finally faced what he had known ever since Sam's return.

Twenty-seven

She would get over this.

She would get over him.

After all, hadn't she gotten over a lot worse?

She tried to pretend the heaviness of her heart and the aching emptiness of her body did not exist.

Friday night was the worst night of Sam's life. Worse even than those first nights after his accident. Then what he'd felt was physical pain. This pain was infinitely worse.

Amy.

It hurt to think of her, hurt to remember the stunned look on her face, the disappointment and betrayal in her eyes.

He told himself he'd done the only thing he could do. By releasing her, he'd ensured her future happiness. He told himself he would get over her. He told himself he had lived most of his life depending on no one, and he could do so again.

Nothing helped.

At 3 o'clock, knowing he would not sleep this night, he got up, dressed in his running clothes, and headed for the hotel's exercise room, which was open twenty-four hours a day. He would wear himself out. And if that didn't work, he'd find an all-night bar.

Amy lay awake most of the night.

She told herself that Sam's decision to take the book deal and leave her should have made everything easier for her. Now, as he'd said, she could marry Justin and live happily ever after.

At 4 o'clock, knowing she wouldn't get any sleep, she got up and walked out to the living room. Shivering a little—she hadn't bothered putting on her robe—she reached for the afghan folded over the arm of the rocking chair and wrapped it around herself. Then she headed for her storage cupboard. Minutes later, the half-finished portrait of Sam that she'd banished so long ago was once more sitting on her easel. Moonlight spilled over the likeness, giving his face an ethereal quality.

She stared at the portrait for a long time.

And as the first blush of dawn tinted the eastern sky, the final truth settled around her with absolute certainty.

She couldn't marry Justin.

It wasn't fair to him, because she didn't love him the way she should.

And she never would.

When Amy called Saturday morning, Justin said, "I was just going to call you."

"Would you like to come over?"

He tried to determine what she was feeling by the tone of her voice, but it told him nothing. He wondered if Sam had told her about the book deal yet. He guessed he'd find out soon enough.

Later, as he drove to Amy's, he felt calmer and more resigned than he'd felt in weeks.

His resolve teetered only slightly when she opened the door to his knock. The impact of seeing her after a week of being away from her was almost his undoing. But he reminded himself of everything he'd been thinking, and within moments, he'd regained control of his emotions.

"I've got fresh coffee. Do you want some?" she said.

He shook his head. He just wanted to get this over with and get out of there.

He followed her into the room. She sat on one end of the couch, but Justin was too edgy to sit. Instead, he walked to the bar and propped one elbow on it.

She bit her bottom lip.

Before she had a chance to say anything, Justin plunged in. "I've been thinking," he said, carefully keeping his voice as free of emotion as possible. He took a deep breath. "And I think you should marry Sam."

Her eyes widened.

"Because he's the one you're in love with," he rushed on. "You've always been in love with him. I just haven't wanted to face it."

"Justin—"

"No, wait, let me finish. I don't want you to feel bad about this. I know this isn't your fault. You can't help how you feel. And I thought I didn't care. I thought I'd take you any way I could get you, but I've discovered something about myself in the past couple of days, Amy. I'm not willing to settle. I want the kind of love you and Sam have. Nothing less is acceptable."

For the second time in twenty-four hours, Amy felt stunned. She knew it was unworthy of her, but she also felt ridiculously hurt. She'd gone from being a woman two men professed to want to a woman that neither man seemed to want. Then she immediately felt ashamed of herself. She should be grateful to Justin. He was making everything so easy for her.

"Some woman is going to feel awfully lucky one of these days," she said softly. "Because she'll be getting one of the greatest guys I know." She slowly removed the diamond ring.

Amazingly, Justin felt no pain as he took the ring and they said their goodbyes.

That, he knew, would come later.

Lark was just getting out of the shower on Saturday afternoon when her doorbell rang.

"Damn you, whoever you are, this better be important," she muttered, grabbing her terry cloth robe. "Or else you're gonna be *dead meat!*"

Charging to the front door, she peered through the peephole. Her heart leaped. Justin! She fumbled with the safety chain, unlocked the dead bolt, and threw the door open. "Hi," she said.

His smile didn't quite make it to his eyes. "Hi."

So Amy had finally lowered the boom. "C'mon in. What brings you here?"

"Oh, nothing much. My life just went down the toilet, that's all." Then he laughed wryly.

"Sounds to me like you need a beer."

"Is beer your solution to everything?"

"You got a better one?"

He laughed again, and this time it had a more genuine ring to it. "I see your point. Sure. I'll have a beer."

Ten minutes later, she'd combed her hair, thrown on jeans and a shirt, and was sitting across from him at her minuscule kitchen table. "Okay, spill it," she said. "Why has your life gone down the toilet?"

He grimaced. "The wedding's off. Amy and I aren't getting married."

His matter-of-fact reaction, the acceptance she saw in his face, in his eyes, in his entire body, surprised her. "For someone who said his life had just gone down the toilet, you don't seem as miserable as I'd have thought you'd be," she said carefully.

He nodded, even smiled. "I know. But see, I'd already decided it was never going to work. In fact, I told Amy so. And you know what?"

"What?"

"It doesn't hurt as much as I thought it would."

"So you didn't come here to cry on my shoulder?" Lark said it lightly and tried to ignore the tiny seedling of hope that wanted to sprout.

His eyes met hers. God, she loved his eyes. A woman could drown in those eyes.

"I don't know why I came here," he said slowly, "I only know you're the person I wanted to see. Do you mind?"

Her smile bloomed slowly, just like the seedling. "No. I don't mind. I don't mind at all."

Late Saturday afternoon, Amy walked over to her parents' house. Her mother wasn't home, but she found her father in his study.

"Hi, Sunshine," he said, looking up from his book. Then he frowned. "Is something wrong?"

She tried to smile, but it wasn't easy. "Justin and I have broken our engagement."

He nodded slowly, his eyes thoughtful. "Does that mean you're going to marry Sam, then?"

"No."

"No?"

Slowly, she told him everything. About Sam's visit. About the book deal. About her decision regarding Justin. And then how Justin had beaten her to the punch.

Alan listened quietly. When she was finished, he said, "Amy, do you love Sam?"

Swallowing against the lump in her throat, she said, "Yes."

"Then why aren't you going with him?"

"But Dad, can't you see? Mother . . . everyone was right. Sam will never change."

Her father was silent for a long time. And then he said the words that changed her life. "If the way Sam is is so bad," he said, "then why did you fall in love with him in the first place?"

Amy's heart beat in slow thuds as her father's question reverberated in the air. "Oh, God," she whispered. "I'm so stupid."

Her father smiled. "No, you're not."

"Yes! Yes, I am!" Amy jumped up, her head whirling. "You're absolutely right! All the things I love most about Sam are all the things I wanted to change. I—I probably wouldn't even *like* him if he were different. Why, all those reasons I gave him for not being able to marry him . . . none of them are really important, are they?"

"I don't know if they are or not," her father said. "Those are things you two need to work out. But I do know one thing. The only safe place to be is with the person you love. Everything else is just window dressing."

"I'm here to see Sam Robbins," Amy told the desk clerk.

"Name?" said the bored-looking man.

"Amy Carpenter."

She listened as the clerk rang Sam's room. "Sorry," he said, replacing the receiver. "There's no answer there."

"Oh. Okay. Thank you." Disappointment rose like bile in her throat.

"Did you want to leave a message?"

Amy was still thinking about her answer when, from the arched restaurant entrance across the lobby, Sam, hardly limping at all, emerged.

Her heart skyrocketed. He looked freshly showered and shaved. His hair was neatly combed, his eyes questioning, his smile cautious as he walked slowly toward her.

"Amy?" he said when he reached her side.

"Hi." She felt suddenly uncertain. Did he still want her?

"What are you doing here? Has . . ." He lowered his voice, taking her arm and moving her out of earshot of the obviously-interested clerk. "Has something happened?"

She smiled up at him, heart in her eyes. "Yes. Something's happened. I—I've finally come to my senses. I was wrong. I love you, Sam, and I want to spend the rest of my life with you . . . wherever that life takes us." She took a deep breath. "Do . . . do you still want me?"

"Still want you!" he shouted, forgetting about the clerk, forgetting about the other people in the lobby, forgetting about everything except the miracle of Amy's presence. Laughing, he swung her up into his arms.

She laughed, too, heart soaring.

He kissed her then, a thousand-watt kiss filled with love and hope and happiness and the promise of all things magical. Neither one of them cared that there were dozens of people looking at them.

They were together, at last, as they'd always been meant to be.

Epilogue

Sam had worried that the hike might be too much for Amy, but she'd proved to be just as game as their two Sherpa guides.

"There it is," he said, pointing to the cluster of huts dotting the tiny valley. "There's the village."

Amy's eyes shone with eagerness as they met his.

An hour later, they were there. The villagers milled around them, all talking at once.

Sam's eyes misted over at the warm welcome.

"Namaste . . . namaste . . ." The greeting came from dozens of lips.

After much hugging and excited babbling, the little knot of villagers parted. Standing a little ways back was a beaming Reena.

"Sam," she said.

Sam's voice caught as he spoke her name. And then he opened his arms, and she came into them. He hugged her tightly, smelling her familiar, not-unpleasant scent, which was a mixture of the soap she made herself and her womanly musk.

When they drew apart, Sam reached for Amy's hand and brought her forward. "My wife," he said. "Amy." He pointed to the plastic-encased photo Reena had seen him finger so many times.

"Amy," Reena said, drawing the name out. Her dark face was wreathed in a smile as her eyes searched Amy's face. Then she put her arms around Amy, and they hugged.

Sam watched them, two women who had so profoundly affected his life. With any luck, he thought happily, there might be a third one of these days, because Amy had confessed just last night that she thought she might be pregnant again.

"I'm a week late," she said, eyes shining. "And I'm never late. Y-you don't mind, do you?"

No, he'd told her, he didn't mind. He was thrilled and knew he was luckier than he had any right to be. There was something else he wanted to tell her, but he decided he'd wait until they were back home again, until she was certain. Then he'd tell her what else he'd been thinking about—asking Justin if he'd consider being the baby's godfather.

Justin might say no; he might say their friendship wasn't mendable. All Sam knew was, he had to try.

As Reena and Amy drew apart, Sam put one arm around his surrogate mother and one arm around his wife.

He was the luckiest man in the world, he thought, as the three of them walked forward together.

And this was only the beginning.

ROMANCES BY BEST-SELLING AUTHOR COLLEEN FAULKNER!

O'BRIAN'S BRIDE   (0-8217-4895-5, $4.99)

Elizabeth Lawrence left her pampered English childhood behind to journey to the far-off Colonies . . . and marry a man she'd never met. But her dreams turned to dust when an explosion killed her new husband at his powder mill, leaving her alone to run his business . . . and face a perilous life on the untamed frontier. After a desperate engagement to her husband's brother, yet another man, strong, sensual and secretive Michael Patrick O'Brian, enters her life and it will never be the same.

CAPTIVE   (0-8217-4683-1, $4.99)

Tess Morgan had journeyed across the sea to Maryland colony in search of a better life. Instead, the brave British innocent finds a battle-torn land . . . and passion in the arms of Raven, the gentle Lenape warrior who saves her from a savage fate. But Tess is bound by another. And Raven dares not trust this woman whose touch has enslaved him, yet whose blood vow to his people has set him on a path of rage and vengeance. Now, as cruel destiny forces her to become Raven's prisoner, Tess must make a choice: to fight for her freedom . . . or for the tender captor she has come to cherish with a love that will hold her forever.

Available wherever paperbacks are sold, or order direct from the Publisher. Send cover price plus 50¢ per copy for mailing and handling to Penguin USA, P.O. Box 999, c/o Dept. 17109, Bergenfield, NJ 07621. Residents of New York and Tennessee must include sales tax. DO NOT SEND CASH.